MATCH RACE

Quarter horse racing presents a thrill few men in the Old West can resist. Dude McQuinn, Coyote Walking, and Billy Lockhart are no exception, riding from town to town, matching and trading racehorses. Dude is the straight-talking front man, Coyote the jockey, and Billy the doctor, concocting potions that can cure a horse of anything — at least temporarily. But Billy is being watched by a strange man in a black bowler hat — a man who knows a secret about his past . . .

FRED GROVE

◆

MATCH RACE

Complete and Unabridged

LINFORD
WESTERN

LINFORD
Leicester

First published in the United States by
Doubleday & Company

First Linford Edition
published 2021
by arrangement with
Golden West Literary Agency

A catalogue record for this book is available
from the British Library.

ISBN 978–1–78541–954–6

Published by
Ulverscroft Limited
Anstey, Leicestershire

Printed and bound in Great Britain by
TJ Books Ltd., Padstow, Cornwall

This book is printed on acid-free paper

To Pauline, Uncle Billy Lockhart's
most ardent champion

CONTENTS

CONTENTS

1

Stranger at the Track

The rain had stopped — that sudden, unlucky rain.

Dude McQuinn groaned to himself, seeing the telltale paint running down Judge Blair's face, revealing the blaze, after the race ended, the speedy Judge seven lengths in front of Roseville's local champion — moments after Dude had hastily collected the bets and hotfooted it to his waiting horse. Behind him the rising cries of 'Ringer! Ringer!' And Coyote Walking tearing on out of town, to the public eye unable to control the runaway bay sprinter. Some playactor, that Comanche jockey.

Dude reined up and looked back, sighting the knot of dogged riders again. The townsmen still pursuing, still pushing their fat horses too fast, their anger and frustration prevailing over the patience required in a drawn-out chase. A kind of weariness bore down upon him. He had the impulse to yell back, 'All we wanted to do was match our horse. Nobody'll run at him under his true name. We still beat you fair and square. We didn't fix your horse.'

The momentary urge passed. After all, the game was the thing. Almost every little town had a local favorite that could 'run a little,' as the old saying went — owned by a cagey horseman quick to take the advantage, if he could, any way he could. Such as the amusing wrinkle attempted last evening, the hayseed slickster drawing Coyote aside and mumbling, 'You heap good Injun — me heap good white friend. Savvy? You like 'em these here purty beads? They're yours if you pull that bay gelding tomorrow and let our horse win,' unaware that he was talking to an honor graduate of Carlisle School in Pennsylvania. And Coyote had replied, 'My dear white man, when attempting to bribe the son of the chief of all Comanches, never stoop to such trilling bagatelles. Proffer something worthwhile.'

'Like what?' the man asked, taken aback.

'Like raw liver, steaming hot from the innards of a two-year-old buffalo bull, spiced with the juice of the gall bladder,' Coyote answered with dignity, and strolled away.

Dude scowled. The townsmen had hung on longer than he had expected, and his rendezvous with Coyote and Uncle Billy Lockhart at the spring south of the county line wasn't many miles away. It was time to draw the pursuit in another direction, to wear down their mounts. Time to play cat and mouse.

Turning west, he rode to a high ridge and dismounted, outlined there against the afternoon Missouri sky. When performing the artful role of a decoy, it was wise to dawdle now and then, to appear in trouble: a loose cinch or shoe, or a spent horse. Yet, staged carefully, beyond rifle range.

After some minutes, to allow them time to draw nearer, he loosened the cinch on Blue Grass, his iron-legged

3

Kentucky saddler, and, bending down, picked up the brown gelding's left front foot as if examining it.

In moments, he heard a flurry of distant shots. When he looked, they were coming on once more, quirting and spurring, their weary mounts scarcely able to hold a ragged trot. Apparently in panicky haste, Dude cinched up and swung to saddle. Riding low, spurring and quirting, he galloped off on the long-striding saddler.

The futile firing died.

Within half an hour, he halted again, this time leading what looked like a tiring horse. Far back there he sighted a straggle of bobbing figures. He waited awhile and they seemed no nearer. Good. They have ridden the bottom out of their mounts, he thought. They have come about far enough now. Darkness will catch them miles from town, walking or leading their worn-out horses. It is time to fade out.

He mounted and gave the eager gelding its head. After that he saw his pursuers no more.

Sundown was an hour away when he marked the limestone hill above the wooded grove that sheltered the sweet-water spring. The sight evoked thoughts of a pull from Uncle Billy's clay jug, of dividing the hard-earned winnings, then a hot supper, with the piéce de résistance the old man's sourdough biscuits and red-eye gravy.

Jogging into the timber, he suddenly halted. The grove was empty. Still, Uncle Billy had left town even earlier than usual, driving the lively sorrel team hitched to the light camp wagon, Texas Jack and the sorry-looking trade horse tied behind.

Dude rode to the base of the hill and back, his concern growing. Had a second posse followed Coyote? That had never happened before. The main impulse of cleaned-out townsmen was always to catch the man with the winnings, one Dude McQuinn. Had Uncle Billy had a breakdown? Or was the old gent playing games again? It had happened more than once. Dude was stumped and not a little concerned.

Going back, he crisscrossed the entire grove, looking for fresh wagon tracks; finding none, he rode worriedly north, the way Coyote and Uncle Billy had come — if they had come this way — his eyes cutting at the sodden prairie.

After covering about a quarter of a mile, he came upon fresh wagon and horse tracks. Here they turned southeast. But why? He followed at a fast trot. Some distance on the tracks bore south toward a low line of wooded hills. Why, why? His puzzlement deepening, he loped the gelding. Now the tracks turned for a narrow gap. As he entered it, riding slower, a raspy voice called from an oak thicket, 'Wondered how long it'd take an Alamo Texan to find us.'

Dude halted with annoyance. 'Just as long as it took to find an old geezer's tracks.' Two figures sauntered from the thicket, Uncle Billy and Coyote, both grinning, a puckishness on the farmer's saintly features. 'Why all the mystery?'

Dude asked. 'Didn't we agree to meet at the spring back yonder?'

'Thought I was being followed, so I just kept on going,' the old man said.

'Somebody trailed you from town?'

'Did, for a spell, or my eyes don't see what they used to.'

'You need glasses, but you're too mule-headed to admit it. And why'd you pull out so early?'

'Figured we's in for that rain.'

Dude drilled him a frankly skeptical look. 'Since when did you tote a crystal ball around?'

'Felt it in my bones. Something you young fellas wouldn't understand. Did you collect the bets?' Uncle Billy asked, pointedly changing the subject.

'Have I ever failed? Managed to — just a shade before the paint started runnin' an' Texas Jack turned into the Judge.' Dude shook his head at the memory. 'That's as close as a man can come an' not get shot.'

'Now, Dude, pardner, everything's jim-dandy. Even found us a nice spring past this gap. Meantime, believe I'll have me a little toddy.' He strolled to the wagon.

Dude dismounted and turned to the Comanche for explanation. 'I still don't understand why he pulled out that early. No sign of rain then. It came up all of a sudden.'

'It was man in black bowler hat, white father,' Coyote said slowly. 'Man whose eyes blink like tree squirrel.'

'Man in the black bowler?'

'Man who got off stage about an hour before the race. Remember?'

That bit came back to Dude, piece by piece. The stage rolling up in front of the hotel and the man getting off just as the outfit rode by. Black bowler, black suit and vest, a gold watch chain across the vest. String tie. A full brown beard. A nondescript-appearing man of compact build, except fur the hawkish face and the piercing blue eyes that were constantly blinking, as if busy setting down for future reference everything within sight. The same man also had been around the finish line.

'Leave pretty quick Grandfather Billy did,' Coyote went on, 'when that man he saw again at the track.'

'I remember him,' Dude said, mulling it over. 'But I don't see the connection.'

Coyote shrugged and between them there passed an unspoken understanding, if not toleration, mixed with affection for one William Tecumseh Lockhart and his sometimes fathomless ways: horseman and veterinarian of the first water, skilled raconteur and scholar of vague academic credentials who could erupt with volleys of creative cusswords without once repeating himself. He could walk around a trade horse and detail its flaws. He could look into a horse's mouth and without hesitation tell its age. He could stir up a 'potion' from his so-called 'medicine chest' in the wagon that would put an ailing racehorse back on the track in a surprisingly short time, a mixture of many ingredients that often had the suspicious smell of sour-mash whiskey. An artist as well — he could take two horses of similar color and conformation, like Texas Jack, who couldn't outrun a fat man, and the hard-knocking Judge Blair, and change their markings so that each looked identically like the other. On a Saturday afternoon Dude had heard him hold a crowd of amusement — starved farmers spell-bound while he lectured on such diverse topics as 'The Salubrity of Dr. Hobson's Hygienic Whiskey' to 'The Downfall of the Roman Empire' — attention-getting ploys leading up to a horse trade or a match race. If his rural audience became bored after too much Julius Caesar, he might demonstrate the intricate looping and tying of Professor Gleason's Eureka Bridle, no more than a strand of stout cord, yet 'designed to hold any horse or mule under any circumstance when properly tied.'

Uncle Billy could speak fluent Spanish, with all the gestures. On a profitable swing through the Louisiana short-horse country, he had spoken Cajun like a native and danced to their wild fiddle music. More surprising, Dude had observed him collecting botanical specimens. When the occasion demanded, he could be a courtly gentleman of the old school: dark frock coat, white shirt, string tie, flat-topped hat and bench-made boots; other times, when his arthritic joints bothered him, as crotchety as a hungry grizzly. Feeling better, he could be as benign as his saintly visage: kindly, clear blue eyes and cherry-red mouth set in a roundish face framed by white whiskers and a distinguished bib beard and a mane of snow-white hair worn long. A spry little man who seemed to grow taller when angered: hands small and deft, as soft-looking as a schoolgirl's, in which a six-shooter could bulge as fast as the blink of an eye.

Dude knew him well, yet knew him not. What was his background? Where was the fascinating and mysterious old gent from? He had never mentioned home. Was Lockhart really his name? Had he ever been on the wrong side of the law, and had he ever been a lawman? There was, and Dude often had puzzled over this, a constant vigilance about Uncle Billy. Or could he be the true, much-quoted Professor Gleason? How old was he? At times he struck Dude as being quite old, which his energetic manner soon refuted, and then again he seemed eternal, animated by his everlasting passion for horses, running horses most of all, with which he had an uncanny communication, and further sustained by frequent toddies and naps. He never took 'a drink of whiskey'; always it was 'a little toddy,' whether taken straight or with water and sugar, as if that term pertained to medicinal use only and entitled him to more than one trip to the jug.

When the old horseman rarely let slip a hint of his past, mentioning a great race or horse he'd seen, and Dude, sensing the opening, would broach a prying question, the reply might be an enigmatic, 'Oh, I've been around the track a time or two,' or, 'That was back in the early days, so long ago I can't rightly remember, Dude, pardner,' or, if out of sorts, a crabbed, 'Now, did I say?'

However, Dude could be certain that his mentor was not a Southerner. No man was who called, with emphasis, the War Between the States the Great Rebellion, and had the annoying habit of whistling 'The Battle Hymn of the Republic.'

The three of them had been through a great deal together: easy times and hard times, when they couldn't match a race, and close times, when steady nerves were required to collect the bets and avoid a gunfight; contesting cagey horsemen from Texas to Missouri, Dude the genial front man, schooled by Uncle Billy at sizing up the other man's horse and how to rock back and forth on race conditions to get the advantage, Coyote whooping the Judge looking like Texas Jack across the finish line.

Now, Dude and Coyote walked over to the covered wagon, where Uncle Billy had the supper fire going and the coffee pot filled. After unsaddling and watering Blue Grass at the spring, Dude tied the gelding with the other horses and fed him oats in a nose bag. Sitting on the wash bench, Dude drew the day's winnings from his coat pockets, wads of crumpled greenbacks, and began counting. On second thought, he rose and took a sack of silver from his saddlebag and started over again.

'How'd we make out?' the old man asked as Dude finished.

'Three hundred even and we earned every cent. Includes the four-to-one money that poor plow chaser bet that his horse would have daylight on the Judge the first hundred yards. Almost hated to tale his money, his face was so honest.'

'Don't ever get softhearted in a horse race,' the old man cautioned, waggling a finger. 'Don't or you'll end up milking cows down on the Brazos.'

'Well, I'd like to see the day when we can match the Judge uoder his own true name and not have to masquerade 'im like some poor ol' packhorse.'

'There's an old saying that still holds true in horse racing as well. 'You have to dance to the tune that's played.' And didn't that simpleton sodbuster try to bribe Coyote?'

'I mean how nice it would be if we could match us a race without all this beatin' around the bush and me gettin' chased all over the couotry two jumps ahead of a hang-rope posse.'

'What you forget is that the Judge, after taking the slack out of everything in south Texas, is known clear up into Illinois.' Uncle Billy's voice had taken on an instructive, almost fatherly, tone. 'Back there where the boss quarter hosses come from. Like Dan Tucker, Peter McCue, Jack Traveler, Hi Henry, Harmon Baker, Hickory Bill and Carrie Nation. When the Judge ran the quarter mile in twenty-one and one-fifth seconds at Juarez and beat Yolanda, the great Mexican speed mare by a neck, he became a marked horse. Has been ever since. He broke most of Mexico that day. Word travels fast where speed horses are concerned. No wonder you can't match him under his true name. Therefore, you have to work the switch.'

'I know. I know.' Rising, Dude handed each partner his share.

'This will come in right handy for my sundown years — you bet,' the old man mused, tucking his away in a money belt around his skinny middle. Lesser winnings he kept in the medicine chest. 'One of these days I'll haul off and buy me that little hotel. Just rock on the front porch and watch folks go by. When the northers hit, I'll have my place by the f'ar.' He was in high humor now. Never keener than before a race, and never happier than after, when the Judge had won, a vindication of his training principles and Dude's matchmaking and Coyote's riding.

A wave of affection and concern for him swept over Dude. 'Why, you'd be bored stiff in a week an' off your feed,' he said. 'You'd get saddle sores from that rocker. You'd just dry up an' blow away.'

'Now, did I say when?' Uncle Billy retorted and looked across at Coyote. 'How'd the Judge do at the break?'

'Took it by one length, Grandfather.

Knew I did then he had it won, that horse.'

'That's line — but when am I ever gonna break you of calling me Grandfather?'

Grinning back at him through coffee-brown eyes, the Comanche went to the wagon to put his share in his parfleche bag, most of which would be mailed to his father the chief in Indian Territory. Coyote was bandy-legged from riding since childhood, and short of stature, yet deep-chested, and appeared awkward when afoot. On horseback he became an integral part of the horse, possessing a horseman's seat and balance and a horseman's capable hands. Furthermore, when mounted, he seemed to acquire the bearing of a warrior: head high, blue-black hair hanging to his shoulders, the eyes steadfast in the wide-boned face, the arch of the aquiline nose proud. In a tight race his primitive whooping, blood-curdling to the ear, seemed to make the Judge run even faster. Strange, Dude thought, how the three of them, each so different, got along and stood together. Come to think about it, maybe that was why they did.

While Dude and Coyote tidied up the camp after supper, Uncle Billy was busy at his medicine chest. Dude could see him holding up a measuring cup to the fading light, squinting, peering; now and then there came the clink of bottles and the rapid stirring of a spoon. Meanwhile, Dude built up the fire, for a cool wind was purring out of the southwest, its damp breath hinting of more rain. Sitting around the fire, Dude whittled while Coyote read from a worn copy of Tennyson's poems.

When the old man joined them, smelling like a drugstore, he said, 'Fixed up another potion for that light bay trade gelding in case he roars with the chronic heaves again. Better swap him off first chance we get. Don't understand how I ever got slickered on that deal.'

'Because,' Dude guyed him, 'you were too busy slickerin' the other fellow, though I figured he got the worst of it by far. That saddle mare will balk ever' time she comes to a steep hill, an' ever' time she comes to a little puddle of water or a creek, she'll want to roll an' waller in it, saddle an' rider an' all. With this heavy rain, I'd say that fellow wishes he had his heaves horse back.'

'Anyway,' the old man continued, smiling, 'I'll give the light bay another dose in the morning. Medicine's no good for man or beast if you don't take it regular.'

'Let's see,' Dude murmured, in mock concentration. 'Two ounces of Spanish brown. Three ounces of resin.' He faltered.

'Two ounces of gentian,' Coyote chimed in, looking up from his book. 'Two ounces of lobelia.' And then he paused.

'You'll never get it down right, neit_ her one of you hoot owls. You left out the eight ounces of Jamaica ginger.' Breathing sarcasm, Uncle Billy said, 'Suppose you can remember how much and how often to give it, the way I've schooled you both, over and over?'

In unison, they recited, serious of face, 'A tablespoonful three times a day . . . and while taking this medicine . . . the horse will show no sign of the heaves.'

'That's a shade better,' the old man said. 'But I believe there's a second remedy.' He folded his arms, waiting.

Dude and Coyote exchanged glances and together began, singsong, 'One ounce of saltpeter . . . one-half ounce of powdered ipecac . . . four pints of rain water . . . mix and give one pint a day.'

To which the old man prompted, 'Although not a permanent cure, is good to trade on,' and, taking a cane-bottomed chair, seated himself by the fire, soaking up the heat, eyes shuttered, at peace with himself and the world.

There followed a run of silence, broken only by the crackling fire and the stamping of the horses and the singing wind.

A feeling of contentment spread through Dude, cut short after an interval when he thought of tomorrow. He said, 'After today's fox chase, I figure we'd be wise to make a circle up into Cass

County. Believe we've worn out our welcome in these parts.'

The old man was still lost in his drowsing.

Coyote said, 'Cass County,' and shrugged. Where made no difference to him as long as he rode the Judge.

Uncle Billy sat up blinking, suddenly alert. 'Cass County, you say?'

'Why, yes,' Dude said. 'Let's make tracks up that way. That's one place we haven't been.'

Refusal began building across the trackless face. 'Understand they're right inhospitable to itinerant horsemen up there. Mighty straitlaced church folks. To them, horse racin' brings in the terrible evils of gamblin'and fitin', not to mention whiskey drinkin'.'

'You've been there?'

Dude wasn't prying,' merely asking, but in return got a snapped, 'Now, did I say? That's only what I've been told by other horsemen.'

Dude had to grin at him, back guarding his past again. 'Just where would you

21

suggest, Uncle?'

'Kansas.'

'Why, Kansas?'

'Grass is at its peak this time of year, and the Judge needs a rest. We've run him pretty hard. You can ride an iron horse down.'

'Missouri has good grass,' Dude said, feeling curious. 'Cass County would be like a bird nest on the ground for us, strangers comin' in with a fast, unknown horse.'

'Kansas is a much better choice in my judgment,' Uncle Billy emphasized, a firm insistence behind his voice. 'Don't worry. We'll match us some races.'

Did where they next ventured really matter, so long as prospects for fresh money were promising? To humor him, Dude spread his hands wide, obliging, and said, 'Kansas it is, Uncle,' yet thinking his old mentor's stand somewhat strange.

2

The Drivin' Horse

Dude had never laid eyes on more pleasing country: fields of wheat making golden waves in the distance, broad pastures rolling rich with bluestem grass, winding creeks, scattered timber, tidy farmhouses and fat smokehouses, hay stacked in portly red barns, windmills pumping stock water, well-kept fences. A land of plenty.

The outfit pulled up on the dusty road and considered the nearby oak grove and its pools of shade, cool and inviting under the hot afternoon sun. Down the road, within walking distance, stood a two-story farmhouse painted a glowing white, as prim-looking as a maiden lady school teacher.

'A good place to camp, but we'd better get permission this close to the house,' Dude said. Early in this touch-and-go game he had learned the benefits of

23

propriety. You avoided clashes over trespassing, and sometimes lucrative match races resulted.

'Ask if we can use that fenced pasture behind the trees,' Uncle Billy said. 'I see a gate.'

Riding ahead, Dude turned into a lane leading to the house. A part-shepherd dog ran out barking. He ignored the dog, dropped the reins on Blue Grass and went to the door and knocked politely. There was a brief delay and then the door opened and a girl, no more than about sixteen, he judged, smiled at him with interested inquiry.

'Good afternoon, Miss,' he said, removing his hat and bowing, displaying his rodeo arena smile. 'My little horse outfit is passing through and I wonder if we could camp in that oak grove up the road?'

Boy, was she pretty! Wide, smoky-brown eyes, auburn hair falling gently past her shoulders, her face full and smooth, tanned by the sun, and a smile that quickened Dude's pulse. Dimples, too. She was wearing a calico dress that sure fit in the right places. Dude thought, Bet her old man has to pour water on the steps to keep the neighbor boys from campin' there all night.

'A horse outfit?' she echoed in an impressed voice.

'We have one ol' runnin' horse that can stir the dust a little when the wind's behind him. Right now, he needs a rest. And we have just one trade horse left, a fine Missouri saddler. My name is Dude McQuinn,from down on the Brazos.'

The smoky eyes danced. 'I'm sure that will be all right, Mr. Brazos. But — '

'McQuinn. Dude McQuinn — from down on the Brazos River,' he said forgivingly. 'That's in Texas.'

'But I'd better ask Daddy,' she said. 'Excuse me. Please wait.'

She vanished into the cool and darkened interior of the house. Shortly, Dude picked up the indistinct murmur of voices, a dialogue that continued at length, longer than necessary, it seemed to him, for her to get a simple 'yes' or 'no.' The voices ceased after some time, a long time, Dude thought. Next he heard the tap-tap of a walking cane on hardwood flooring, and an elderly man limped out on the porch, followed by the girl.

'I'm Lum Mayhill,' he said, friendly enough, offering his hand while leaning on his knob-handled cane. He wore faded blue overalls with square patches on the knees.

'Dude McQuinn, sir.'

'This is my youngest daughter, Dolly. Got five girls. She's the only left at home.'

Dude bowed from the waist in open appreciation. 'Pleased to meet you, Miss Dolly, I'm sure.'

Lum Mayhill was a rather small man, on the verge of slightness, yet he imparted the impression of lean strength despite his years and reliance on the cane. One lock of stubborn white hair, which hung over his right eye, gave him a youthful look. His eyes, wide in a clean-shaven face, were of the same smoky-brown texture of his fetching daughter, and his

26

handshake was as firm and cordial as his voice.

He said, 'Dolly tells me your horse outfit would like to camp in the oak grove off the east road?'

'Yes, sir. We'd appreciate that. As I told Miss Dolly, we're traveling through, on our way back to Texas.'

'You carry a running horse?'

'Happens we do, sir. An ol' quarter horse called Texas Jack.' You never carried a young quarter horse. Yours was always old with the telling, on the chance that might encourage race talk.

Instead, Mayhill said, 'And you trade horses, Dolly says?'

'Yes, sir, though right now we're down to just one. A smooth saddler we traded for back in Missouri. Our last bunch of trade stock, which included some draft horses as well, went fast. Dr. Lockhart is a great judge of racehorses, saddlers, trotters or what have you.'

'Dr. Lockhart?'

'A well-known horseman back in Kentucky and New York, sir. He's traveling with me for his health. Has the catarrh and arthritis. I'm pleased to say that living in the open has done wonders for him. He's feeling much better of late.'

Mayhill cleared his throat, adding, 'I can sympathize with the doctor,' and gestured toward a straight-backed wicker chair. 'Make yourself comfortable, Mr. McQuinn.' He turned to Miss Dolly. 'Daughter, fetch us something cool from the cellar. Mr. McQuinn must be thirsty.' When Dude was seated, his host settled in a rocker and sighed, 'Just not the man I used to be. Now the only problem with the grove is water. You'd have to water your horses at our windmill.'

'Be fine with us, sir, and we'd like to buy some oats and hay, if you have any for sale?'

'That we have in abundance, Mr. McQuinn. Whatever you need. Our prairie hay is the finest you can find in this section of the state.'

'Mighty fine, sir. May we also use the little pasture behind the oak grove? I noticed it is empty.'

'Indeed you may, Mr. McQuinn. Turn all your horses out there. The fencing is tight, so you need have no fear of a breakout.'

Dude thanked him and thought, My, how obliging the old gent is and how proper we both are. Me with my 'sirs,' and him with his 'Mr. McQuinns.' He said, 'We'd like to stay a few days, if that's all right? Need to rest our runnin' horse before we go on. We campaigned him pretty hard in Missouri.'

'You are welcome to stay as long as you like, Mr. McQuinn. And how did your racehorse fare?'

Ah, Dude thought, he's got a runnin' horse stuck back in that big red barn somewhere, and he'll match us if he thinks he can get the advantage. 'Well, sir,' said Dude, looking down, 'best I can say is that he won some an' he lost some. Had his good days an' bad days. Sometimes he's just fast enough to lose money. As tard as he is right now, I wouldn't match him against a milk cow.'

That drew a half-smile from Mayhill,

but nothing further about racehorses, and Dude wondered whether he had laid on the buildup too much and scared him off.

Just then, Miss Dolly brought pitcher and glasses on a tray and poured what looked like apple cider and handed Dude a glass. As she started to pass her father his, a look of concern clouded her pretty face. 'Daddy, did you take your medicine when you got up from your nap? You're so forgetful.'

Lum Mayhill scratched his head. 'Let's see, did I?' Finally, he said, 'Yes, I did. I remember now.'

'That's better,' she said firmly. 'You know what the doctor said.'

'What we need around here is more good horse doctors,' her father grumbled and raised his glass. 'Here's to your racehorse, Mr. McQuinn. May he bring home the bacon.'

Murmuring his thanks, Dude raised his glass and sipped. It was apple cider, sweet and cool. Again, he waited for his host to make the first approach leading up to a match race, and again nothing happened as they sipped in silence.

It was Miss Dolly who spoke first, looking up at Dude with that sidelong way she had as she took a chair between him and her father. 'I'd like to see your saddler, Mr. Brazos — I mean Mr. McQuinn. I just love a good gaited horse. The last one we had on the farm, Buster Boy, lived to be twenty-five years old.'

'You just come right over, Miss Dolly. I'll give you a firsthand look.'

'May I come over this evening'?'

'You bet. Anytime.'

'This Dr. Lockhart,' her father asked, 'is he a veterinarian?'

'That he is, sir. Dr. Lockhart is the resident veterinarian of the Cedar Crest Farm of Kentucky, now on leave for his health, like I told you.' Dude could not recall having seen a diploma confirming Uncle Billy's qualifications, nor had he heard him make such claims as a graduate of a school of veterinary medicine. His past was a guarded blank, always.

Whatever, an ounce of performance beat a pound of diplomas. The old man had a remarkable gift, self-taught or not. He was constantly mixing new potions and reading large, scholarly looking books which he kept in his medicine chest, books that Dude and Coyote had yet to see close up, books that Uncle Billy called 'tomes.' As for the title of doctor, Dude could blame himself for tacking that on while acting as front man and match-maker for the little outfit, though the old man didn't seem to mind, and certainly he looked like a doctor. The results spoke for themselves. As for the fictitious Cedar Crest Farm, Dude had used that before; it sounded impressive and Uncle Billy had not protested and who would ques-tion a nonexistent horse farm?

'Well, then,' Mayhill was saying, 'do you reckon he would look at one of my horses?'

Seeing the opening at last, Dude replied, 'One of your runnin' horses, sir? You bet he would.'

Again that slow half-smile as Mayhill

said, 'One of my workhorses.'

'Makes no difference. Dr. Lockhart will be glad to look him over and mix up something. He carries his medicine supplies with him.'

'It's Old Ned,' Mayhill told his attentive daughter. 'He's off his feed. I didn't tell you, knowing he is one of your favorites. Meanwhile, Mr. McQuinn, I'll be looking forward to making the good doctor's acquaintance. And call me Lum. Everybody calls me Lum.'

'And I'm Dude.'

With that, Dude took his leave, saying he would bring the horses back for water, and reminding Miss Dolly to be sure to come over that evening.

'Took you long enough,' Uncle Billy fretted. 'Did you stay for an early supper?'

'Now, Uncle, you know these things take time. We have permission to camp here and use the pasture and we can water the horses at the windmill. Is that trade horse still roarin' with the heaves?'

'Just now and then. Don't recall that

I promised a permanent cure. I'll doctor him again in the morning.'

'Better do it now. That farmer's daughter is in the market for a good saddler. She'll be over this evening for a look-see.'

Nodding, the old man went to the wagon and soon Dude could hear him mixing.

Not much time had passed when a wagon came creaking along the road from the Mayhill farm, piled high with baled hay and sacked feed. The driver, a husky, jovial-faced man whose long black hair hung below his straw hat, stopped and got down, nodded genially all around, and said, 'Mr. Lum sent over some feed.'

'That's fine,' said Dude, surprised, and relieved that the trade horse had stopped roaring. 'But about how much is Mr. Mayhill gonna charge us for all this? That's quite a load you got there.'

'Not one cent. Just Mr. Lum's way of bein' neighborly. I'm Homer, the hired man.' He shook hands with everybody, pumping so hard that Dude's knuckles cracked.

Dude and Coyote pitched in to help, and when all the feed was unloaded and stacked, Homer took a hitch at his overalls and said, 'Miss Dolly tells me you got a saddler you might want to trade for?'

'Might,' said Dude, cautious. 'Which horse is it?'

'That light bay tied to the wagon.'

Homer strolled over there and eyed the gelding back and forth, up and down. Of a sudden he moved closer and opened the bay's mouth, curled his lips back and inspected his teeth.

'About how old is he?' Homer asked, stepping bade.

'Six years and approximately four months,' Uncle Billy replied distinctly, not about to get caught.

'Just wondered. Miss Dolly kinda likes my opinion about stock.' He kept pushing at his long hair.

'A horse,' Uncle Billy took over, and Dude sensed a coming lecture, 'has forty teeth — twenty-four grinders, twelve front teeth and four tusks, whereas a mare has thirty-six, the same number of grinders and front teeth, sometimes tusks, but not often. The teeth grow in length as the horse advances in years. At the same time his teeth are worn away by use about one twelfth of an inch every year. Therefore, you will note that the cups are worn from the saddler's two middle teeth — in other words, that the black cavities of the center nippers have disappeared — and the cups are shaded in the next tooth on both sides of the middle teeth.'

'Uh . . . huh, I see,' said Homer, buffaloed. 'Well, he looks right nice. I'll tell Miss Dolly.'

'And thank Mr. Lum for the feed,' Dude said. 'He sure is neighborly.'

'A little more than neighborly,' Uncle Billy observed suspiciously as the hired man drove away. 'A bale or two of hay and a sack or so of feed — that's neighborly. But this is enough to start a feed store.'

'Grandfather Billy, wise he is like Owl

Person,' Coyote joined in. 'Once Utes brought gifts of blankets to Comanche war party. Next morning Comanche horses all gone. Much face those warriors lost walking back many days to our tribe. Even white man's medicine book warns, 'A gift doth blind the eyes of the wise.' Remember, white father?'

'Not exactly,' Dude hedged. 'You two beat all. Lum only wants to share some of his plenty.'

As the afternoon lengthened into the first dimness of evening, Dude caught sight of Miss Dolly approaching. She carried a basket and a pail. He strode out to meet her.

'Daddy thought you would like some fresh eggs and milk,' she said. 'Nothing we'd like better, Miss Dolly,' he assured her, relieving her of the milk pail, and escorted her into camp and made the introductions. 'Dr. William Tecumseh Lockhart and Mr. Coyote Walking, our jockey, who is the son of the chief of all the Comanches.'

Miss Dolly curtsied and shook hands

with both, smiling all the while. She had changed into another calico dress and brushed her long hair. A bouncy, fetching girl, growing prettier by the day. A walking picture, Dude thought.

Uncle Billy was likewise visibly impressed. He and Coyote both bowed.

'Daddy would have come,' she said, 'but he's poorly this evening.'

'I regret to hear that, young lady,' the old man said.

'I'm so pleased to meet you, Dr. Lockhart,' she exclaimed. 'Mr. Brazos tells us you are from Kentucky and New York?'

'Brazos?'

'I mean Dude — Mr. McQuinn, who's from down on the Brazos. He told us all about you.'

'Sometimes these Alamo Texans, coming from that windy section of the country, think they're back in Texas and tend to stretch the blanket.'

'I hope your catarrh is much better this evening, Dr. Lockhart.'

'My catarrh?' An oblique glare in Dude's direction, then, 'Why, much better, thank you.'

Turning to Coyote, she exclaimed further, 'And you are a Co manche. A real Indian. I suppose you speak some English?'

'I speak it fairly well,' Coyote said, sober of countenance. 'I also read fairly well. My favorite author is the Bard of Avon, and I have a fondness for Tennyson.'

'Pardon me, Mr. Coyote!' she apologized, flustered and awed.

'Not necessary, Miss Dolly. And the name is Coyote Walking. My father the chief gave me that name the morning of my birth, in the Wichita Mountains of Indian Territory, when he looked out the door of our lodge and observed a coyote walking by.'

'Oh, I see.'

'We Comanches, who are very brave, regard the coyote as a brother who often warns us of impending trouble, also if good times are ahead. Coyote power or medicine is for knowing things in the future. You savvy, Miss Dolly?'

'I . . . I believe I do, and I like your name very much. It is so . . . unusual.'

'Thank you, Miss Dolly. Saying that, you also honor my father the chief.'

Dude, deciding it was time to rescue Miss Dolly, said, 'Would you like to see our saddler? He's right over there.'

She drew a long breath. 'You bet I would.'

She went wide-eyed at first glance, and kept nodding while she walked around the light bay. 'What's his name?' she asked.

'Rambler,' Dude replied, thinking fast, because the gelding was nameless. 'He comes straight down the ladder from good Missouri saddle stock on both sides. In fact, from Audrain County. No doubt you've heard of Audrain County saddlers?'

'You bet I have.'

Seeing that she was swallowing everything he said, he began to feel the first stir of a disquieting guilt. He wouldn't mind spieling at a man, but a mere girl, so innocent and trusting? He could feel himself backing off.

But when she asked, 'I suppose you have his papers?' he could only reply, 'It was a fast trade, Miss Dolly. The trader liked our smooth saddle mare, which he wanted to take to the court of a friend's fancy saddle sire, and we liked Rambler. We'd tried him out. He's a fox-trottin', head-noddin' road dog. The trader didn't have Rambler's papers with him, but promised to send them to me down on the Brazos.'

'I see.' She sounded disappointed, but convinced.

'You can't always get papers. Papers aren't important unless you're raising saddlers to sell.'

'May I try him out now?'

Dude hadn't expected that request so soon and his conscience suggested that, in all fairness, he discourage her and put her off. 'Afraid I don't have a sidesaddle,' he told her.

'I can ride a stock saddle.' He saddled the gelding.

She mounted before he could give her

a hand up, as agile as any boy, her long skirt covering all but her pretty ankle as she hooked her right leg around the saddle horn, à la sidesaddle, and reined the light bay toward the road. There he struck away into the shuffling fox-trot, the hind foot hitting the ground a trifle before the diagonally opposite forefoot, his head nodding in time to the easy movement. She rode to the house, reined him through a figure eight and fox-trotted him back, her oval face Hushed and pleased when she rode up to the wagon.

'It's like sitting in a rocking chair,' she bubbled. 'He changed leads nicely too. How much do you want for him?'

'I'd have to ponder on that a little,' Dude said, hoping to dampen her enthusiasm for a saddler with the chronic heaves. 'Also, you'll have to remember that Rambler's no cow horse. He's just a gettin' down-the-road horse. He'll stumble when you ride him across a pasture. If you noticed, he doesn't lift his feet high.'

'Neither did Buster Boy. I could just

ride him to town.'

'That's up to you, Miss Dolly.' Dude's tone was dissuasive.

'Well,' she said, 'I like Rambler a lot and I'll see what Daddy says.' After Miss Dolly had gone, Uncle Billy, his voice heavy with sarcasm, said, 'That was some show you put on, *Mr. Brazos.* You did your best to talk her out of buying the saddler.'

'Just tryin' to he honest was all.'

'Well, remember this: All's fair in love and war and horse racin' and horse tradin'.'

★ ★ ★

Next morning, while Dude and Uncle Billy cleaned up around the wagon after breakfast, Coyote, who was standing near the road, called sharply, 'Comes big horse! Like this horse you will, Grandfather. Look!'

Dude turned to see.

From the direction of the farmhouse stepped a blue roan pulling an open-top

43

buggy. Head reined high, the horse moved at a powerful rate on a straight and true course. As horse and buggy swept by, the driver nodded briefly, eyes fixed ahead, mouth set in concentration, both hands tight on the reins.

'That's Lum Mayhill,' Dude said.

'He's behind a sure-enough drivin' horse. Shows breeding and speed.'

'Surprised he'd drive a horse like that, as old as Mr. Mayhill is.'

'It's not the years that make a man old,' Uncle Billy snorted. 'It's his attitude.'

'He walks with a cane and takes medicine.'

'Cane or not, that old man's a horseman. And I'd like a close look-see at that blue roan.'

They watched the buggy speed out of sight behind a distant rise. Dude was busying himself around camp a little later when Coyote called, 'Comes big horse again!'

Indeed he was, Dude saw, hurrying out to the road. Coming at the same ground-eating pace.

'Like an arrow from a bow,' Uncle Billy sang out. 'Boys, that horse has been on the track. My, how he can move!'

Slowing down, Lum Mayhill pulled on the reins and stopped, nodding neighborly as the outfit came out.

The big horse, a gelding, stood at perfect ease, head nodding, breathing evenly, his heavily muscled body glistening with sweat. He wore blinkers and shiny black harness.

'This is some harness horse you are driving, sir,' Dude said.

'Amos is feeling his oats a mite more than usual this morning,' Mayhill said. 'He didn't hanker to reining in and turning around. Wanted to keep on going over hill and dale. Sometimes he's almost too much for me.'

'Mr. Mayhill,' Dude said, 'we want to thank you for all the feed, and I want you to meet Dr. Lockhart and Coyote Walking, our Comanche jockey.'

'It's Lum, remember? You are more than welcome. Folks are neighborly around here.'

After the handshaking, Uncle Billy said, 'Your harness horse is the finest specimen of the Standardbred I've ever seen, Mr. Mayhill. May I look at him?'

'Go right ahead, Doctor. Amos is a kind horse, though spirited, but by now I've taken some of the morning spark out of him.'

Murmuring to the horse, Uncle Billy stroked his sleek neck and shoulder, inspected him from both sides, eyed his feet, stood back and rubbed the horse's nose and looked into his face and said, nodding, 'He looks as good up close as he does from a distance. There's a lively sparkle to his eyes, and the eyes are the inner mirror of a horse's health and disposition. A balanced horse. His legs are straight and sound. He is long in the shoulder. Powerful in the forequarters, with remarkable muscular development in the gaskin and stifle areas.' Uncle Billy stood farther back, cocked an eye and said, 'I would say he stands sixteen hands.'

'Sixteen, two,' Mayhill said.

'Right at fourteen hundred pounds.'

Mayhill smiled. 'Fourteen, thirty-five. You have a keen eye, Doctor. He's bigger than he looks.'

'I would be interested in knowing his breeding, Mr. Mayhill.'

'It's Lum. Everybody calls me Lum. Amos is by the trotting champion Nelson, known as the Northern King, and his dam is Hulda, who goes back to the mother of trotters, the famous Flora Temple, who coursed a mile in 2:19.'

'Aw, yes,' Uncle Billy followed him, knowing. 'Then surely he has been on the track?'

'Was — in Illinois and Missouri. I wanted him the first time I saw him on the track at Sedalia. Guess my eyes got mighty big that day. Reckon you know how that is, Doctor?'

'A man's eyes always get big when he sees a truly fine horse like this one.'

'Amos was a little past his prime, else the owner, who is an old friend of mine, wouldn't have let him go. Even then, my friend took hide and hair in the deal. Amos is now nine years old, and although he's lost some of the edge off his go, he sometimes makes me think he's more horse than an old man needs.'

'You had him under tight control all the time. I could see that.'

'But it is tiring for me at my age.'

'A man's no older than he thinks he is.'

'That's the problem, Doctor.'

They both guffawed, and then Lum Mayhill, wincing as he shifted on the buggy seat, said, 'Dude told me about you and I would like to ask a favor of you, Doctor.'

'Shoot,' Uncle Billy obliged.

'Could you take the time to look at one of my old workhorses, which I believe has the thumps. I haven't been able to relieve him at all, and there's not one reliable vet in the whole county.'

'I am at your service, friend Lum. Say when.'

'Say two o'clock this afternoon?'

'I'll be there.'

'My hired man, Homer, will have Old

Ned out in the corral.' Mayhill tightened the reins; still, Amos did not move, which caught Uncle Billy's instant approval. 'I've never seen a drivin' horse stand any quieter while awaiting his driver's command. He is beautifully trained.'

'He was not this obedient when I first got him. Spirited as he is, accustomed to the excitement of the track . . . other high-strung horses and the noisy crowds . . . it has taken time and patience to train him down to an old man's slower tempo.' Sighing, he took a thick, silver-plated watch from the breast of his overalls, opened the case, glanced therein, and said, 'The ache in this demned old leg o' mine tells me it's time to get back to the house and take my medicine, else Miss Dolly will be after me again.'

He snapped the reins, chirruping, 'Giddup,' and Amos moved off at once.

'You know, Dude, pardner,' Uncle Billy mused, watching, 'it does occur to me how much more comfortable a buggy seat is behind a good drivin' horse than bumping along in this wagon of ours.'

49

At two o'clock Dude and Uncle Billy
walked down to the corral by the big red
ham where the hired man had a stout
gray workhorse tied on halter.

'Mr. Lum will be out in a little bit,'
Homer said. 'He's just gettin' up from
his nap. Has to have his rest and medicine reg'lar at his age.'

'Meanwhile, I'll take a look at the
patient here,' Uncle Billy said. He folded
his arms and studied the horse for a
while. Then, nodding to himself, slowly,
step by step, he circled the animal, which
stood with head hanging. He then placed
a hand against the throbbing flank and
held it there half a minute. Next, he
stepped to the head of the animal, listening to its breathing; next, he felt under
the lower jaw for the pulse, found it, and
drew his watch to check by.

'Here comes Mr. Lum now,' Homer
said.

Leaning on his cane, Lum Mayhill
limped from the house to the corral,

struggled some moments with the gate's heavy wooden bar and eased in. 'Well, Doctor,' he said, 'have you found out what's wrong with Old Ned?'

'Your diagnosis was correct, friend Lum,' Uncle Billy said, putting away his watch. 'Old Ned has the thumps, characterized by violent beating or throbbing in the Ranks. It is properly a palpitation of the heart. Now, the rate of pulse in a mature, healthy horse while resting is from thirty-six to forty-eight times per minute, and any variation from that number indicates excitement, disease or suffering of some sort. Old Ned, I'm sorry to report, has a pulse of seventy-four.'

Mayhill looked woebegone. 'What can I do?'

'How is his appetite?'

'Poorly.'

'Well, then, put half a pint of raw linseed in his feed. Linseed acts as a digester. An excellent food to open the pores, hence a good spring tonic.'

'Remember that, Homer,' Mayhill said.

Uncle Billy continued, 'Give Old Ned plenty of salt and rest. If he doesn't come around, give the following prescription three times a day. No, in his case, four times.'

'Hold on,' Mayhill said. 'I want to take this down.' He took a small memorandum book from his overalls, fumbled for a pencil stub, found it, and said, 'Go ahead.'

'Spirits of camphor, one ounce,' Uncle Billy began. 'Muriate of ammonia, ten grains . . . sweet spirits of niter, one ounce . . . water, one pint . . . mix and give as a drench. That should put Old Ned back in harness.'

'Would you say it's a permanent cure, Doctor?' Mayhill drawled, grinning like a tomcat.

Uncle Billy did a great deadpan, harrumphed and said, 'I'll lay it out like this, friend Lum. It's always good to trade on.' And they both guffawed, knowing smiles wreathing their sly faces.

Two of a kind, Dude thought. Two cagey old codgers, one as slick as the other. A perception that carried its subtle caution, if they came to a trade or match race, though by now Dude had decided Mayhill had no racehorse.

'Homer,' Mayhill ordered, 'stall Old Ned and bring Amos out. While the Doctor is here, I'd like for him to look at Amos's right foreleg, which he got nicked this morning when the buggy threw up a rock.' His tone was apologetic when he said, 'Hope you can spare the time, Doctor. I want you to add this to your fee.'

'Fee? I should say not, after that feed store you had Homer deliver. Let me see that big boss.'

Homer took Old Ned away and led out Amos, whose large, dark-colored eyes, set wide apart and well to the outside of his head, sparkled like pools in the afternoon light. He stood like a champion, a sculpture of smooth muscle and speed.

One look and Uncle Billy jerked around to Mayhill. 'He's still got blinkers on. He's no bad actor, no nervous horse. Why?'

'I figured you would ask that,' Mayhill

chuckled. 'It's like this. When Amos was first on the track, he acquired the bad habit of trotting with his head cocked, curious about his surroundings. He watched everything, even when a bird flew by. He lost every race. So the trainer put blinkers on him — that cured him. He started winning right away. I've continued the blinkers to this day because he's used to 'em and seems to like 'em. Guess you observed how straight down the road he travels? All business? Eager to get somewhere?'

'I did.'

'So why change a piece of equipment that makes for a better performing horse?'

'If it works, it works,' Uncle Billy shrugged and bent down to pick up the right foreleg. After peering intently and feeling around the nick, he said, 'It's just a scratch. There's no soreness along the cannon bone. Wash it thoroughly with warm, soapy water, then apply a mixture of equal parts glycerine and water and add a few drops of carbolic acid. Morning and evening should be enough.' He let the leg down gently and stood off to admire the trotter. 'You have a fine animal here, friend Lum. A blue roan's base color is black. It's the intermingling of white hair that gives the handsome blue appearance. All roan horses — including the red roans and the rose grays — have solid-colored heads and the legs are likewise from the knee joints and hock joints to the hoof. Manes and tails correspond to the same color.' He left off to let his appreciation deepen. 'Look at the way Amos stands, barely moving a muscle, in complete control of himself. As well-mannered as a country schoolgirl at her first pie supper. You could drink a cup of coffee on him and never spill a drop. I like the way he stands there gazing off, eyes sparkling, head high. You'd think he owns the whole farm. A truly noble horse.'

Except for Judge Blair, Dude had not heard Uncle Billy heap such eloquent admiration on a horse. Amos was exceptional and Dude's old mentor was impressed.

'That saddler you call Rambler is another fine horse,' Mayhill said, pleased. 'Miss Dolly keeps telling me how easy riding he is. She's wanted another fox-trotter ever since Buster Boy died. However, this is no time to talk about a trade. Not the way this demn leg is acting up again. Well, I am much obliged to you, Doctor, for seeing about my horses. Good afternoon.'

Wincing, Lum Mayhill made his slow way to the corral gate. Leaning with one hand on the cane, he pushed at the gate's bar with the other.

Seeing that, Homer dropped Amos's halter rope and hurried over to help. Whereupon, Mayhill growled, 'I'm still man enough to open my own gate. Stand back!' He forced the bar clear, swung the gate open, limped through, closed the gate, rammed the bar home and limped on to the house.

'That bum leg sure makes Mr. Lum crotchety,' Homer muttered, hurt.

Uncle Billy was uncommonly thoughtful on the way back. He did not speak until they neared the camp. 'I keep thinking that maybe Lum might swap or trade that Amos horse,' he said. 'What do you think?'

'He'd want some boot,' Dude said. 'A fine trotter like that. Are you serious?'

'Oh, it just now crossed my mind, is all,' Uncle Billy said airily.

'Just now? It's been on your mind ever since this morning. Uncle, you want that drivin' horse.'

★　★　★

The old man had the supper fire going when Miss Dolly brought two loaves of bread, still warm from the oven.

'Young lady,' he said, beaming, 'you are an angel on earth. I haven't smelled such bread since I was a boy. I was just getting ready to mix up a batch of sourdough biscuits, of which my two friends have been complaining of late, though they'd rather kick about mine than stir up something they claim is better.'

She curtsied her thanks and asked,

'How is your catarrh this evening, Doctor'?'

'Much improved, thank you. And how is friend Lum?'

Her fresh young face darkened. 'He's down in the back from handling Amos on that long drive and his leg pains him.'

'I am sorry to hear that.'

'Sometimes I wish he'd trade Amos off,' she burst out, gazing down at her hands.

'Amos strikes me as an exceptionally well-behaved horse.'

'When not in harness he is. It's all Daddy can do to hold him when they start down the road. Then Amos thinks he's back on the track again. You've noticed how fast he goes. Why, he fairly flies!'

'Yes, he can move. He's a powerful horse, but your father handles him quite well.'

'But what if something frightened Amos and he ran away? What if a rabbit jumped up in front of him or some quail flew up beside the road? Daddy couldn't hold him, I know.'

'Amos is no skittish colt, spooking at every new thing he sees. He impresses me as remarkably cool-headed.'

'I wish I felt that way, Dr. Lockhart.' Her voice trailed off.

All at once she was brushing at her eyes and looking down, and as suddenly the whole outfit crowded around to comfort her. Uncle Billy put an arm around her and patted her shoulder. 'There, there, Miss Dolly. Don't worry. Your father is a natural-born horseman.'

'Grandfather Billy, wise he is like Owl Person,' Coyote assured her, awkwardly shifting his feet.

'Have no fear, Miss Dolly,' said Dude, just as awkward.

'Excuse me for going on like this,' she said, gazing up at them through misty eyes. 'But it's worried me from the time Daddy bought Amos two years ago. You see, I really want Rambler for Daddy's sake, so he'll have a gentle saddler to ride. I want him to sell Amos.' She brushed at her big eyes again, favoring the outfit an apologetic smile, and when Miss Dolly smiled her dimples showed to appealing effect.

'We understand,' Uncle Billy said. 'But don't worry.'

'I'd better get back to make sure that Daddy takes his medicine,' she said. 'Thank you, Doctor. And you, Mr. Coyote Walking. And you, Mr. Brazos — I mean Mr. McQuinn.'

'We thank you for the bread, Miss Dolly,' Dude said gallantly, 'and you may call me anything you wish.'

They watched protectively after her, until she turned in at the lane. There she looked back and waved, and they waved, watching until she entered the house.

'Did you ever see a sweeter little country girl?' Uncle Billy said, touched.

At that moment a peculiar roaring and heaving sounded from behind the wagon. Uncle Billy spun around. 'Thunderation! That trade horse! I forgot to doctor him this afternoon!' He sprang into action with his words.

3

A Trade's a Trade

Lum Mayhill did not drive past the camp the following morning, an absence that caused Dude to remark, 'I guess friend Lum is still under the weather. Miss Dolly may be right. That big horse is more than he can handle, the way he's ailing.'

Uncle Billy had no comment. He seemed reflective and as usual when he had something on his mind, he went to his medicine chest and started mixing and perusing the books that he had yet to allow his partners to see, as if the tomes contained occult mixtures that he guarded as carefully as his past.

'Maybe we should get on down the road today,' Dude said, a restlessness to his voice. 'I'd like to reach Texas by fall. We still haven't traded off Rambler. Lum has no racehorse to match, and the Judge is beginnin' to look rested.'

'He's picking up a little flesh, but needs more,' the old man said, peering hard at his measuring cup, held high against the light. 'Give him a few more days here.'

'I'll tell you one thing,' Dude said, watching Uncle Billy squint while he moved the cup back and forth, 'first town of any size we come to I aim to buy you some glasses.'

'When I don't need 'em?'

'Bet you're just guessin' at that potion.'

There was a cackling 'heee — heee.'

'How can you measure without glasses?' Dude went on.

'Practice, practice, practice.'

Upon which the loyal Coyote, speaking solemnly, slowly, interposed, 'Grandfather Billy, wise he is — '

'Like the Owl Person,' Dude said and threw up his hands in surrender.

That afternoon, while Dude and Coyote were watering the horses at the windmill behind the house, Miss Dolly came to the kitchen door and smiled and spoke to them.

'How's your father?' Dude asked.

'Still down in his back. But he won't give up. Insists on taking Amos out in the morning — and he will!'

'I'd say that's a sign of recovery.'

'You don't know my Daddy. Older he gets, the more stubborn he is,'

'I know another old gent who's the same way.'

Since she didn't mention Rambler and how nicely he rode, Dude guessed the deal was off. Well, he wasn't about to push off a chronic heaver on a sweet little country girl like her, unless, of course, she just had to have the horse!

★ ★ ★

The outfit set an early watch next morning for horse and buggy.

But not until ten o'clock past, true to Miss Dolly's prediction, did Lum Mayhill head the fast-striding Amos out of the lane and along the road toward the camp. Upright, face stubbornly set, hands held high as he gripped the taut reins, Mayhill drove past with a brief nod.

Uncle Billy could have been a track steward observing every step of the big blue roan. 'If Amos has lost his edge like friend Lum says,' the old man marveled, 'think what he was in his prime. There goes a hoss!'

The three continued to watch as the buggy grew rapidly smaller and smaller, shrank to a mere dark wedge, and vanished over the distant rise.

They were still watching minutes later when the big horse bobbed over the rise, moving like a dark storm, much faster than his usual gait, as he took the buggy down the slope and reached the flat.

'Look at that stride!' Uncle Billy flung out. 'Lum ought to match that horse!'

'He's too fast to match around here,' Dude said.

In a very short time, horse and buggy burst into close view. Amos was striding flat-out at top speed, Dude saw, and instead of holding the reins high, Mayhill was now tugging on the lines, struggling to slow Amos down. Was the big horse running away, out of control?

Just as Dude feared that, he saw Mayhill take his horse in hand and draw him down, little by little, the mark of a true horseman. By the time they drew near the camp, Mayhill had tight command. Instead of driving on by, however, he pulled up and stopped. He was puffing hard. Strain laid a stain across his face. He lay back against the cushions several moments, too spent to speak. Reviving, he looped the reins around the whip socket and, wincing, rubbing his leg and back, he eased himself out and down.

'Doctor,' he said, shaking his head, 'I've just come to a very reluctant decision. Miss Dolly is right. Amos is too much horse for this old farmer, who's used to plow horses. He almost got away from me back there as he came down the rise. All I could do to hold 'im.' He tucked in his lips and sighed. 'I might listen to a trade for that saddler you call Rambler. Not only for Miss Dolly, for myself as well. She says it's time to switch to a gentle saddler.'

Uncle Billy eyed him.

Mayhill cocked his head, his eyes as keen as any traveling horse trader's. 'I might — that is — if you're of a generous frame of mind this morning'?'

'I'm always generous, friend Lum,' Uncle Billy said, as obliging as could be. 'What say we trade even, horse for horse?'

Mayhill's face changed. 'I said a trade, not a giveaway.'

'Like what, good neighbor?'

'Some boot. Something fair. You know Amos is fast enough to go back on the track. You could campaign him with your running horse. Or am I on the wrong slant? Maybe Rambler is Dude's horse?'

'He's Dr. Lockhart's,' Dude covered up, deciding he would stay out of this. 'He traded for Rambler. The runnin' horse is mine.'

'All right, then. But I won't trade without some boot. That's only fair for an outstanding trotter.'

'How much is fair?' Uncle Billy parried, genially, shrewdly.

'No piddling amount.'

66

'I might, just might,' Uncle Billy said, looking generous, 'give you twenty-five dollars to boot.'

Lum Mayhill tossed his head, a gesture of indignant refusal. 'You're not even close, Doctor. A hundred would be more like it.'

'A hundred? I'm no trottin' horse man,' Uncle Billy snorted, and walked away from him, whistling 'The Battle Hymn of the Republic.'

'I might shave that a little, Doctor.'

Uncle Billy drifted back, his face smoothing. 'What do you call a little, friend Lum?'

'Down to ninety.'

'You're way over me.'

'Tell you what I'll do, Doctor, to be fair. I'll take seventy-five dollars. No less.'

'Twenty-five,' Uncle Billy held. 'Seventy-five!' Mayhill shouted. 'Twenty-five!' Uncle Billy shouted.

'Now, gentlemen,' Dude broke in. 'Let's be reasonable.'

'I will not go one cent below seventy-five,' Mayhill said, folding his arms.

'And I will not go one whit higher than twenty-five,' Uncle Billy declared, jaws set.

Dude, knowing a stalemate when he saw one, said, 'You both have good horses. Why not split the difference between twenty-five and seventy-five? That way one comes down and one comes up,which breaks off at fifty dollars.'

Neither antagonist spoke.

Mayhill fidgeted for the first time, as if uncertain. He took a plug of tobacco from his overalls, rummaged for his knife, cut off a wedge and conveyed it to his mouth off the blade, and wallowed the piece around in his mouth until settling it in his jaw as if it were hard candy. After a moment or so he spat deliberately, neatly, struck an imposed-upon stance and said, 'Here I am asked to trade off the finest trotter in this part of Kansas for a Missouri saddler of vague breeding — all for fifty dollars.'

'Vague?'Uncle Billy shot back. 'Do you have the registration papers on Amos?'

'Well . . . no. But you know what he can do. Do you have the papers on Rambler?'

'Well . . . no. But Miss Dolly has tried him out.' They broke into simultaneous-guffaws.

Two of a kind! Dude grinned at them.

'Fifty dollars is agreeable with me, friend Lum,' Uncle Billy said, rather fast, which told Dude the old man would give more if Mayhill held out, for Uncle dearly coveted the big horse.

'It's a deal,' Mayhill said, equally fast, and held out his hand. They shook.

'And you'll throw in the blinkers, friend Lum?' Uncle Billy coaxed, giving him a sly look.

Mayhill smiled his half-smile. 'The blinkers too. You'll need them if you put him on the track. As a matter of fact, I would keep the blinkers on all the time, since he is used to such. They tend to keep him calm, Amos being a spirited horse.'

'Let's have a little toddy on that, then I'll get your money,' Uncle Billy said, nodding toward the wagon.

They drank from the jug and strolled back, chatting like two neighboring farmers. Mayhill was saying, 'I'll have Homer groom Amos and bring him over right away.'

'Fine. We'll tie Rambler to the buggy and you can take him home now.'

Once a trade was agreed on, the sooner one carried it out the better. So without delay, Dude led Rambler forth and tied him behind the buggy.

That done, Mayhill limped to the buggy. An abrupt thought seemed to occur to him, and he turned and said, 'You have a line trotter and no buggy, Doctor. I'll sell you this one, since I won't be needing it anymore.'

'Hadn't come to that, friend Lum.'

'I bought it when I got Amos two years ago. It's in good condition. I'll sell it cheap.'

'What do you want for it?'

'Seventy-five dollars.'

'You are stuck on that high figure, it seems. I won't deal.'

'Seventy?'

'Think not.'

'Sixty-five?'

Uncle Billy stood his ground in silence.

Mayhill's face reddened. 'Then fifty, demn it, and I'll throw in the harness to boot. I'm too tired to haggle with you.'

He did look somewhat worn out, Dude thought, leaning there on his knob-handled cane.

'Friend Lum,' Uncle Billy said, 'you have just made yourself another good trade,' and he turned to the wagon for more money, his step light.

When he returned, Mayhill said, 'There are some things I need to get out of the buggy and leave at the house, such as my old water jug and my old buffalo robe I used to keep this demn leg of mine warm on a cold morning. Homer will be right back. Good afternoon.' With effort, he climbed to the buggy seat, took up the lines, chirruped, 'Giddup,' and drove away.

Well, Uncle,' Dude said, 'you've got yourself a real drivin' horse, a good buggy and harness. Guess we can pull out pretty soon.'

'As soon as Homer brings my horse and buggy. No big hurry, however. I figure the doctoring I gave Rambler will hold till this afternoon.'

They had no more than begun packing when Homer drove Amos up to the camp. Curried and brushed, the big horse looked sleek and powerful. Homer hung his head and said, 'We're sure gonna miss Amos. Mr. Lum, most of all. It's like sellin' a member of the family.'

'Same here for Rambler,' Uncle Billy said, putting on a sad face. 'We've grown powerful fond of that saddler.'

After Homer left, Uncle Billy couldn't keep his booted feet still as he regarded Amos. 'Just look at him! How nobly he stands. Like a statue in a park. I tell you this horse has superior breeding. What do you really think of him, Dude, pardner?'

'He's a dandy, all right.'

'And what do you make of him, Coyote?'

'Big horse great horse is, Grandfather.'

'Glad you agree. But don't call me Grandfather. Now, note if you will,' the old man said, off on a rhetorical spiel, 'the noble head and the faraway look in his sparkling eyes. The long shoulder and the straight forelegs. The overall muscular development. Many horsemen are ignorant of the fact that the position of the head and the forelegs greatly determines the balance of a horse, and good balance is essential to a horse's speed. Furthermore — '

'Uncle,' Dude broke in gently, wanting to humor him, 'we'd better finish packing so we cao get down the road. Homer said the next town is Clover Springs. Don't know how far it is.'

'No matter. Be there in no time, with Amos leading the way.'

Dude and Coyote had the cooking utensils and bedding packed when Uncle Billy, perhaps a hint of conscience in his voice over the horse trade, said, 'Dude, I got to thinking maybe friend Lum may not be able to get that prescription filled in Clover Springs for his Old Ned horse.

May be too complicated for these little hayseed towns. So I've written out a simpler one he can get filled anywhere theres a drugstore. Will you hurry it down to Lum before we leave?'

'Glad to,' Dude said, thinking of one more sight of fetching Miss Dolly.

He saddled Blue Grass and rode to the house. No one came when he knocked. He knocked again, more loudly. Still no one. When he knocked a third time, Miss Dolly opened the door.

'Did you knock before?' she asked, smiling up at him. 'I was busy in the kitchen.'

'Just once,' Dude storied, hat in hand 'Dr. Lockhart sent another prescription for Old Ned, in case your father can't get the first one filled in town. Is Mr. Mayhill in?'

She hesitated for scarcely an eye blink, gone so quickly he hardly noticed. Yet why should she hesitate? 'Daddy's . . . resting,' she said. 'I'll give it to him. Thank you very much.'

'We're breaking camp. Be down in

Texas by fall. Sure been nice knowing you and Mr. Mayhill, Miss Dolly.'

'Same to you, Mr. McQuinn.' She gave him a delightful laugh. 'Got it right that time, didn't I'

Although a horse trade was a horse trade, each side taking its chances, her melting smile made him wish otherwise. But hadn't she said she really wanted Rambler for her father's safety, Dude rationalized, and couldn't Rambler be used if doctored, and hadn't the outfit taken the spirited Amos off Mr. Mayhill's hands? Dude felt better then.

He mounted and saddled out to the road and glanced back for one more look at Miss Dolly. But the door was closed. At that moment movement caught his eye. A man hurrying briskly from the barn to the rear of the house. Dude got just one glimpse, no more.

He rode on, hurrying. Hewas at the edge of camp, seeing that Coyote had the sorrels hitched and Texas Jack and Judge Blair haltered behind the wagon, when his mind seemed to call him back to the house and the man he'd glimpsed there. Was he white-haired?

Uncle Billy was calling to him. 'Dude, we're all ready to pull out. I'll go ahead with Amos. This hoss already makes me feel ten years younger. See you in Clover Springs!' He seemed on air as he took the high step to the padded buggy seat. Shaking the lines, he spoke an exuberant 'Giddup!' and Amos took him down the road at a fast clip, the buggy's wheels spinning dust.

'Reminds me of some kid,' Dude said.

'Of some young Comanche with first buffalo runner,' Coyote said, and sent the sorrel team off in lively pursuit.

Uncle Billy soon outdistanced them, Amos striding with his head extended like a chaparral cock. Horse and buggy disappeared around a timbered bend.

Clover Springs turned out to be about six miles away, another little Kansas farm town arranged in neat order on the boundless prairie.

A fast-moving buggy took Dude's eye as he and Coyote followed the road into town. People were standing outside the stores watching. Now the buggy turned at the other end of the broad street and the driver, snapping his whip, drove his horse at astonishing speed past the stores.

It was Uncle Billy and Amos.

'Showin' off,' Dude said, disgusted, halting beside the wagon. 'Takes the cake — at his age!'

Uncle Billy flashed by them with a carefree wave, the light of boyish excitement on his whiskery features. Driving on, he drew up in front of a grocery store, next to a farmer loading supplies. Coyote drove the wagon alongside Uncle Billy, who hopped nimbly from the buggy. The years seemed to fall away from him when he said, 'That sure beats riding in a wagon. Amos never let up once. I tell you he's a distance hoss!'

As Uncle Billy finished speaking, the farmer mounted the seat of the wagon, backed his horses out into the street, turned them, barked, 'Giddup!' and the team stepped away.

At that exact instant there also came the clatter of hooves on the boardwalk in front of the store.

Dude and Uncle Billy whirled to look.

Amos was up on the plank walk, heading for the open door of the store. Inside, men shouted. Women shrieked.

Uncle Billy bounded to the head of his horse, taking him by the bit and backing him clattering off.

A portly, aproned man dashed out of the store and stood on the walk, amusement slowly spreading across his round face. Suddenly he began roaring and shaking with laughter and whapping his thick thigh. He burst out, 'Don't tell me you fellows just traded for Lum Mayhill's blind trotter!'

4

Open to the World

Too embarrassed to linger in Clover Springs any longer than it took to get out of town, the outfit camped some miles away by a clear-running creek in rolling country.

By then Uncle Billy had regained his composure enough to talk and even smile a little. 'I've been outslickered before and I've done my share of slickering the other fella,' he admitted ruefully. 'But this is the first time I ever traded for a blind horse.' He kept shaking his head. 'And those blinkers! Lum Mayhill was slick, all right. He had the blinkers shined so they would reflect light and Amos's eyes would always sparkle. When you take off the blinkers, his eyes look dull. That's a new wrinkle. William Tecumseh Lockhart learned something today.'

'Cheer up, Uncle,' Dude said. 'That's not the first time a man's been skinned in a horse trade. Talk about wrinkles. What pulled the wool over our eyes as much as anything — me in particular — was Miss Dolly. Miss Dolly an' her fresh eggs an' milk an' fresh-baked bread, an' her smile. Sweet sixteen!' Thinking back, he saw again the figure striding briskly from the barn to the house. 'An' don't forget Lum's fake limp. As I rode away from the house after leaving the prescription for Old Ned, I noticed a man coming from the barn. Just a glimpse was all I got. Maybe he spotted me. Anyway, he was walkin' fast. He had white hair. It was Mr. Mayhill, I know.'

'That squares with the blinkers,' Uncle Billy said, returning to his principal mortification. 'I should have caught that right off. No man leaves blinkers on all the time. Only on the track or when working a spooky horse.'

'Yet Lum made it sound logical and don't forget you traded off a horse with the heaves. Also, you have to admit that Amos has perfect manners.'

'Because,' the old man lectured, 'a

blind horse depends entirely on his driver for every move he makes. A blind trotter — or blind saddler or workhorse for that matter — that's used a good deal soon learns patience and complete obedience. The driver's voice is the horse's eyes. Naturally, he develops an extra keen sense of hearing. Hence, when that fool farmer hollered, 'Giddup,' Amos simply obeyed as usual.' A knowing came into his eyes. 'I figure Amos was blind when Lum bought him off his so-called friend. Else why would a man let go a fast trotter, one that can move like Amos? So Lum got stung too. Like me, all he could see was that perfectly trained speedy trotter. I'll have to trade him off first chance I get.'

Coyote, who had said nothing to this point, went to the motionless blue roan and stroked the dark face and neck. 'Big horse brave horse is. Goes where see he cannot. In olden days we Comanches buffalo runner would make. Keep big horse, Grandfather Billy. Brave he is. Kind he is.'

'Don't try to sway me and don't call

me Grandfather.'

'He's an easy keeper — no trouble,' Dude sidled in. 'Amos is as good a drivin' horse as you'll ever have, and that padded buggy seat is mighty comfortable on a long ride.'

'It's a disgrace for a horseman to trade for a blind horse, and a greater disgrace to keep a blind horse,' Uncle Billy said, resolved. 'I'll have to trade him off somehow. Maybe throw in the buggy and harness.'

'It won't be easy,' Dude said to discourage him, 'unless you keep the blinkers on.'

'Those cussed blinkers,' the old man lamented, let down. 'Guess I've lost my eye for horses. Means I'm getting old. Maybe it's time for me to take my place by the f'ar.' Morosely, shoulders slumped, he went to his medicine chest for solace and started moving bottles.

Both Dude and Coyote watched him with sympathy bordering on alarm. The Comanche eased over and said, low, his keen face concerned, 'Grandfather

Billy's heart on the ground is.'

'I've never seen him like this,' Dude worried. 'If he quits the track an' buys that hotel an' sits down, he won't last anytime. We've got to do something.'

Coyote seemed to search the far comers of his mind, and then he said, 'Race he needs. Against slick white man. Better if slick white man mean and bad is.'

Dude stared at him. 'You're right, Coyote. Uncle thrives on competition, the give and take. He needs the challenge of a tough match race, of rocking back and forth for the advantage. Meanwhile, on guard against somebody tryin' to fix our horse.' He slapped Coyote on the back. 'Let's see what we can find down the road.'

★ ★ ★

The rolling country gave way to long sweeps of prairie as they traveled westward, and the little towns grew farther apart. The outfit stopped only for supplies and went on, Dude and Coyote deeming that time was needed to heal Uncle Billy's shattered self-esteem.

One afternoon the outfit came to a large wooden sign beside the road. Painted black on white, it read:

OPEN TO THE WORLD

The Honorable Gideon Lightfoot, formerly of Roanoke, Virginia, offers to run his celebrated stallion Old Dominion against any horse in the world, with catch weights, at any distance up to one mile for $500 or $1,000, half forfeit. The race to be run on the Lightfoot Paths. Challenges may be received at the Lightfoot Bank, in the town of Lightfoot, between the hours of I and 3 pm. Monday through Friday. Only gentlemen horsemen will be considered, and the challenging horse or mare must be of unqualified breeding with valid papers.

Dude and Coyote swapped conspiratorial glances — *this was it* — after which

Dude said, 'Mighty interesting and unusual. What do you make of it, Uncle?'

'I've seen such before.'

'Where was that?'

'Now, did I say?' came the bristling reply. Besides his unchanged crestfallen mood, he was very tetchy. 'But if you have to know, it was in Van Buren, Arkansas, and the horse was the great Cold Deck. I remember the sign. It read: 'Cold Deck Against the World.' Cold Deck was by the great Steel Dust, out of a lightning-fast quarter mare from Missouri. I don't recall that Cold Deck was ever beaten. They always matched him at the shorter distances.' At mention of Cold Deck his face seemed to light up momentarily, then become dejected again. He went on crossly, 'All this sign amounts to is some town fella with a fast horse wants to outslick some poor outfit passing through. However, he won't get many takers at five hundred or a thousand dollars. That's a pile of money these days.'

'We could rake up the five or so,' Dude

said. 'Maybe get odds, if he figures he's got advantage.'

'Dude,' the old man said, out of patience, 'as much as I've schooled you and here you'd fall for this Gideon Lightfoot fella's come-on. He's got a scorpion horse or he wouldn't be open to the world.'

'Judge Blair is no slowpoke. This sign interests me, Uncle. Makes me want to see what the Judge could do against this Old Dominion. Sounds like a Thoroughbred. What do you think?'

'Let's go on. I'm feeling poorly today.'

'Poorly on that soft buggy seat behind Amos? Why, you're on easy street.'

They drove on.

Time passed slowly and the day turned hot. When Dude rode back to ask Uncle Billy if he wanted a drink of water from the wagon, the old man snapped, 'Do you pamper the Judge?'

'A man never pampers a runnin' horse. Might spoil 'im.'

'Same goes for me. If I want a drink of water, I'll get it myself.'

Close on three o'clock Dude noticed a wagon stopped on the road ahead. Nearer, he saw a bonneted woman on the wagon seat impatiently cooling herself with a round-shaped paper fan such as church folks used, while she watched a man working on the harness of the right-hand horse.

'You folks need some help?' Dude called.

The man looked up and said, 'Wouldn't happen to have an extra piece of harness leather, would you? Breast collar's busted.'

'Believe there's some in the wagon.'

Coyote, anticipating, passed across a wide strip of tanned leather to Dude, who handed it down.

The man was fifty or upwards, thin and hard-used, shoulders sloping, a gray, stubbly beard prickling out around his pinched face. His blue eyes, though watery, were mild and patient, set wide under sparse brows. He cut off a piece of leather, stopped, made a gesture of disgust, and asked, 'Wouldn't happen to have an awl, too, would you?'

Dude also fetched that from Coyote.

While the man worked fast, punching holes through which he pulled leather laces cut from the borrowed piece, the woman called, shrill of voice, 'Hurry, Cy. It's almost three o'clock. The bank will be closed.'

'We'll make it, Abby. I'm just about finished, thanks to these folks.'

'We should've started earlier.'

'There's a world of things I should've done earlier. Like staying away from Gideon Lightfoot.'

Dude asked, 'Is Lightfoot the next town?'

'It is.'

'How far?'

'Just over the hill.'

The man finished and stuck out his hand. 'Name's Cy Kirby. We're sure obliged to you.'

He was moving before Dude could give his own name, Kirby mounting the wagon seat and charging off at a jingling trot.

'We'd better tidy up before we go into town,' Dude said.

Nodding, Coyote drove off the road, and for the next ten minutes the two groomed Texas Jack, brushing and currying the dark bay with the four white-sock feet. Meanwhile, Uncle Billy waited in the buggy, moodily staring into space.

Seeing his lack of interest, Dude felt the sudden grip of concern. Uncle was getting old; no douht about that. But far worse, he had lost heart. Always before he had relished the steps preparatory to setting up a match race: grooming their slow horse to look fast, disguising their fast horse to look slow. Riding into a strange town. Entertaining the local hayseeds with wit and knowledge. Later, judging the other man's horse, whether to run at him short or long, while Dude jockeyed to make the match.

To stir the old man's attention, Dude said in a loud voice, 'Texas Jack looks almost too smooth to match. The spittin' image of the Judge except for no blaze. He'll draw some stares when we show 'im off. A pity he can't run fast enough to scatter dust.' Satisfied with the handiwork, he said, 'Uncle, we need the peroxide for the Judge,' expecting Uncle Billy to fetch it.

'It's in the front there. In the big green bottle. You can get it.' He not only sounded old, he sounded tired and defeated.

Another bad sign, Dude thought, and further reason for worry. Until this moment, the medicine chest had been off bounds, as untouchable as a Comanche's medicine bag.

Reaching in, breathing the mingling odors of turpentine, white pine pitch, camphor, hoof ointments, sulphur, sweet oil, iodine, Jamaica ginger and other scents he couldn't identify, Dude found the green bottle next to the jug of sourmash whiskey. Pouring peroxide on the Judge's neck, he rubbed and rubbed. Next the shoulders, back and hindquarters. The result was what looked like harness streaks on the dark bay hide, indicating that the Judge was a work animal.

That done, Dude unharnessed one of the sorrels and tied him behind the wagon alongside Texas Jack. He then led the Judge forward and hung an oversized collar on him and harnessed him beside the other sorrel.

This was another exceptional quality about the Judge. He seemed to know what was expected of him. Slap on a stock saddle and he became a cow horse or saddler, though limited to an easy trot. No fancy gaits for a runnin' horse. Cinch up a light racing saddle and he changed character, tensed for the upcoming sprint. When standing harnessed, he would actually droop his head and let his lower lip hang, looking bored and put-upon, a deceptive appearance that often led an unsuspecting sodbuster to dig for his money when Dude said, 'If you don't want to run at Texas Jack, we might match that of plow horse there, just to make a race. He can run a little when the wind's with 'im. But I'll have to have odds.'

Now in his prime at six years of age,

Judge Blair was a picture of the complete running horse: the handsome head with the distinctive blaze coming to a point between the nostrils. The fox ears and the wide-spaced eyes, the big jaws and large, sensitive nostrils. Four white sock feet. Legs straight and squarely set for soundness, a balanced horse, well-proportioned. Short cannons and pasterns. A short topline and a long underline. Powerfully muscled in the front and hindquarters, which accounted for his rapid starts. Fifteen hands at the withers. Drawn down to run, weight 1,250 pounds. He looked big but measured small. He could run short or long and he had boundless heart. Only the Lord knew his breeding.

Won in an all-night San Antonio poker game when Dude's luck ran high, the Judge — claimed the bragging Texas cowman-loser, who had won the horse the previous night off an Arizona cowman — was sired by the 'famous Buck Shiloh,' none other than a son of the legendary Shiloh, and was out of the 'unbeaten Mexican sprint queen Lolita.' Hadn't Dude heard of those two greats? Dude had smiled, figuring the man was putting up a plain ol' cow horse. Sure enough, later, Dude could find no trace of a Buck Shiloh or a Lolita. But, to his amazement, he soon discovered that he owned a once-in-a-lifetime racehorse, besides being a mystery horse, also an iron horse, who could run twice the same afternoon and win. Not that breeding mattered on the Texas bush tracks — performance was all that counted. Even so, the little outfit often lamented that its consistent winner had been gelded, his speed, conformation, soundness, disposition and heart lost to posterity.

Unable to match his runner after the classic victory over the true Mexican champion, Yolanda, Dude had moved operations to other parts. Down on his luck until meeting a roguish old codger with the face of a saint, one William Tecumseh Lockhart, who demonstrated how to work the switch, using a look-alike slow horse. This intriguing game called for a certain finesse and timing: matching the slow horse, knowing he would lose unless the opposing runner fell down or broke a leg, then matching again and getting odds, then switching to Judge Blair, painted to look like the slow horse, who was in turn painted to look like the speedy Judge. When the race was over, collect the bets and head out of town. Looking for fresh money and using pick-up jockeys, they had made their way across Texas to Indian Territory. When Coyote Walking joined them — longin to ride a horse that ran 'like old-time Comanche buffalo runner' — the outfit was complete.

'We're ready,' Dude said. 'Uncle, why-don't you take the lead when we get in town? You know Amos is an eye-catcher.'

'I'm still feeling poorly. I'll just pull off and wait while you and Coyote make your little sashay.'

Dude let out a loud groan. When was Uncle going to come out of the dismals?

5

One Man's Town

The town of Lightfoot was built around a square, in the center of which rose a three-story building of weathered gray limestone. Over its entrance Dude read: Lightfoot County Courthouse, 1880. Somehow it struck him as cold and unfriendly. Yet around the courthouse lofty elm trees spread pools of shade, and spitters and whittlers overflowed the long wooden benches, and games of checkers were in progress. Four oldsters pitched horseshoes and raised shouts of triumph when one tossed a ringer.

Dude grinned. Good. *We've got an audience.* And today was Saturday. He could tell by the number of people going in and out of the stores, and the wagons and buggies crowding the streets, and the kids running loose like spring colts in a pasture.

When reaching a new town, it was

always a cagey idea to advertise that you carried a racehorse. No better way than to parade him down Main Street or around the square. As a matter of fact, people in the little towns were starved for entertainment, something besides grim-faced preachers shouting the threat of hellfire and damnation to sinners. An unknown racehorse provided an object of mystery and a direct challenge to local pride, which demanded that townsmen back their champion to the hilt. If the moral element had banned racing in town, you could always stage the event beyond the city's limits on a level stretch of prairie. Then watch the prudish elders sneak out to watch!

Reining Blue Grass into his easy running walk, Dude led off with Coyote close behind, the smooth Texas Jack trailing the wagon beside the sorrel, arching his neck and dancing a little, looking fast and dangerous. Uncle Billy had halted Amos.

Saddling around the square, Dude noted the Lightfoot name more and more: the Lightfoot Mercantile, which occupied half a block; Lightfoot Drug Emporium, Lightfoot Cash Grocery, Lightfoot Saddle Shop, Lightfoot Hotel & Barber Shop, Lightfoot Cafe and the Lightfoot County Bank, the Honorable Gideon Lightfoot, president. There were two exceptions: the *Pioneer Courier*, Van Vinson, editor, and the Jayhawk Saloon, Big Boy Brody, prop. Tied in front of the bank was the bay team belonging to Cy and Abby Kirby.

A man stepped out of the Lightfoot Hotel & Barber Shop to observe the outfit. This man was as lean as a rail and his high-crowned hat made him appear taller than he was. He wore a big star on his calfhide vest and a six-shooter wobbled on his right hip. He kept stroking the wings of his handlebar mustache.

Other eyes followed as the outfit moved by again. Now and then Dude tipped his hat. In turn, that attracted some friendly nods. Approaching the benches again, he heeled Blue Grass into a rhythmic fox-trot, the gelding's prettiest gait of all, because it brought out his Kentucky breeding all the more, accenting his proud head and carriage and the ease of his going. The idlers paused in their loafing to view the head-nodding saddler and the dark bay Texas Jack. The checker players looked up. The game of horseshoes ceased.

None of this escaped Dude. *Now is the time to break off, when they're all gawking at good-lookin' horseflesh.*

Therefore, he swung off along the broad street on which they had entered town, looking for the wagonyard. There it was, within easy walking distance from the courthouse. He rode past the post office, past the Lightfoot Livery, Hay & Grain, past the noisy Lightfoot Blacksmith Shop, and drew rein under an elm tree by the wagonyard.

'Texas Jack is the honey that will draw the bees,' Dude assured Uncle Billy when he stopped Amos. 'Ever see a smoother-lookin' racehorse?'

The old man gave him a bleak look. 'First thing I plan to do is sell or trade

Amos off to one of these simpleton sod-busters.'

'What about matching that Old Dominion, if we can? Bothers me to let a brag like that go by.'

'You Alamo Texans! Now, Dude, I warned you about that slick come-on. Don't expect me to help out on that. Besides, I'm still feeling poorly. Mighty poorly.'

'Maybe you'd better have yourself a little toddy right now?'

'Believe not. I'll just rest here in the buggy till these hick loafers start congregating.'

Dude stared at him, first in surprise, then outright concern. Uncle was poorly! Never before had Dude known him to refuse a toddy. 'I'll get the jug for you,' Dude said. 'You can have a nip here.'

'No, Dude,' the old man said, weak of voice. 'I'll just rest awhile.'

Dude left him to help Coyote unharness the other horses and tie them around the wagon, disturbed by the uneasiness he felt for Uncle Billy, though still convinced that a challenging race was the needed cure. But how could they match a race without the old man's canny help? Maybe the answer was to get rid of Amos first?

A man came strolling up, the angular man with the star. He stood a moment, roving his eyes about, before he said pompously, 'I am Marshal Columbus Epps. Come to check the brands on your horses.' He had a deep voice, sepulchral in tone. He stroked his mustache with his left hand while keeping his right free should Dude cause trouble.

Dude rubbed his nose to help cover his grin at the show of official self-importance. 'Go right ahead, Marshal,' he said, gesturing.

Methodically, Epps looked at each horse, checking against notations in a little brown notebook, strolled back and said, 'You're all clear, mister. Been considerable amount of horse stealin' east of here. How long you plan to be in town?'

Dude shrugged. 'Depends. Few days, I guess.'

'Well, it's a nice town and we aim to

keep it that way.' Thus, Marshal Epps left them.

'What would he do if the James boys came to town?' Dude asked, shaking his head.

Coyote struck a pompous pose and stroked his upper lip. 'Chief Big Wind check brands on James boys' horses only one time he would.'

Within minutes, the first loafers began gathering to eye Texas Jack at close range. Dude nodded to them, but said nothing, making himself appear busy around the wagon. The time for palaver would not come until somebody voiced an interest. Proven strategy dictated that an itinerant horseman never acted eager to sell or trade or match a race.

More idlers gathered, until a small, curious crowd had collected.

Wearily, Uncle Billy got out of the buggy and shuffled over to the wagon, his step labored.

Then a young, red-faced farmer, strapping and bumptious, asked, 'You gents carry a racehorse?'

Dude, who customarily opened the ball for the outfit, held back, hoping, and Uncle Billy, after hesitating, straightened and answered instead, 'That's just one of the line horses you see here, young fella.'

'All I see is a sorrel tied by the front wagon wheel, and an ol' bay with harness marks tied by him, and tied on behind another sorrel, and a fairly nice bay by him, and that fox-trotter that went around the square, and that ol' blue roan in the buggy shafts.'

'By that,' said Uncle Billy, 'I can see that you haven't been farther from home than the county fair maybe. You been too long out where the hoot owls holler all night and the coyotes sing.'

Snickers rippled through the crowd. The young man's red face was now a beet red.

'He's got you there, Rufus,' a man bantered.

The show was about to start, Dude sensed from long experience. The farmer called Rufus was a smart aleck, there being one in every hick town, and Uncle

Billy was tetchy today. Dude almost felt sorry for the young sodbuster, the way the old man would cut him up verbally.

'Oh, I don't know about that,' Rufus said. 'I been to Kansas City and St. Joe.'

'All by yourself? Did the street cars scare you?'

'Nothin' scares me, Grandpa.'

'How many times did you get lost, sonny boy?'

'Nary once — and I took in some trottin' races, too.'

'No doubt that makes you an instant authority. Now, among these fine horses is a fast racehorse and a champion trotter. You tell me which is which.'

'Go on, Rufus,' the same bantering voice urged. 'Tick 'em out for us.'

When Rufus hesitated, his eyes moving from Texas Jack to Amos and back without decision, Uncle Billy said, 'I'll let you off the hook. Did you ever see a racehorse pulling a light buggy? The blue roan you see is none other than the well-known Missouri trotting champion, Avalanche. The first trotter in the 'Show

Me' state to course the mile in two minutes flat. He was a big winner on the Grand Circuit.'

'So? I had me a trotter once. Better lookin' than him.'

'Mule or plow horse, sonny?'

'He's got you again, Rufus!'

Dude could see the young man straining for a clever parrying retort. Rufus's attention settled on Amos for a moment before he said, eyes cutting at Uncle Billy, 'If this Avalanche is so fast, how come he's not on the track now?'

'Because he's my personal drivin' horse. I like fast horses.'

'So you say,' said the doubting Rufus. 'Well, he may be your drivin' horse, but I'll bet he's old enough for the glue factory. What's his true age?'

Uncle Billy laid a relishing smile on Rufus. Jousting with the young farmer, he seemed almost himself again: alert and vigorous and convincing. He said, 'The only way to tell the true age of a horse is by his teeth. However, since I see that you wouldn't believe me if I told you, I'd like to call on one of your good neighbors here to confirm what I'll presently tell you. Some gentleman who's had considerable experience with horses. Will one of you please come forward and examine Avalanche's teeth?'

When an elderly farmer stepped out at the urging of his friends, Uncle Billy said, 'Mr. McQuinn, give the gentleman a pencil and a piece of paper from your memorandum book so he can write down the age.'

Dude complied and the farmer walked over to Amos, opened his mouth, peered for long moments, wrote down his finding, and returned the pencil to Dude.

'Now,' Uncle Billy said in a voice meant for the crowd, 'I think it only proper that friend Rufus do the same. What do you think?'

When Rufus balked, the same ragging voice rose again, 'Sure, Rufus. That's only fair. Go on.' Other voices joined the urging.

Caught, Dude thought. Uncle's hogtied him again.

Dude handed Rufus paper and pencil and he sauntered over to Amos, cocky and unhurried. He fussed with the bridle and he fussed with the bit, and when he did look into Amos's mouth, he would stand up close and then stand back, as if pondering, meanwhile turning his head from side to side. At times he appeared to be looking more into Amos's throat or nose than at his teeth. The needless maneuverings told Dude something: Rufus was faking. He couldn't read a horse's teeth. Many farmers could not. It required study and practice. A true horseman like Uncle Billy could.

'Now,' Uncle Billy said when Rufus stood back, 'write down the age and hand the paper to your neighbor.' Rufus did that and Uncle Billy said, 'After I write down Avalanche's age, we'll compare our findings. Paper and pencil, please, Mr. McQuinn.'

Dude did so, feeling like a stage assistant in a magic act.

Scribbling with a flourish, Uncle Billy handed the paper to the elderly farmer and said, 'Now, sir, will you first read aloud for us the age you ascertained?'

'Nine,' the man said.

'Nine. You found Avalanche to be nine years old?'

'I did.'

'Now, if you please, read the age I put down.'

'Nine,' the man said, looking down.

'Now, if you please, tell us what Rufus found.'

The man looked at the piece of paper, broke into a broad smile, and said, 'Eighteen.'

The crowd exploded into hooting laughter. Rufus set his jaw and glared at Uncle Billy, who said, not unkindly, 'Truth is, friend Rufus, not everybody possesses the scientific knowledge of how to read a horse's teeth. You were basing your guess on suspicion alone, because in the past some unscrupulous horse trader has hornswoggled a trusting soul in your nice town of Lightfoot. Such as trading off a doctored horse with the colic or heaves — even a blind horse.

I believe it was Diogenes who remarked that honesty has never been the long suit of the human species.' He paused to look out over the crowd, his saintly features expressing repugnance. 'Therefore, when an honest horseman comes to town with good stock, he meets with understandable suspicion . . . But I'll let you in on a little secret, friend Rufus. How your good neighbor and I can tell that Avalanche is nine years old. You see, cups are black spots in a horse's teeth from three to nine years. At nine the cups leave the two center nippers, and each of the two upper corner teeth has a little sharp protrusion. Now, you know.'

'Is Avalanche for sale?' Rufus asked, still not appeased.

'At a fair price.'

Rufus sneered. 'Reckon you want a heap for 'im?'

Dude sighed. This Rufus was a stubborn one. The two were going another round.

'If you are thinking of purchasing this fine champion trotter,' Uncle Billy said,

'I suggest that first you go to the bank to see if your credit is good for more than a couple of bales of hay. Say in the vicinity of three hundred dollars.'

Rufus blinked. 'I didn't say I wanted him, Grandpa. Another thing. How come you got blinkers on 'im? In K.C. they blinker a trotter only when he's rambunctious and on the track, not off've it.' He glanced around at his cohorts for endorsement. Let the old codger answer that!

'Avalanche is a spirited horse, on the track or traveling a country road,' Uncle Billy replied easily. 'He has just covered some fifteen miles or so today. You should know that blinkers keep a horse's eyes fixed straight ahead on the business of going.'

There were nods and murmurs to that logic. Rufus said no word. He was silent so long that Uncle Billy said, 'Something else got you stumped, sonny?'

'If this Avalanche is so fast,' Rufus said, a bucolic cunning transparent in his round, reddish face, 'how come he's up for sale, Grandpa?'

'Are you implying, because he is for sale or trade that he is not a sound horse? That I have concealed a physical defect in this fine animal?'

Rufus let his smirking silence speak for him.

'Tell you what,' Uncle Billy continued, his tone amiable, 'will you oblige me by driving Avalanche around the square as a sort of demonstration of his class and obedience, his speed and soundness? There is no truer test of a horse than to try him out. Will you do that, friend Rufus? But remember, now, he is spirited and full of go.'

Dude had to grin at the tableau. Uncle was playing poor Rufus like a fiddle again, pulling him this way and that, first taking him down notch by notch, now jockeying him around to show off the horse.

The ragging voice prodded, 'Go on, Rufus. Show us you can.'

Rufus stood fast until hands pushed him forward. A few steps and he checked himself, an inner struggle perceptible on his face: The desire to prove he could handle the trotter versus the fear of making a fool of himself again.

'Show us, Rufus!'

'Oh, aw right,' he gave in and went clomp-clomp to the buggy and mounted the seat and took loose the reins. He said, 'Giddup,' and Amos moved out obediently. The onlookers turned as one to watch. Rufus now had Amos turned around headed for the square. Taking the whip, Rufus popped it once over Amos's hindquarters and instantly the big horse shifted into his ground-eating trot.

Down the street, Rufus reined right to go around the square, there lost from sight until he made the next turn left, the blue roan striding smoothly. Another left turn and he came in on the broad street leading to the wagonyard. Instead of turning in that direction, however, Rufus headed out of town. By now the big horse was traveling full speed, head thrust in that characteristic way of the crested chaparral cock.

'Look at him go!' Dude heard a farmer exclaim.

At the edge of town, Rufus wheeled and started back.

'See that?' somebody said. 'Turned him on a dime!'

'Here they come! That big horse can pick 'em up and put 'em down, believe me!'

'Straight as a string!'

'Look how he lifts his feet!'

A farmer leaving the square in his wagon did not see the fast-moving trotter and buggy until late. He yanked his team up sharply.

Amos sped by without swerving an inch.

'Why, he pays no attention to other horses,' a man in the crowd marveled.

'It's them blinkers,' another man said. 'Proves they work.'

Rufus pulled to a halt, looped the reins around the whip socket and got down, his face alight, free of the peevish suspicion with which he had begun the tryout.

'What do you think of him?' Uncle Billy asked.

'He's a stepper. Never been behind a horse like him before.'

As gracious as a body could be, Uncle Billy said, 'I am indeed obliged to you, friend Rufus, for trying Avalanche out for everybody to see. You handled him well, quite well.' Then, turning, 'And now, friends, I am going to answer a question which I know is on all your minds. Why is Avalanche for sale? This line Standardbred? He is because I am getting on in my sundown years, though I hate to admit it in public, and I'm lighting the afflictions of old age, arthritis and catarrh. I can't handle a spirited horse the way I could a few years ago.'

That evoked head waggings of sympathy from the oldsters.

Dude kept his face expressionless. Uncle was laying it on extra heavy today, trying to unload poor Amos, even resorting to Lum Mayhill's convincing put-on of physical infirmities, the limp excepted.

At the same time, Dude noticed more

men coming from the square, apparently curious after Amos's fast-stepping performance. One man, distinguished by stovepipe hat and frock coat, stood at the edge of the crowd, a tall, dignified figure, apart from the farmers.

'So there he stands like a statue in a park,' Uncle Billy was saying, pointing to Amos, evidently fancying the repetition of his own phrasing, first used at the Mayhill farm. 'Where . . . where in this great world of ours can man find such nobility without arrogance, such steadfast loyalty without recompense other than a meager bundle of hay or a measure of grain . . . such grace and power and speed of movement? I ask you, gentlemen, where do we find these grand traits but in the horse. The most beautiful animal the good Lord has put on this weary earth to serve ungrateful Homo sapiens. We are his heirs. Therefore, let us show humane conscience for his welfare.'

As he carried on in that rhetorical vein, the crowd commenced to fidget, and

Uncle Billy, sensing that, said, 'Besides being the outstanding speed trotter you have just witnessed, Avalanche is not too proud to pull a plow. Remember, gentlemen, the plow is the beginning of civilization. Without it, we would all be barbarians, living in caves or — for better or worse — swinging from trees.'

Hearing chuckles, he paused at exactly the right moment, as Dude had seen him do so often, timing his windup as if he were on a stage, leaving the matter of the horse sale dangling like a prize. He coughed and said tiredly, 'Thank you, gentlemen. My name is William T. Lockhart. If any of you have sick horses or mules, I'll be glad to visit with you individually after I've rested a bit.'

'It is Dr. William Tecumseh Lockhart,' Dude filled in quickly, loud enough for all to hear, going along with the ploy. In these little out-of-the-way towns, nothing seemed to impress the yokels more than the title of 'Doctor.' 'Dr. Lockhart,' Dude said again, 'is on leave from Cedar Crest Farm of Lexington, Kentucky, where he is the resident veterinarian. Under his direction, Cedar Crest has become the fountainhead of the best Thoroughbred blood in the country. Dr. Lockhart is traveling withus for his health. We aim to go on downthrough Texas to New Mexico — if he can stand the trip.'

Dude then brought a cane-bottomed chair from the wagon,and when Uncle Billy was seated, the alert Coyote hustled him a dipper of water from the barrel. Leaning back, eyes half closed, the old man murmured his thanks and sipped gratefully, while the crowd looked on with sympathy.

In a short while, he blinked his eyes and sat up, apparently revived, his expression benign and inviting talk.

A middle-aged farmer said, 'I might be interested in your trotter, but the price is too steep.'

'I might treaty with you,' Uncle Billy said amiably, but skirting eagerness. 'Give a little, take a little.' Seated there, he made Dude think of a kindly potentate bestowing favors.

'My old buggy horse is way past his prime,' the farmer went on, 'and he's lame right now in both front feet. Walks like he's treadin' on eggs.'

Uncle Billy snapped to attention. His voice struck an accusing ring. 'Have you been trimming the frog?'

'Well . . . yes, I have,' the man admitted, dipping his chin and shuffling his feet. 'How did you know?'

'Symptoms, my friend, symptoms. You know the old tried-and-true saying of our horsemen forefathers that has come down throughthe ages: 'Leave the frog alone.' '

The other smiled guiltily. 'And another old standby saying: 'No foot, no horse.' '

'You have it exactly. Now, has your horse been standing a great deal in a stall with shoes on?'

'He has. Reckon I've kept him up too much because he's old.'

'You can do something about that. Many experienced horsemen cure lameness simply by removing the shoes and turning the horse out to pasture on soft ground or a sandy pasture. You see, at every step the horse is then putting pressure on the frog and the bars of his foot. This restores the natural circulation of the foot. I strongly recommend that'

'I'll sure do that, Doc. Thank you.'

'Here's something else. Mr. McQuinn, kindly jot down the following hoof ointment ingredients for this gentleman.' Dnde opened his memorandum book, wet a pencil stub on the tip of his tongue, and readied himself as Uncle Billy began to dictate in a staccato voice:

'Balsam fir . . . oil of hemlock . . . white pine pitch . . . honey . . . Venice turpentine and beeswax . . . each one and three-quarter ounces. No more, no less.'

'Hold on, Doctor,' Dude protested. 'Let me catch up. Was that Venice turpentine and beeswax?'

'It was,' came the crotchety reply. As Dude nodded, catching up, Uncle Billy resumed:

'Lard . . . one-half pound. Fine-ground verdigris . . . three quarters of an ounce.

Simmer all together over a slow fire. When melted, take off the fire and stir until cool. Apply generously.'

Dude finished, tore out the small sheet of paper and handed it gratuitously to the farmer, who said, 'Sure much obliged, Doc. Is there any charge?'

'None a-tall. Just take care of your horse.'

'You can bet I'll do that, And I'll keep your trotter in mind. Will you be here long?'

'A few days, while I rest up.'

Another farmer stepped up, somewhat hesitant and sheepish. 'Doc, my old saddle horse Prince is off his feed. Won't hardly touch fresh prairie hay or grain.'

'Remember, a horse will not eat from a sour trough.'

'It ain't that.'

'Is he coughing?'

'Nope.'

'Is his mouth sore?'

'Nope.'

'Does he stand straddling, or walk

in that manner, which would indicate a lame back or some kidney or bladder ailment?'

'None of that. Just noses his feed.'

'I see. I see. Is his hair dry, standing straight out, indicating indigestion, glanders, worms, skin disease, or possibly the condition of being hidebound or consumptive?'

The man shook his head in relieved negation.

Uncle Billy reflected a long moment. 'How old is your saddler?'

'Going on twenty-two.'

'Hmmnn. I hesitate to doctor a horse without seeing him. However, taking into consideration his advanced age, I recommend a good conditioner. Professor Gleason's Sure-Shot Conditioner.'

'Professor Gleason?'

'An old and trusted colleague of mine back in Kentucky, now passed on to his just reward, free at last of worrying about man's inhumanity to *Equus caballus*, better known as the horse. This conditioner is guaranteed to make an old horse get up and howl.' He winked roguishly. 'The same might be said for some of us older gentry when you hear what's in it. I gave it to an old gentleman back in Missouri at his insistence and not long af ter that his wife ran him out of the house with a broom. Made him sleep in the ham.'

That roused some chuckles and elbow nudgings.

'I'll try anything for old Prince,' the man said earnestly. 'All my kids learned to ride on him. He's one of the family.'

'This can't fail to help him. Here it is. Are you ready, Mr. McQuinn? I'll go slower this time.' Dude nodded, pencil stub poised, and Uncle Billy said, 'Tincture of asafetida . . . tincture of Spanish fly . . . oil of anise . . . '

'Hold on, Doctor,' Dude interrupted. 'How much?'

'Now, did I say? I'll come to that in due time. Oil of cloves . . . oil of cinnamon and fenugreek. One ounce each of the aforementioned. Antimony, two ounces, and half a gallon of brandy, hundred proof. Mix well and let stand ten days, then give ten drops daily in a gallon of water. That ought to bring old Prince back to the feed box with a smile on his face.'

After the farmer thanked him and turned away, frowning over Dude's scribblings, there was a lull and Uncle Billy said, 'Now, Mr. McQuinn, I didn't mean to talk all day. No doubt these gentlemen would like to hear about your racehorse. That smooth dark bay tied to the wagon.'

Dude quirked his mouth. 'I wouldn't say Texas Jack is a racehorse today, since he's just gettin' over the colic. Maybe he can run a little before long.'

'He was kicking up his heels this morning after I doctored him.'

'That was this morning,' Dude said, remembering his schooling. You never said a horse was sharp, ready to run. Instead, you said he was about to come down with something, or had something, or was just getting over something. Sometimes the hint of a slight edge was all the other man needed to start talking match race.

'He'll leg up fast once you start working him,' Uncle Billy said.

The loafers drifted across to look at Texas Jack, studying him from his head to the point of his shoulder to his withers, from hooves to back and stifle aod hip, nodding and swapping comments among themselves.

'What's his best distance?' Dude was asked.

'Sometimes he runs long. Sometimes he runs short. He: can reach out there a little bit when he's on his feed.' Most match races were over the standard shorter distances: 220, 250, 300, 330, 350 yards, with occasional sprints up to 400 and the classic quarter mile. But now and then a local sharpy with a distance horse, figuring your horse hadn't much bottom, would try to match you over a longer route. That was where Judge Blair was deceiving. He didn't have the long-legged look of a Thoroughbred, he was all quarter horse; but he could lengthen out when trained. As

Uncle Billy pointed out, 'Speed always helps out bottom.'

'Where you been runnin' him?'

'Back in Missouri.'

'How'd he do?'

'He won some when the wind was with him. He lost some when it was against him.'

'You don't brag much, I see.'

'I figure it's brag enough when I put up my money,' Dude said, smiling back. He waited for somebody to make the opening pitch for a match race, but nobody did. They only stood around and sized up Texas Jack some more, their interest general. Glancing about, Dude happened to catch sight of the man in the stovepipe hat walking back to the square.

The show was about over, Dude realized, and before long the lookers started straying back toward the square. Only Rufus tarried. He asked Uncle Billy, 'Did I hear you right when you said three hundred dollars for the trotter?'

'Thereabouts,' the old man replied, hoping to draw him on. 'I might throw in the harness to boot.'

Rufus jogged his head, as if making a mental note of that concession, and followed the others, musing as he went.

Uncle Billy whapped his leg and groaned, 'I've never talked so much and so hard in my life and had less to show for it.'

'You had a couple of nibbles, I'd say.'

'Nibbles don't always bring in the fish. I may have to come down on my price.'

'Neither did anybody say they had an ol' horse that can run a little. There's something odd about this town, Uncle. I tell you there is.'

'That's because Gideon Lightfoot has the only racehorse in these parts,' said a breezy voice behind them.

They whipped about and Dude saw a man whose eyes were cynical but friendly, whose face was extremely angular but genial, fringed by a brown beard that thinned out at the snip of a goatee. He stood as if unhinged, his appearance one of careless disarray: baggy gray pantaloons, sleeves rolled up to his skinny elbows, a soiled vest which sprouted a cluster of pencils, an askew bow tie, and a jaunty derby. He looked past forty, but not much.

'I happen to be Van Vinson,' he said, 'editor of the weekly *Pioneer Courier*, published every Thursday, the Lord willing. We also make up the snappiest ads you ever saw and do a wonderful job printing — campaign cards, placards, broadsides, posters, wedding announcements and reward posters — when we can get any. I also take in chickens and eggs and hams and butter, in trade for space and subscriptions, and whatever vegetables are in season. Once I took in a sway-backed horse, which I traded off for a milk cow that didn't give milk.'

He held out his hand and they shook.

'Glad to know you,' Dude said. Uncle Billy gave him a tired nod.

'Dr. Lockhart,' Vinson said, waving an ink-smudged hand, 'I want you to know that your spiel — if I may call it that — was just about the best I've ever heard. Beats any medicine show, including the governor's speech, when he came through here kissing babies and making promises he wouldn't or couldn't keep. I heard you from the very beginning when you put Rufus Hubbard in his place. Rufus is a good boy, just a little smart-alecky. Been through the eighth grade twice. If you don't mind, I'd like to run a little piece in the paper about you and where you're from and so forth. It's news when anybody new comes to Lightfoot or even passes through.'

Uncle Billy's gaze on Vinson was weary and discouraged. 'I'm too played out to talk to you now,' he said.

'A story might help you sell or trade that fast trotter,' Vinson suggested.

'He's right, Uncle,' Dude said.

'Then you talk to him. You know how poorly I am.'

'Sorry to hear that, Doctor,' Vinson said. 'Now, there's a nice wooded camp-ground on down the street at the edge of town. Plenty of good spring water. Hope you can stay awhile.'

'We're in no hurry,' Dude said, thinking of a salutary match race for his old mentor. 'I was hoping maybe Gideon Lightfoot would show up today, since he's a big racehorse man.'

'Oh, he did, all right. He was the man in the stovepipe hat.'

'I saw him. But he didn't come over to size up our horse.'

'That's not the way the game is played in the fair city of Lightfoot,' Vinson said, assuming an exaggerated air of propriety. 'It's just like it says on those signs that the Honorable G.L. has posted on all roads leading in here. You have to go to the bank and challenge him there. He would not deign to challenge you. T'wouldn't be proper, my deah suh.'

Dude raised a dry grin. 'Sounds like a real back-slappin' fellow.'

'He can be sociable when he gets his way, which he pretty much does in Lightfoot. Maybe you've noticed the Lightfoot name on everything in town except the Courier and the Jayhawk Saloon? He'd own me if it wasn't for printing the county's legal notices, for which I am paid in that scarce commodity known as cash, and for swapping subscriptions and ads for vittles. Truth is, the Honorable G.L. owns the Jayhawk, though it's run under Big Boy Brody's name. Public image, y'know. The honorable name of Lightfoot must not be associated with the evils of demon rum.'

'How good is his Old Dominion stud?'

'He's never lost a race.'

'You mean around here.'

'Around here and elsewhere in Kansas. It's got so the Honorable G.L. can't match Old Dominion anymore, hence the reason for the signs. G.L. bought him back East two years ago as a three-year-old.'

'A quality Thoroughbred, eh?'

'And some left over. He's got a pedigree a mile long. All kings and queens. I've seen the papers on him.'

'What's his best distance? Not that poor ol' Texas Jack would have a chance against him.'

'Any distance up to a mile, like the signs say.'

'Remember any of the times? Just

curious, is all.'

'He has run the half mile in forty-six flat from a standing start on a heavy track.'

Dude's eyes flew wide at such speed. 'When was his last race? Not that I'm really interested.'

'Two months ago. A horse trader came through here with a fine looking race mare called Missouri Belle. It was thought she had a chance to take Old Dominion at five furlongs. I saw her work. She could fly. A beautifully formed sorrel. The farmers dug down in their overalls to bet her.' His face clouded as he thought back. 'But come the race she didn't seem the same. Never got untracked.'

'Somebody fixed that mare,' Uncle Billy snapped.

Dude regarded him with surprise. *At last, Uncle was taking an interest.*

Vinson shrugged. 'Horsemen like to say that when something goes wrong.'

'Something was wrong if the mare didn't run her usual race,' Uncle Billy disagreed. 'Was she limping or coughing?'

'No.'

'Did she look sleepy? At times fidgety? Pawing with one foot? Did she try to lie down and roll? Was her breathing labored?'

'Dr. Lockhart, only the trainer could tell you that. So far as I know, she didn't.'

'I have just enumerated the principal symptoms of the colic. If she showed none of these, she was fixed.'

'You seem mighty certain, Doctor.'

'Editor Vinson, there are three rules you can follow about a horse's behavior on the track. If he doesn't seem himself, he's either sick or hurt or been fixed. Another tried and true way of winning, of course, is to buy off the jockey, so he'll pull the horse or maybe shift his weight at a crucial moment, thus causing the horse to break stride or veer. Those are just two of the cute little stunts a jock can do. There are others.'

'There couldn't have been any skulduggery. Missouri Belle's jockey was the son of the owner.'

'Then the mare was fixed,' Uncle

Billy said flatly. He coughed weakly and touched his throat, by which Dude suspected the old man was giving in to himself again.

'Excuse us, Mr. Vinson,' Dude said, worried. 'Believe we'd better make camp!'

'I'll go along with you. After you've set up camp, I hope you'll tell me about Dr. Lockhart?'

'Glad to,' Dude said, thinking ahead. This one-man town had the earmarks of a tough lay, yet what Uncle needed to pull him back to the track and feeling himself again. The outfit would have to stay here longer than it usually did in a town, if it sold or traded one blind horse and matched a race. A story in the paper would create interest and possibly rouse the avarice of Gideon Lightfoot. Another point of view opened in his mind, steadying as he fairly beamed at Vinson. 'You said you would like to run a little piece in the paper. Is that like what we call an item down in Texas, where somebody's Aunt Nell comes to visit?'

'More than an item, Mr. McQuinn.'

'In that case, it's no more than fair if we take out a good-sized ad on Texas Jack bein' here, and maybe you could mention Avalanche in your story.'

Vinson thumped the brim of his derby. 'A brainy idea. What do you want to swap? Right now I'm long on chickens and early spring vegetables.'

Dude smiled. 'I was thinking of cash.'

'Cash! McQuinn, a newspaperman could make a better living by devoting the same talent and time to chasing coyotes. But when he hears the word 'cash,' he becomes a demon newspaperman again. You'll be astounded at the story you'll get. Just start talking!'

6

The Honorable Dude McQuinn

Obeying a hunch, Dude decided to start training Judge Blair over the longer routes, from half a mile to seven furlongs. Before daybreak on alternate mornings he and Coyote would ride around town to the east road and work the horse and circle back soon after dawn. Otherwise, the outfit rested and waited for something to happen. Occasionally a talkative oldster from town would drop by, more to pass the time of day than to look at the horses or to buy a trotter. When Uncle Billy, discouraged because Amos remained unsold, suggested they go on to the next town, Dude said, 'Wait a few days. I think somethin's gonna pop.'

'What do you mean?'

'We'll know after the paper comes out — maybe.'

Thursday afternoon a breathless boy delivered a newspaper at the camp. 'Just off the press — compliments of Mr. Vinson,' he said and took off running.

Dude's eyes bugged when he saw the story on page one of the *Pioneer Courier*. He read it through rapidly. 'Uncle,' he called, 'you and Coyote just listen to what Van Vinson wrote up on us. Here's the headline: NOTABLE HORSEMEN COME TO LIGHTFOOT.'

'Now what have you and that Vinson fella cooked up?' Uncle Billy growled. He was grumpy this morning, still feeling 'poorly,' he said, which he would be until he rid himself of Amos, Dude knew.

'You two listen to this,' Dude said. Clearing his voice, he read:

'Dr. William Tecumseh Lockhart, the distinguished Kentucky horseman, internationally known as a breeder, trainer, veterinarian, scientist and author of nnmerous books on the development of the Thoroughbred and the Standardbred, is in our fair city for an extended stay at Lightfoot's imposing community campground.

'Not one to mince words of praise

when praise is so nobly derved, Dr. Loclchart described our progressive city in these glowing terms: 'Of all the cities and settlements I have visited in the West, Lightfoot is the fairest of the fair. Never have I been so cordially received and so impressed with citizenry dedicated to the advancement of its city, county, state and nation. Lightfoot can be proud.' '

'Now when did I say that?' the old man barked.

'You just did, though friend Van might have stretched the facts a trifle.'

'And when did this hayseed town become a city?'

'Quit interrupting and listen. Van is only tryin' to help you sell Amos and me match a race. This gets better as it goes along.' Dude began reading again:

'The esteemed Dr. Lockhart, whose family tree dates back to the Plymouth Colony of Massachusetts, is traveling with the Honorable Dude McQuinn, a direct descendant of the great Sam Houston on his maternal side of Texas pioneers.'

136

Uncle Billy sprang out of his chair, storming, 'The Plymouth Colony! I never claimed that!'

'Calm down, Uncle. A little molasses never hurt anybody.'

The old man rolled his eyes. 'And the 'Honorable Dude McQuinn.' '

'I can say that if Gideon Lightfoot can. Don't you see, he won't match anybody but quality folks.'

'But a descendant of Sam Houston? You never told me that.'

'Now, did I ever say I wasn't? Van also writes that Mr. Coyote Walking is with the outfit. That Coyote is a full-blooded Comanche, the son of the chief of all Comanches ... is the West's leading quarter horse jockey, an honor graduate of Carlisle and speaks five languages fluently.'

'Five languages? Whoa again.'

'Correct, that is, Grandfather,' Coyote said. 'Besides English and Comanche, I speak Kiowa, Cheyenne and Arapaho. Those Indians used to come to our camp. Stay they would, for days. Feed them he would, my father the chief. They still come. My relatives too. Why my father is poor. Why I send him money.'

Shaking his head in resignation, the old man went back to his chair, and Dude resumed reading:

'Dr. Lockhart, who is on a tour of the Southwest for his health, reports that although in Lightfoot but a few days, the climate has improved his well-being considerably. He says, 'I find the salubrious air hereabouts not unlike that of California, constant in its sunny euphoria, conducive to the relief of arthritis and catarrh and other ailments.'

'Needless to report, where Dr. Lockhart leads others follow. Long identified with the fountainhead of Thoroughbred racing in Kentucky, he is the recognized author of a score of scholarly tomes, among them *Lockhart's History of the American Turf, Lockhart's Horse Breeders' Guide, Lockhart's Horse and Horsemanship, Lockhart's Training the Thoroughbred, Lockhart's Equine Ills and Cures,* and others too numerous to mention. He is a frequent contributor to Cadwallader's widely circulated scientific journal, *The Herbivorous Mammal*, and was an intimate colleague of the late Prof. P. D. Gleason, inventor of the famed Eureka Bridle.'

Dude paused, set for another howl from Uncle Billy; instead, he was leaning back, listening intently, a rather mollified expression on his face. Dude went on:

'The party is carrying two valuable horses. One is Avalanche, the Missouri trotting champion and the personal driving horse of Dr. Lockhart, the other Texas Jack, a Thoroughbred of impeccable breeding which Mr. McQuinn, an eminent judge of equine class, bought in the Lone Star State.

'Mr. Rufus Hubbard, who resides north of town on Bug Creek, gave Lightfoot residents something to talk about last Saturday when he demonstrated Avalanche's astonishing speed around the town square and up and down Main Street. Regretfully, Dr. Lockhart announced that the speedy trotter is up for sale. 'Although this great horse is close to my heart,' Dr. Lockhart said, 'I must let him go to some deserving person because of the state of my health. The buyer will have to be of established Christian character and a lover of horses. Teetotalers of public witness will be given preference.' '

'Teetotalers be damned!' came the roar. 'That's the last species I'd give preference to!'

'Hold your fire, Uncle. The idea is to bring in the church folks to look at Amos. I mean Avalanche.' Uncle Billy calmed down on that logic, and Dude read on:

'As a contribution to the public good, Dr. Lockhart generously volunteered to give a free diagnosis of any ailing horse or mule brought to the Lightfoot campground between ten and three o'clock this coming Saturday. In addition, he will prescribe the proper medication and demonstrate the safety of Professor Gleason's remarkable. Eureka Bridle.'

The old man leaped out of his chair, growling, 'They'll bring in every broken-down nag and lop-eared mule in the country. As poorly as I am, I won't survive the day.'

'More people the better,' Dude said, 'to help you sell your horse. Listen to the rest of this:

'Mr. McQuinn also had an interesting announcement. He will run the noted Texas Jack, short or long, against any horse in the world. The editor of this great newspaper urges its many loyal readers to turn to page three for more details of Mr. McQuinn's startling news of the turf.'

Dude opened the newspaper and saw the full-page ad. The top line, a single word centered in huge black capitals, seemed to fly at him. He read with an amplified expression:

'CHALLENGE! I, the Honorable Dude McQuinn of Live Oak, Texas, on the Salt Fork of the Brazos, will run mygreat Thoroughbred, Texas Jack, against any horse at any distance, catch weights, for $500 and up. Texas Jack can beat anything alive and above ground. Challenges will be received officially at the Lightfoot camp-ground between the hours of 9 A.M.and 5 P.M. any day except Sunday.'

'No sodbuster would bet five hundred on a horse race,' Uncle Billy contradicted. 'Only Lightfoot has that kind of money.'

'That's what I'm counting on,' Dude said.

'As snooty as he is, he'll expect you to challenge him.'

'And I'll expect him to challenge me.'

'If he doesn't?'

'Then we'll have to do some tall maneuvering.'

'We? Dude, I told you to leave me out of this. I'm too poorly to stand the strain of another tough match race.'

Dude let the matter rest at that point.

★ ★ ★

That afternoon a buggy drawn by a plodding gray horse drew up and Dude saw two women peering curiously at the camp. He went out to them, swept off his hat, bowed and said, 'Good afternoon, ladies. What can I do for you?'

'We are looking for Dr. William Tecumseh Lockhart, the distinguished Kentucky horseman,' said the one at the reins. 'I am Mrs. Levi Haley and this is Mrs. Dewitt Wheeler — the widow Wheeler.'

'I am Dude McQuinn. Pleased to meet you, ladies.'

'Oh, we've read about you too, Mr. McQuinn,' Mrs. Haley said, impressed, all twinkling eyes.

Dude hung his head as a manifestation of modesty. 'Afraid your editor's pen got away from him just a little. Dr. Lockhart is over there, resting in the shade. He's been a bit poorly.'

'May we speak to him?'

'Certainly. You will find him a true Kentucky gentleman.'

Mrs. Haley, a plump little woman with a girlish face and lively brown eyes, secured the reins around the whip socket, and Dude assisted her down, then Mrs. Wheeler. The latter's sharp expression and the set of her jaws told him that she was a no-nonsense person and not likely to fail once embarked on a mission. She was tall and bony and a long way from being a beauty. Both were in their middle years.

As Dude escorted the women into camp, Uncle Billy looked startled for an instant. Quickly recovering, he rose to meet them and took off his hat, his face smoothing, his manner genteel and dignified.

After Dude made the introductions, Mrs. Haley offered her hand to Uncle Billy and said, 'We are very pleased to meet you, Dr. Lockhart. We are from the ladies' auxiliary of the Lightfoot County Historical Society and we read with great interest of your Plymouth Colony antecedents. Mrs. Wheeler, who is president of the society, is related to no less than William Brewster, a founder of the colony, on her paternal side.'

He bowed low, an old-school bow. 'Pride in one's founding fathers is worthy of note, indeed it is.'

Mrs. Wheeler seemed to relax her aggressive features. She shook hands like a man, heartily, her grip so forcible that Dude saw the old gent wince.

'We want you to address the society at our meeting Tuesday next,' Mrs. Wheeler said, barging straight to the point.

He coughed weakly behind his hand. 'I am flattered that you ladies would ask me. However, I've been unwell lately and must respectfully decline your gracious invitation.' Turning to Dude, at the same time sending him a murderous look, he said, 'I'm sure Mr. McQuinn will be honored to speak in my place. After all, he is a direct descendant of the immortal Sam Houston. No doubt you ladies read that in the *Pioneer Courier*?'

Dude said at once, backing off, 'I believe the Plymouth Colony far surpasses in importance General Houston, great as he was.'

'Indeed it does,' Mrs. Wheeler said, her tone decisive. 'Dr. Lockhart, we insist that you address the society because of your Mayflower ancestry. It is so remarkable to find another person of early American lineage comparable to my own. It is even thrilling.'

The old man had acquired a suddenly cornered look. 'Speaking of quality folk,' he said, gesturing toward Coyote, busy attaching a new girth on the light racing saddle, 'over there is a fella who traces back to the first Americans with plenty to spare — Mr. Coyote Walking. His ancestors met the boat. He'd make an excellent speaker for you.'

Coyote, already alerted, said, 'Me Comanche — no savvy much white-man talk,' and, picking up the racing tack, retreated behind the wagon.

Growing more firm, Mrs. Wheeler said, 'Dr. Lockhart, you cannot afford to disappoint the society, especially the ladies of Lightfoot, who do all the society's work. Never again will such a coincidence of historical significance as this occur in Lightfoot. Imagine, meeting another person with Plymouth Colony antecedents! We could even be related.' She gave him a little tweak on the cheek. 'Can't you just picture our brave people standing on the deck of the Mayflower, gazing toward that distant shore of freedom?' She swung her shoulders, a gesture of decision. 'We'll expect you at the town hall over the bank come Tuesday evening at seven o'clock sharp. I myself shall assume the honor of introducing you personally. Refreshments will be served after your lecture. Thank you.'

Before he could refuse again, she and Mrs. Haley marched shoulder to shoulder to the buggy, climbed in and drove off waving, especially Mrs. Wheeler.

'Uncle, I do believe that Mrs. Wheeler has taken a shine to you,' Dude guyed him. 'She could be draggin' her rope to catch a man. Mrs. Haley called her the widow Wheeler.'

'Widow!' Uncle Billy glared at Dude. 'You and that Van Vinson, if you didn't get me hemmed in!'

'Uncle, you know it would have been ungentlemanly to refuse. Keep in mind that some sweet little lady might be in the market for a blind trotter Tuesday evening.'

* * *

At midmorning next day a man coming from the square nodded and said, 'Saw that piece in the paper. Like to look at your horses.'

'You are welcome to,' Dude said. 'The blue roan is Avalanche, the trotter, the bay is Texas Jack, the Thoroughbred.'

He had the two horses tied nearby for easy display. Judge Blair was haltered between the two sorrels behind the wagon.

'Avalanche has coursed the mile in two minutes Bat,' Dude said, first planting the idea of speed. 'He's as gentle as any kid pony and handles well, is an easy keeper and can go all day in that hurry-up trot of his. Any little ol' lady would find him an ideal drivin' horse.'

'Why the blinkers?' the man asked.

'He's always wore 'em. Does better that way. Keeps his mind on where he's headed.'

The visitor made a quick look-see around Amos and no more. A dismissal. He wasn't interested in a fast trotter. Going over to the racy-looking Texas Jack, he stood still and studied the gelding for fully two minutes. 'So this is your racehorse?' he said.

'He's it. Texas Jack. Just gettin' over the colic and not long ago he bruised his left knee. I might run him like he is for a short go.' *Let this bird jaw around and match us long, figuring he's got the advantage. The Judge will be ready.*

'Easy now . . . easy,' the man said, bringing his hand along the point of the gelding's shoulder and chest, arm and forearm, down to the knee. He studied the knee and examined it gently. 'There's no swelling,' he said. 'Does he seem to favor it?'

'Not that I can tell. Maybe it's like the old saying, 'He only hurts when he runs.''

The man stood and ranged his eyes over Texas Jack from tail to head. After a wait, he said, 'He looks a little short-coupled for a Thoroughbred and is not rangy like a distance horse. His tail is a shade lower than the point of his hips and he stands higher behind than in front. But he is well-fanned. A nice-looking horse. Good muscles. Heavy shoulders and muscled rear quarters. Long underline. Nice.'

Dude knew immediately this was no ordinary loafer from the town square, come to idle away time. This man knew horses. He was short and stocky, as thick across his middle as he was at the shoulders, eyes pale and bold. He had the weathered skin of a man who spent much time outdoors. He said, 'So you would run him short?'

'Might.'

'Good idea, if he's hurting.'

'You got a racehorse?'

'Not me. A friend does.' He circled Texas Jack again, slower this time. 'Mind telling me how far you like to run him when you do match him long?'

Now, that's a slick one, Dude thought. He grinned and said, 'That depends on what the other hombre agrees to, but most times four furlongs,' continuing to fix the notion of a Thoroughbred that usually ran short.

'You got a real nice horse,' the man said, leaving. 'Real nice.'

Dude watched him go. *The first nibble. It was about time.* However, he could not but feel a degree of wariness. The man was cagey.

Watching, Dude saw a horseman rein out from the square and head this way. He passed the man leaving the camp. Neither spoke. Dude recognized the rider as Cy Kirby, who waved and looked troubled when he rode in. He dismounted and shook hands, saying, feigning need, 'Thought I'd borrow some more patchin' leather. Remember me?'

'I remember you, Cy Kirby, and we've got leather left. I'm Dude McQuinn and that's Dr. William Tecumseh Lockhart and that's Mr. Coyote Walking.'

Shaking hands, Kirby was obviously glad to meet the outfit. The harried stamp on his face left him and when Dude offered him coffee, he accepted and squatted down on his heels to visit.

'What I really came for,' he said, 'was to thank you again for your help that day. I hurried off pretty fast. Also wondered if you'd matched a race yet? We get the paper. Years ago, back in Illinois, I had a mare that could run some. She had Shiloh blood.'

'Not yet,' Dude said, 'though the man that was just here seemed interested, close-mouthed as he was.'

'Mean you don't know who that was?'

Dude looked blank. 'He didn't say.'

'That was Stub Tate, Gideon Lightfoot's jockey and trainer and general all-around handyman, bank guard and collector on old notes.'

'The first part figures. I could tell he knew horses, the way he went over Texas Jack.'

'They say Tate used to ride on the big Eastern tracks — New York and New Jersey, and down in Maryland. A top jockey. He came out here when Gideon Lightfoot bought Old Dominion some years back.'

Uncle Billy, slumped in his chair, sat up suddenly and asked Kirby, 'Tate, you said — Stub Tate? Know his given name?'

'He's always gone by Stub around here.'

Dude slanted an eye at Uncle Billy. 'Does the name ring a bell?' Dude was thinking it might be a window on his old partner's past.

'Now, did I say? It just struck me I'd heard it somewhere — that was all.'

'Tell us more about this Stub Tate,' Dude said. 'I noticed you two didn't speak or nod when you passed.'

Kirby's face was rueful. 'I told you Tate is a collector. He's been out to see me more than once. The mortgage on my place is past due. Gideon Lightfoot' — his lips thinned — 'the Honorable Gideon Lightfoot — has given me a month to pay it or he'll foreclose. We've had two lean years in this section of the state, but this season looks good. Plenty of rain for a change at the right time. Trouble is, Lightfoot won't extend my mortgage till I get my wheat in.'

'So that's why he owns most of the town and probably most of the county?'

'It's all legal. He's always within the letter of the law.'

'There's no other way you can raise the money?'

Kirby smiled dryly. 'No way that's honest.'

'Ever think of bringing in a horse that can run a hole in the wind, bringing him in under another name? Get odds, then dust Old Dominion?

'Would if I knew one. You got one in mind?'

'Oh, it's just a thought,' Dude said, shrugging, shying away from saying too much. 'Naturally, I'll run Texas Jack at him if Lightfoot takes my challenge.'

'Texas Jack had better be fast.'

'What's the lowdown on Old Dominion?'

'A big, powerful chestnut. A little slow on the break, but once under way he runs like a singed cat. He's plenty horse.'

'Where does Lightfoot stall him?'

'At one of his farms south of town.

Keeps a man at the barn around the clock.'

'Guess he's afraid somebody will slip in and fix his horse.'

'Gideon Lightfoot never takes a chance on anything. For instance, he won't match his horse short, no distance under half a mile, because Old Dominion is a slow breaker, and everybody knows the break is everything in a short race.'

'Van Vinson told us the farmers bet on the Missouri mare that got beat. How come? Most people back the local champion?'

'Not if they don't like the owner. We figured the mare could take Old Dominion. Lightfoot even gave odds. He cleaned up.'

'Van said the mare didn't run her race. Didn't look right. Any idea what happened?'

Kirby shook his head.

'She was fixed, wasn't she?'

'Something was wrong. A stranger thing happened when some cattlemen in Indian Territory brought in a sure-enough fast stud called Midnight. Like the mare, he looked lightning fast working out.' Kirby sipped his coffee before continuing. 'It was Saturday and folks for miles around came to see the race. What happens? The cattlemen forfeited five hundred dollars. Said Midnight couldn't run, that he was off his feed.'

'There are a lot of ways to fix a horse,' Dude said, all innocence. 'You have any suggestions for us, if we do match Lightfoot?'

'You bet I have. Sleep with your horse. Don't leave him day or night, and check any feed you buy in town.'

'You are suspicious!'

'I picked up a few wrinkles back in Illinois when I had a fast mare, but lost more times than I won. Tell you what. If you match this race, let me furnish the grain. That way you won't have to worry.' He put down his tin cup and stood.

'Thanks, Cy. We'll remember that, if we match the race.'

As Kirby rode off, Dude said, 'What

do you think, Uncle?'

'I don't like the looks of this setup. You can't win here. Stay out of it.'

'I hate to see a good man like Cy Kirby lose his farm.'

'Don't start getting softhearted now, Dude. We could end up in a switch ourselves. But knowing one Alamo Texan like I do, I can see that you'll ignore good advice and match this race.'

A little later Dude saw the old man pondering over a letter, the first Dude had seen him pen, for he never spoke of family or old friends. Finished, he folded and sealed the letter carefully before addressing it, stuck it inside his coat pocket, rose and without explanation walked to town.

★ ★ ★

By ten o'clock Saturday morning the campground was beginning to fill with farmers bringing ailing horses and mules. Van Vinson was among the early arrivals, chatting for news.

157

'Dude,' Uncle Billy said, 'I could hang you and that editor fella. But I'll do what I can, poorly as I am.' He moved to his medicine chest and Dude heard the corncob stopper on the jug go thung. Afterward, quick of step and bright of eye, the old man stepped out to the milling crowd and, rising to the occasion, said cordially, 'Which one of you gentlemen is first?'

After some looking around and holding back, a bearded farmer led out an aged mule, saying, 'Jasper's got the staggers.'

'Fortunately,' Uncle Billy said, peering intently at the mule, 'it is not the blind staggers or Jasper wouldn't be here. Take one-half gill of melted lard, which is equal to two fluid ounces, one-half gill of strong sage tea-mix and pour down his throat. That will effect a cure in thirty minutes.'

'Is that all?'

'That's all. You have a fine old mule there, sir.'

The next farmer said his workhorse

had an 'outbreak of warts.'

'Saturate with spirits of turpentine three times a day for a week,' Uncle Billy said. 'This remedy has never been known to fail. Who's next, please?'

Another man's horse had the itch.

'Itch or mange, it is one and the same,' Uncle Billy lectured, taking a close look at the miserable animal. 'It is a contagious disease caused by parasitic mites burrowing under the skin.' Sighting Vinson visiting with a farmer, he called out as a teacher might an inattentive pupil, 'Mr. Vinson, take down the following treatment for this gentleman, and write so he can read it:

'Wash the horse thoroughly all over with castile soap. Then apply this mixture — four ounces of sulphur, four ounces of green copperas, four ounces of white hellebore root in powder. . . . I thought you called yourself a newspaperman, Mr. Vinson? Why, you write no faster than a fumbling schoolboy . . . Mix together in two quarts of fresh buttermilk and rub the affected parts freely twice daily. That should give this fine animal rapid relief . . . . Next gentleman step right up.'

Not once going to his medicine chest to look up a mixture, Uncle Billy reeled off remedies through cures for the glanders, nasal gleet, stifle-joint lameness, hidebound, fistula, heaves, thumps, harness and saddle galls, sweeny and bone spavin, barking the prescriptions so fast that Vinson scribbled furiously to keep up.

Then a farmer — thin, stooped, tottering — led up a sleepy-looking, venerable bay saddler whose breathing was labored.

Uncle Billy observed the animal at length and said, 'I see he has the colic.'

'Old Dan has,' the man replied laconically.

'Have you tried the olden-day home remedy of two common tablespoonfuls of saleratus — not heaping — mixed with one and one-half pints of sweet milk, given in one dose?'

'Have. Didn't work.'

'By chance, have you tried one ounce each of chloroform, laudanum, sulphuric ether, and eight ounces of linseed oil?'

'Have. Didn't work.'

'I see that you have done your best for your old and trusted friend, good neighbor.' Uncle Billy stepped to the horse and squinted into the drowsy eyes, listened to the ragged breathing and felt of the pulse, and turned to the owner. 'I'm afraid this calls for Professor Gleason's One-Shot Remedy. It is drastic and may not be a permanent cure — but is always good to trade on, if you get my meaning?'

'Do,' the elder said and grinned knowingly, as did the appreciative watchers.

Uncle Billy looked around, searching, and Dude felt the old man's eyes fix upon him.

'Mr. McQuinn, hustle uptown and get three ounces of gunpowder and one pint of Kentucky sour-mash whiskey. Hurry, now.'

Dude took off, striding fast. When he returned with the gunpowder in a small sack and a pint of whiskey, Uncle Billy looked critically at the label on the bottle and said, 'Guess I failed to tell you the whiskey must be hundred proof — this is only eighty-six. Hustle, now. This old horse is hurting.'

Again, Dude hurried, but when the old man read the label on the bottle, his mouth squeezed in self-reproach and he said, 'Tarnation, if I didn't forget to tell you the whiskey has to be six years old. This is a mere four.'

'Won't four do?'

'Mr. McQuinn, for a remedy to be effective the ingredients must be exact. No more, no less. Hustle, now. Let's do this right.'

Dude got it. The old coot was getting even.

He went for the whiskey and hurried back, by now breathless.

Uncle Billy checked the label and said, 'Very good, Mr. McQuinn. Six years old.' Turning to the wagon, he let down the tailgate and reached inside the medicine chest and took out a fruit jar, an empty quait whiskey bottle and a tin funnel. He poured the whiskey into the fruit jar, then the gunpowder, sloshed thoroughly, funneled the contents into the bottle, and ambled back to his audience.

'And now, gentlemen,' he said, off on one of his lectures, 'I shall demonstrate how to give a horse medicine. The old practice of forcing the head of a horse by tile halter over a beam or pole to administer medicine is as cruel as it is absurd. The lower jaw of the horse should remain perfectly free while taking medicine. Remember that. . . . What you do is take a forked stick or a common pitchfork and run it through a small strap fastened to the upper jaw of the horse. No strangling or struggling will take place, if done correctly. Remember, neither man nor beast can drink unless the lower jaw is free to move. My friend, Mr. McQuinn, can give a testimonial to that.'

Once more Dude could feel the boring eyes as Uncle Billy said, 'I now call on my two able assistants to join in the demonstration. Mr. McQuinn, fetch the equipment from the wagon.' Arms folded, the old man waited like a performer on stage, and when Dude brought a buckled leather strap and a long, forked stick, 'Mr. Vinson, you will affix the strap to the horse's upper jaw.'

'Me?' Vinson quailed, taken by surprise. 'I've never done that.'

'Then now is a good time to learn what any schoolboy can do. Come forward, please.'

Sheepishly, Vinson took the strap from Dude and advanced uncertainly to the saddler; fumbling, he tried to force the strap between the horse's jaws and could not.

One man laughed. Another and another, until there was a ripple of laughter.

'Mr. McQuinn, lend Mr. Vinson a hand. Obviously he's a city boy.'

Dude laid down the forked stick and, pulling on the horse's upper and lower lips, pried open his mouth. Vinson slipped in the strap.

'Now, Mr. Vinson,' ordered the

authoritarian voice, 'while the gentleman holds the halter, you slip the fork under the strap and elevate the horse's head. You — Mr. McQuinn — administer the medicine I am about to hand you.'

Vinson, after almost jabbing the poor animal's eye, forced the fork under the strap and pushed the horse's head upward.

'Medicine, Mr. McQuinn! Medicine! Be quick!'

Perhaps it was the smell of the whiskey and gunpowder, or the discomfort of the strap and the stick, or the way Vinson and Dude kept jumping around. Whatever, of a sudden the old horse started rearing and kicking and lunging just as Dude was pouring the medicine.

It spilled, all of it, even though the elderly owner still held the halter rope.

'You'll have to go for more whiskey and more gunpowder, Mr. McQuinn,' Uncle Billy said, concealing a smile. 'Hurry. We can't let this poor horse suffer any longer.'

'On one condition,' Dude panted.

'That you give the medicine . . . while I put a rope around this critter's neck.'

'Very well.'

Dude hurried off for the ingredients, and Uncle Billy mixed them as before.

When the old man approached, the saddler began acting up again. Hiding the bottle behind him, murmuring all the while to the wall-eyed patient, Uncle Billy then said, 'Gently, Mr. Vinson, with the fork,' and as the horse's jaws opened and Dude steadied the rope, the old man swiftly poured the contents of the bottle down the animal's throat.

'Remove the fork and strap, Mr. Vinson, and the rope, Mr. McQuinn.'

A swell of spontaneous applause followed, which Uncle Billy recognized with a modest little bow of his head. He said to the saddler's owner, 'Unless you want to keep Old Dan out of sentiment, I suggest that you trade him off to the first stranger you meet.'

No more ailing animals remained, and when no one voiced an interest in buying Amos and the crowd showed sigus of breaking up, Dude feared another fruitless day. He caught Van Vinson's eye. An understanding passed between them, whereupon the editor spoke up in a loud voice, 'Dr. Lockhart, I wish you would demonstrate Professor Gleason's famed Eureka Bridle. I understand it is sensational and new to this part of the West.'

There was an immediate stirring toward Uncle Billy. Farmers leading off their stock turned around and waited.

'I might — if there is sufficient interest,' Uncle Billy said coyly, not unlike a musician who must be begged before he will play.

A voice jeered, 'Fessor what's-his-name's Eureka Bridle? Never heard of it.'

The scoffer, Dude saw, was none other than the smart-alecky Rufus Hubbard back for more punishment.

'There's a great deal in this old world that you haven't heard of, friend Rufus,' Uncle Billy said. 'Professor what's-his-name happens to be the late Professor P. D. Gleason, who knew more about horses than any man, past or present, in the United States of America.'

'I don't see no bridle, Grandpa.'

'You won't see the conventional bridle, sonny. Mr. McQuinn, please go to the wagon and fetch me the Eureka.'

Dude did so, dangling a length of stout cord with a slip noose in one end that he handed over ceremoniously.

'That's a bridle?' Rufus scoffed and winked around.

Uncle Billy ignored him, waiting until more onlookers had crowded about before he replied, looking straight at the doubting Rufus. 'To get the attention of a horse or mule, I trust none of you first hit the poor creature over the head with a club.' He displayed the piece of cord as one might an object of great mystery. Everybody stared. Then: 'Professor Gleason devised the Eureka Bridle after years of trial and error for only one purpose — the prevention of cruelty to animals and for the safety of mankind. Its very simplicity is mystifying. Yet, it will hold any horse or mule under any circumstances.'

'Will it hold a mean stud horse?' Rufus jeered.

'It will hold a bull elk, if you can get close enough to slip the noose over his antlers and around his neck.'

Everyone laughed except Rufus, who only glowered. 'How much you gettin' for it?' he asked suspiciously.

Uncle Billy was offended. 'You don't think I'm traveling about the country peddling bridles, do you? This piece of common cord is ten feet long and one eighth of an inch in diameter. It can be purchased for a few cents at any general store.'

'How's it work?' Rufus was still unconvinced and expecting a 'catch,' Dude saw.

'Simple. First, slip the noose around the neck, pass the cord through the mouth over the tongue from the off side; then through the noose on the near side, and pull forward firmly. Next, over the head just behind the ears, from the near side; then under the upper lip, above the upper jaw from the off side, pass through a second time and tie. Now, that sounds a little complicated. Would you like me to demonstrate this on your horse? Or did you ride a mule to town?'

Rufus glowered. 'A good saddler. I'll bring him in.'

The 'good saddler' turned out to be a gentle individual whose extremely heavy frame and plate-sized feet suggested draft horse ancestry.

'Remove the bridle, friend Rufus.'

That done, Uncle Billy slipped the noose over the large head and slowly went through the passes, explaining each as he progressed, ending with the tie and the reins.

'Now, take him off and back,' the old man instructed. 'Don't be afraid to turn him. He will obey you for a reason which I shall presently explain.'

With a skeptical wink, Rufus mounted and rode out to the street. There he turned in a circle to his left, then in a circle to his right. He pulled on the reins and the horse halted. When he gave the horse slack and clapped his heels, it moved ahead. 'Well, it does work,' he admitted as he rode up. 'But why?'

'The key is the leverage against the upper lip, which is quite sensitive. So you try tying the bridle. I will leave only the loop around the neck You take it from there.'

Rufus began, but was soon lost in loops and tangles. On his second attempt, while Uncle Billy coached him, step by step, he completed the intricate weavings, as pleased with himself as a country boy solving a riddle.

'You are to be congratulated, young sir,' Uncle Billy said, whapping him on the back, 'on being the first man in Lightfoot County to tie Professor Gleason's Eureka Bridle. Would someone else like to step up and learn how?'

After that, it was like a new game as the farmers pressed in, talking and joking, eager to take their turns. During this time, Dude happened to see a man watching from the edge of the road. It was Stub Tate. The bold eyes seemed more than curious. Discovering Dude's eyes on him, he turned and walked away.

Cagey, Dude thought. Cagey.

One by one, the farmers left. After the last demonstration, Uncle Billy freed the cord, coiled it neatly, bowed graciously, and presented it to Rufus. He mumbled his thanks, kicked at a clod, and asked, 'Is it still three hundred for Avalanche?'

'It is — he's such an outstanding trotter — and for you throw in the harness.'

'I'll think about it. Would you come down a little?'

'I'll think about it.'

Each had a laugh at that, and the deal hung there.

When the young man had gone, Uncle Billy sighed and told Vinson and Dude, 'Rufus is the only prospect I have and he can't rake up the money. That's plain.'

'And I got stuck for the whiskey and gunpowder,' Dude moaned. 'Not a match race in sight, though I did spot Stub Tate eyeballing us.'

Vinson said, 'That means the Honorable G.L. is interested.'

'I think we need to stir the pot,' Dude

said. 'Uncle, remember that wrinkle we pulled in the Lone Star Saloon in Fort Worth?'

The old man was silent. Gradually, the discouragement faded from his face and Dude saw a puckish twinkle. 'How could I forget it? Proved there's more than one way to match a horse race.'

'It takes two to set it up.'

'Oh, I'll side you. But poorly as I am, don't expect me to do any more. Right now I need a little toddy and nap.'

7

As the Bard Quoth

Midaftemoon had come before Dude and Uncle Billy and Coyote Walking ventured into the Jayhawk Saloon, thronged with farmers and townsmen. Pool and card games were going at the rear of the long room, while a tired-looking little man in gartered sleeves toiled listlessly at the off-tune piano on what sounded like 'The Blue Tail Fly.' On the nearest wall, through the coils of smoke, Dude saw the familiar lithograph of 'Custer's Last Fight,' and the fistic likeness of 'The Great John L.' stripped to the waist, wearing the heavyweight champion's belt, and a print of Dexter, the great trotting sire of long ago, a son of the famed Hambletonian, pulling a high sulky at ground-eating speed. The time of 2:17¼ by his name.

They shouldered through to the mahogany bar, Dude noting also the picture of the customary buxom nude reclining on a tiger-skin covered couch above the tiers of murky glasses and bottles. Mottoes abounded alongside the mirror: DON'T ASK FOR CREDIT — WE'RE FRESH OUT. THINK OF HOME AND DEAR OLD MOTHER WHEN YOU HAVE A DRINK — THEN HAVE ANOTHER. IF DRINKING INTERFERES WITH YOUR BUSINESS — YOU'RE IN THE WRONG BUSINESS. IF YOU WANT TO FIGHT GO OUTSIDE — BUT REMEMBER TO COME BACK IN.

Dude and Uncle Billy ordered their 'usual,' Old Green River, and Coyote had a sarsaparilla.

'I perceive that you gentlemen are good judges of good whiskey and your Indian friend is a model of abstinence,' said the gravel-voiced bartender, a man of intimidating physical dimensions — pomaded hair parted in the middle, a gold chain draped across his vast middle, lodge emblems bedecking his jacket of stained white duck — sliding glasses toward them, uncorking a bottle of Bourbon, and, last, in disapproval, serving Coyote's sweet soft drink. 'As the bard quoth, 'Strive mightily — but eat and drink tidily.' '

'Thank you, sir,' Dude responded, sliding silver across the bar. 'It is an honor to be in your high-class establishment.'

The bartender grinned and moved down the bar, and the partners swapped nods of agreement based on Van Vinson's prior briefing: Big Boy Brody, the Jayhawk's affable tavern keeper and bouncer and one-time prizefighter back East, earthy and unpretentious, qualities that endeared him to his rural patrons. And a good deal more. A well-read man for these distant parts, quick with quips, who on request would recite 'Shamus O'Brien' with great feeling, and who liked to quote (and misquote, Vinson said) the classics — a bit or two here and there, though a bit of learning went a long way out here. Brody also started local horse races, which gave Dude pause for thought. *Tsssk. Tsssk. The Honorable G.L.'s man starting races in which G.L.'s horse is running? Now isn't that sweet?* Not every itinerant horse outfit had the benefit of a forewarning Vinson.

Uncle Billy tasted his drink and ut it down, muttering, 'If this is Old Green River, it's changed course.'

'Been watered down,' Dude said, likewise sampling. 'But don't say anything. Brody's our man.'

As the afternoon wore on and the outfit had another round of drinks, the place filled and the clamor grew louder. A row started at the gaming tables. Angry voices exploded. Two men stood, spilling cards and poker chips. They started swinging.

Brody rounded the end of the bar and bounded over there, surprisingly quick for a big man. He tore the two adversaries apart, and a hand clutching the collar of each, marched them to the door and outside.

Brody returned to his station behind the bar, shaking his head tolerantly, full of high humor, evidently having enjoyed the brief set-to, and when a tipsy customer asked him if he knew that an acquaintance had been kicked by a mule, Brody affected a dramatic stance, hand inside his white duck jacket, and commenced reciting loudly, 'As the bard quoth, 'Alas, poor Yorick! I knew him well! A feller of much pleasin' tomfoolery, of most excellent taste in whiskey and women. He hath toted me on his back a thousand times, and now how terrible in my imagination it is! My gorge rises to think that he ayproached a mule from the back instead of the front. Alas, poor Yorick!''

The bleary-eyed rubes along the bar howled with coarse laughter and gave him whapping applause and ordered another round.

Coyote flinched at the paraphrase and into Dude's ear, he whispered, 'All wrong, white father. All wrong. Hamlet says, 'Let me see,' and takes the skull and then he says, 'Alas, poor Yorick! I knew him, Horatio: a fellow of infinite jest, of most excellent fancy: he hath borne me on his back a thousand times; and now how abhorred in my imagination it is! My gorge rises at it. Here hung lips that — ' '

'Never mind, Coyote,' Dude interrupted. 'Don't say anything. We don't want to rile 'im.'

Marshal Columbus Epps strolled through the crowd and up to the bar. Brody was quickly there, deferring to him.

'Any trouble tonight?' Epps asked in that deep and official voice.

'The good ship Jayhawk rides a calm sea, Marshal. Everybody's behavin' like little lambs. How about some drinks on the house?'

'Might have one. Have to make my rounds, you know. Keep an eye on things. Been a passel of strangers about lately.'

'How well I know. As the bard quoth, 'Your rounds you make — to keep our fair city safe.' ' Brody set out a bottle and glass.

Epps poured his own, downed it, roved his eyes about, and departed.

After him, Coyote puffed out his cheeks and slowly exhaled.

Now and then a farmer who had been at what one called 'the doctorin' session' would come up to the outfit and speak.

'Dr. Lockhart,' said the man whose mule had the staggers, 'why don't you settle here in Lightfoot. We're sorely in need of a good vet.'

'I'm too poorly. Thank you just the same.'

'Dr. Lockhart has to get back to his duties in Kentucky after he tries the salubrity of the climate in Texas,' Dude explained. 'Will you all have a drink with me?'

They would.

Brody was all ears when he served the drinks. His attention seemed to redouble, Dude thought, when the farmer asked, 'Have you sold your trotter or matched Texas Jack?'

'Not yet,' Dude said.

'He's a smooth-lookin' horse, that Texas Jack. Guess he's ready to run or you wouldn't have made the challenge in the *Courier*?'

'I'll let you in on something, my

friend,' Dude said, easing his voice to a confidential low, but not too low for the listening Brody. 'Truth is, he's just gettin' over the colic.' *Let Brody pass that on to the Honorable G.L.* 'But we'll match 'im if the distance suits us.'

'Which means what?'

'If it's not too yonder for us.'

The farmer displayed a toothy grin. 'How much yonder is to your liking?'

'About half a mile.'

Brody, who hadn't moved, suddenly began blowing on a murky glass and polishing it

Another man whose face looked familiar to Dude pushed through to slap Uncle Billy on the back. It was none other than the elderly owner of the colicky saddler.

'Doctor', the old gentleman said, beaming, 'I want you to know that professor what's-his-name's remedy of gunpowder and whiskey worked like a charm. I just sold Old Dan to a stranger who seemed in an awful hurry and kept lookin' behind him. Got a nice price, too.'

'I am pleased to hear that.'

'Let's all drink to Old Dan.'

They did.

Presently, two ranks down the bar, a smallish farmer complained, 'Big Boy, what's wrong with the whiskey? Don't taste right. Tastes weak.'

Brody's face tensed, close to anger, and then he grinned and said, 'It's your taster. As the bard quoth, 'One swallow don't make a summer.''

At that, Coyote, no longer able to restrain himself, chimed aloud, 'I believe it was Miguel de Cervantes who said, 'One swallow never makes a summer,' and John Heywood, who also said, 'One swallow maketh not summer.''

Brody's veneer of house camaraderie vanished. He slanted an eye at Coyote and set another bottle before the complainer and said, 'The bard had another saying along that line. 'You can lead a horse to water, but you can't make 'im drink.'' He swung around, daring Coyote to top that, upon which Coyote replied distinctly, 'Heywood said, 'A man may well bring a horse to the water, but he

cannot make him drink without he will.'
I believe the bard put an e on the end of drink. Old English, you know.'

Dude said aside, 'That's enough, Coyote. Don't make him mad. We want him to listen some more.'

'White-man bards write well, they do,' said Coyote, shrugging, 'but white men quote well, they do not,' and he left them to watch a pool game.

To Dude's relief, a fleshy woman wearing enough paint for a Plains Indian chose that moment to emerge from a back room and stand by the piano. She spoke to the weary little man, who promptly spanked the ivories and she swung into the lyrics of 'Oh, Mr. Bartender, Has Father Been Here?'

Not too bad, Dude thought.

When she finished, her onetime soprano drew only a spattering of applause. Apparently sensing the need for something more suited to her worn voice, she spoke again to the accompanist and they quickened into the lively 'Little Brown Jug.'

Much better, Dude judged, and joined in the applause as she took her bow.

'Better spring it pretty soon, if we're going to,' Uncle Billy said at Dude's ear. 'I'm still feeling poorly. I hope you've picked a road where there's brush.'

Dude nodded and, catching Brody's eagle business eye, waved genially and turned again to the old man, timing his conversation just as Brody moved down the bar to them. 'All right. We'll blow Texas Jack out Monday morning before daybreak north of town.' And as if he had said too much and been overheard, he faced hastily about to Brody and said, 'Another round of Old Green River, Mr. Bartender.'

Brody leaned in. This close, Dude saw details he had not before: Brody's gray eyes, set deep and hard, around them the scars of many ring fights and brawls. His broad nose was bent. His mustached mouth looked battered.

'That Indian friend of yours is mighty free with his lip,' he said, bringing up a bottle and setting it down with a thunk, and with an oversized right hand pulling the cork.

'He savvies American pretty good,' Dude said, smiling. 'He meant no offense. That's what they teach reservation Indians at Orrlisle School in Pennsylvania.'

'They oughta teach 'em manners and send 'em back to the reservation and keep 'em there.'

Dude let it go by without comment and paid for the watered whiskey.

They were heading for camp with Coyote soon afterward when Uncle Billy asked, 'Think Brody heard it?'

'I'm sure he did. The question is will he pass it on and will the Honorable G.L. take the bait?'

⋆　⋆　⋆

They rode north at a steady trot through the filmy darkness of early morning, dawn minutes away, the sweet scent of dewy grass on the mewling wind. Dude astride Blue Grass, Uncle Billy on one of the sorrels, and Coyote Walking mounted behind them. Dude had chosen the north road because of the scattering of underbrush and timber on both sides, noticed when he and Coyote were looking for a likely stretch on which to work Judge Blair, a level road free of concealment from which they might be spied on, hence their choice of the open east road.

Earlier, Coyote had scouted along the north road on foot, carefully lteeping to cover, posting himself there and waiting.

'Two white men,' he reported back at camp. 'One little man, one very big man. I could hear them talking. Big man said, 'I understand they'll work that horse half a mile. It's about that far to where the road makes a bend. You take cover along here and see where they start from. I'll ride to the bend and start my stopwatch when I hear the horse break. Way the wind is blowing, I should be able to pick it up. They won't hang around long because they're working their horse on the sly. When it's good daylight, we can go over the ground and figure the distance fairly close.''

'Tate and Brody,' Dude said. 'We're all set, Coyote.'

'You two hoot owls hold on,' a raspy voice called behind them.

Dude was surprised, thinking Uncle Billy still in his bedroll under the wagon. Standing there in his long underwear, which he wore winter and summer, with his white bib of a beard and his mane of white hair hanging to his shoulders, he reminded Dude of a ghostly patriarch.

'Hold on,' he said again. 'Poorly as I am, I didn't want to get into this. But I can see that you two have overlooked an important fact that could squelch the whole match. Sure, they've taken the bait — so far. But if Texas Jack runs half a mile like a hoptoad, which he will, and you try to match this G.L. fella, they'll smell something right away. Who would put up money on a horse that slow? That half a mile will have to be run in forty-nine or fifty flat or it won't look right. Remember, Cy Kirby said Old Dominion has run the half in forty-six flat.'

'I figured we'd just gallop Texas Jack

pretty good,' Dude said. 'Won't do. Not after you let fall to Brody you planned to blow the horse out. That means a speed work. So we'll have to make the switch now to make this look convincing. We've no other choice.'

Dude looked at Coyote. Each feeling the same, but saying nothing. *At last, Uncle Billy was beginning to sound like his old self.*

'There's not much time for that,' Dude said.

'There's enough, poorly as I feel. Too early for coffee and not late enough for whiskey.'

While the old man dressed, Dude bridled Judge Blair and slapped on blanket and the light racing saddle. By then, Uncle Billy was at the medicine chest. He took out a can and a small paintbrush and led the Judge behind the wagon, even now guarding his artistry. Neither Dude nor Coyote had yet to witness the changeovers.

When the old man led the Judge out a short while later, the gelding's broad blaze was gone. 'I'm glad he's not a bald-faced horse and that both horses have identical white socks on all four feet. I'll remove the marking when we get back. Just gave him a light touch-up. Too early in the game to start the switch and hold to it. Things can happen.'

'Like rain,' Dude said, making a wry face.

'Or some bird snooping around camp. The switch is a great deal like the duration of a country girl's kiss — short and sweet. Now, Coyote, you will have to hold the Judge in, and that won't be easy. You know how he likes to run. So keep in mind forty-nine or fifty flat. If Old Dominion runs it in forty-six — let's say forty-seven or forty-eight, since he hasn't been out lately — and I calculate one second equals one length — that means the other side will figure an advantage of two to three lengths. Think you can hold the Judge down?'

'Whoop, I will not, Grandfather.'

'That's the difference of a second or two right there,' Dude said.

'Another thing,' Uncle Billy warned. 'Do not use the swinging break. That will tack on a little time. Just heel the Judge straight off. Besides, why let them know how we start our horse? The advantage we have at the break?'

'Grandfather Billy, wise you are like Owl Person.'

Uncle Billy replied, in a tone of exasperation, 'How many times do I have to tell you not to call me Grandfather? But nevermind — go on.' He waved his arms.

Dude and Coyote mounted and were turning their horses when the old man said suddenly, 'Poorly as I am, I see I'd better go along. You'll both forget everything I've schooled you on.'

'Think you can make it?' Dude asked, laying on the challenge.

His reply was a jerk of his head. He grabbed a bridle and legged it for the sorrels.

They trotted past the first growth of thick underbrush, continuing a short distance until Coyote, riding between his partners, nudged Dude with his foot.

At that signal Dude said, loud of voice, 'We'll start from here,' and halted.

'How far?' Coyote asked as loudly.

'Blow him out to the bend. That's a good half mile. Dr. Lockhart and I went over the ground Friday, furlong by furlong. Half a mile is about what we guessed.'

'Mr. McQuinn,' Uncle Billy said, taking the cue, his voice indignant, 'I'm not about to 'guess' any common distance. I want you to know I've marked off more than a few racing paths in my day. I can come within a yard of measuring a furlong with the naked eye as I ride over the ground. It is one-half mile to the bend — or four furlongs or four eighths, whatever you wish to call it — no more, no less — give or take a foot or two.'

'That's what I mean, Doctor. A good half mile.'

'If you prefer to run your horse over five furlongs,' the old man went on, still sounding ruffled, 'I should be pleased to go back down the road and mark off the correct distance.'

'Not necessary, Doctor. Half a mile will tell me what I need to know about his condition. Texas Jack is a funny horse. He's no faster over the second furlong than the first, nor the third than the second, nor the fourth than the third. Runs the fifth same as he does the fourth. He wins races on consistency. He's no scorpion, but he's steady.'

'You mean he's more like what the British call a stayer than a sprinting Thoroughbred?'

'You hit it right on the nose, Doctor. All right, Coyote. Take Texas Jack back there a little way and walk him up to me and talce off. This is a speed work. Let's see what he can do.'

Coyote did so and brought the Judge forward. Reining to a halt, he held there a moment, then away they tore.

The break, Dude saw, watching horse and rider growing dimmer in the muddy light, was slower than the usual swinging getaway.

Several minutes passed before Coyote rode back, the horse blowing and capering, full of himself.

'How did he do?' Dude asked.

'He took to the round. I let him out. I believe over the colic he is.'

'Good! Then he's ready to run. Let's go get some breakfast.'

★ ★ ★

Other than the daily drift of loafers from the town square coming to the camp to loaf some more, nothing happened throughout the day.

'I figured we'd have a nibble from the Honorable G.L. by this time,' Dude said that evening, winking, 'now that he knows his horse has got us daylighted.'

'Give him a day or two to ponder on it,' Uncle Billy said. 'He's cautious. Cy Kirby said he never takes a chance.'

'What say we amble into enemy territory this evening, wet our whistles and listen around?'

The old man was for that!

Surprisingly, the Jayhawk was almost as crowded as on Saturday. 'Welcome back, gentlemen,' Big Boy Brody greeted them. 'Will you have the same as the other evening? Old Green River and a sarsaparilla?'

'The same,' Dudesaid, and complimented him. 'You have a remarkable memory, sir.'

Brody smiled. 'You develop that in this business. Some of it you wish you could forget.'

'He wasn't this friendly when we left the other night,' Uncle Billy said, when Brody went to the other end of the bar.

As the evening advanced, the woman came out and to the listless accompaniment, played pianissimo, sang 'I'm Goin' Away' and 'Nobody Knows the Trouble I've Seen' and 'Home on the Range,' familiar weepers guaranteed to spur the trade. In the ensuing crowding along the bar, two men pushed in next to Dude.

'I tell you Old Dominion can daylight anything in Kansas,' declared one. Boastful and overbearing, he was squat and cocky, as erect as a banty rooster. He had a hard little mouth and a cranky face set amid a tangled thicket of reddish whiskers.

'But he's never been matched against the Topeka mare,' replied his companion. There was a drollness about him: the lazy, indolent eyes reflecting an inner amusement, enhanced by a scraggly mustache over loose lips, hat pushed back over a round, balding head, and a bulky body overflowing his greasy shirt and greasy, loose-fitting overalls.

'The Topeka mare — what's she done?'

'Just cleaned out everything east of here — that's all.'

'And Old Dominion's warped everything around here.'

'Tell me this. Why don't Lightfoot campaign his horse, if he's so fast? Why don't he take his horse east? He won't run 'less it's on his own track. Answer me that.'

Their voices were rising, louder and louder, even above the din of the saloon. Suddenly the cocky one pushed the droll one.

Brody was there in an instant, looming over them, clamping a big hand on each man's shoulder. 'As the bard quoth, 'Do not swing or be profane — else no longer in the Jayhawk will you remain,'' he said, and turned to Coyote to top that if he could.

Coyote grinned and shook his head, saying, 'That bard I know not,' and shrugged.

The pair quieted down, but continued to glare at each other.

'Mack,' Brody said, addressing the cocky individual, 'I think you and Lon had better have another drink to cool off' on.' He set out a bottle.

Each poured his own, Mack spilling some of his, and Brody grunted sarcastically, 'Would you like a towel, sir?' And when neither man paid, each waiting on the other, Brody said, 'As the bard quoth, 'Pay on time — or you won't like the rhyme,'' and folded his thick arms, waiting for them to divvy up.

Mack paid for his, though reluctantly. 'All I said was that Old Dominion can beat anything in Kansas.'

'So what?' Brody replied. 'Everybody knows how fast he is.'

'And all I said was that he can't shade the Topeka mare,' Lon said, paying.

'A matter of opinion, which is what makes a horse race.' Looking at Coyote, Brody said, 'You're a good sport, redskin. Here's one on the house for you and your friends.' He served the drinks with a flourish, his air that of the benevolent host. A moment later a fight broke out at the far end of the bar and he rushed there.

'I wonder if all that generosity is not somewhat out of character for one Mr. Brody?' Uncle Billy asked.

Coyote nodded. ' 'For a gift doth blind the eyes of the wise,' Grandfather.'

'Not to forget Miss Dolly's fresh eggs an' milk an' bread fresh from the oven,' Dude recalled with a painful grimace.

Mack and Lon were arguing again. As Dude looked around, Mack muttered, 'I still say no horse in the state can come close to Old Dominion,' and elbowed away from the bar.

'Even though he's got leg problems?' Lon called after him.

'Leg problems?' Dude asked.

'Don't know much about it,' Lon said. 'Something I just heard. Seems he's been doctored for a swelling in one leg.' He shrugged and finished his drink. 'You can hear anything in here.'

Dude glanced in question at Uncle Billy, who nodded that he had heard what was said. Dude, hoping to draw Lon out some more, turned to find him gone.

'Uncle,' Dude said, 'what do you make of that?'

'I'd have to see Old Dominion before I believed saloon gossip.'

★ ★ ★

Tuesday likewise passed uneventfully.

Early that evening, bathed, beard trimmed, boots shined, attired in brushed frock coat, white shirt, string tie and flat-topped hat and exuding the strong aroma of bay rum, Uncle Billy glumly announced himself ready for the meeting of the Lightfoot County Historical Society.

'Dude,' he said, the clear blue eyes accusing, 'you got me into this, you and that Vinson fella, so you have to go with me. That's only fair.'

'Want me to lead the applause after your lecture on the Plymouth Colony and your antecedents — that it?'

'I want you to suffer with me.'

'Why don't you take Coyote?'

'He wouldn't go. Besides, he wasn't the windy hombre that got me into this box canyon surrounded by females.'

'You keep forgettin' this may be a good chance to peddle Amos to some sweet little lady in need of a good drivin' horse.'

'You're talking about a long shot. Come on. We can pick up Vinson on the way. I understood him to say he lives over the print shop.'

Vinson was just leaving to cover the meeting, he said, when they arrived. 'I guess you've boned up on the Plymouth Colony, eh, Doctor?'

'As much as you and Dude did when you cooked up that folderol about me,' the old man replied, casting him a remembering glance.

They climbed the creaky wooden stairs over the bank to the town hall, where they found Mrs. Haley and the widow Wheeler stationed at the door. Mrs. Wheeler went straight to Uncle Billy. 'We are delighted to see you, Dr. Lockhart. We are all anxiously awaiting your lecture on the history of the Plymouth Colony and our mutual antecedents.'

'Indeed,' beamed Mrs. Haley.

The widow Wheeler, her hands suddenly fluttering, stepped in and straightened Uncle Billy's tie, and gave him that little tweak on the cheek.

He bowed gravely. 'Don't you ladies expect too much. I am still under the weather. I may have to cut this short if I feel weak or start coughing.' He cleared his throat as if to remind them.

The two women led away into the

meeting room, which Dude saw was filled with old ladies and a sprinkling of elderly gentlemen, the ladies busy chatting and fanning themselves. As Dude and Vinson took seats in the front row, the editor whispered, 'Has Doc worked on his speech or not?'

'Didn't see him reading anything. But don't worry. He'll think of something.'

When Uncle Billy was seated next to Mrs. Haley at the speaker's table, on which sat a glass and a pitcher of water and a bouquet of wildflowers, the widow Wheeler strode to the lectern.

When the chatting continued, she frowned and rapped hard on the lectern for silence. Immediately the voices subsided. In her resonant voice, she then said, 'It is a great and lasting honor for me to introduce our esteemed speaker of the evening. A true Kentucky gentleman, he is a doctor, scientist, author, world traveler and horseman of international repute. I know all of Lightfoot was thrilled by the performance of his personal driving horse, Avalanche, as reported in the

Pioneer Courier by our ever-alert editor, Mr. Van Vinson. I am further honored to inform you that our distinguished guest's ancestry, like my own' — hand pressed lightly to her ample bosom, she inclined her head in a bow intended as a gesture of modesty — 'goes back to our nation's founding fathers. So it is with great pride that I present Dr. William Tecumseh Lockhart, who will address us on the 'History of the Plymouth Colony.'' Her hands then beat a vigorous welcome.

Dude and Vinson and Mrs. Haley were already clapping, and forthwith the entire audience was applauding.

Calm and dignified, Uncle Billy rose and bowed slowly, left and right and center, on his face that beguiling look of a saint that Dude knew usually presaged the unexpected. The old man cleared his throat and said, 'Thank you, Mrs. Wheeler . . . gracious lady that you are . . . .for that charitable, if not over-charitable, introduction. It is likewise a signal honor for me to address such an august group dedicated to the high moral aims of our abstemious forefathers.' His voice softened, on the verge of breaking. 'I also thank you for your reference to my beloved trotter, Avalanche, the Missouri champion, from whom I must regretfully part company because of the declining state of my health.'

Dude nodded. *Smooth, the way he's bringing Amos to their attention. Smooth.*

Then, facing the audience, seemingly overcome by his sense of loss, the old man said, 'I am pained when I ponder the noblest creature bequeathed man to mistreat and place in unremitting toil until the end of his days. I am humbled when I consider this creature whose strength is boundless, whose grace and beauty are beyond compare, whose blinding speed and fiery spirit are tempered with heartwarming gentleness and undying loyalty. This creature who has carried our nation's destiny on his stout back without complaint. He is truly our cherished national inheritance. For we are the heirs of *Equus caballus* — the horse.'

Led by Mrs. Wheeler and Mrs. Haley, the audience broke into applause, and Uncle Billy bowed his snow-white head in dignified acknowledgment.

'I did not intend to wander so far afield,' he began, and paused strangely. A puzzled expression passed over his features. He seemed to grope for words. His left hand went haltingly to his throat, and all at once he was coughing and gasping for breath. The audience froze.

'I fear . . . I can't go on,' he managed to utter between gasps.

Mrs. Wheeler, there in a flash, guided him to his chair. Mrs. Haley poured water and held the glass to cherry-red lips. He took a slight sip, murmuring in a weak voice, 'Sorry, ladies.' Another sip. 'I'll have to turn the program over to my associate . . . Mr. McQuinn. I know he'll be glad to speak in my place.' He closed his eyes. His bearded chin sank to his chest.

By this time the audience was on its feet and pressing forward in concern.

'Mr. McQuinn?' Mrs. Wheeler

repeated, disappointed. 'Why him? What can he talk on?'

The old man's lips barely moved. 'On Sam Houston. Don't you know he's a *direct* descendant?'

So that was it! The old codger had pulled another slick one. Thinking fast, Dude stepped behind the speaker's table to Uncle Billy. 'I'd better take him outside,' he told the two hovering women. 'He needs fresh air. He gets like this some-times . . . has spells. Van Vinson is here. He can speak to the society.'

Not hesitating, Dude lifted Uncle Billy to his feet and made for the door-way, hearing the widow Wheeler tell Mrs. Haley, 'Fannie, you take over!'

Down the stairs and outside, Dude growled into the old man's ear,

'That was sneaky. You oughta be ashamed, the way you led everybody on.'

Behind them came pounding foot-steps. Mrs. Wheeler charged up, shrilling, 'How is he? How is he?'

'He's coming out of it,' Dude said. 'I'll take him back to camp.'

'You'll do no such thin. My house is close by. Dr. Lockhart needs . . . a bracer or something.'

'A little toddy would be most welcome,' Uncle Billy said, keeping his voice weak.

With the old man between them, the widow Wheeler and Dude walked him to the west end of the square. A block onward she opened a picket gate and showed them into a lamplit house. In the parlor she turned up the wick of a vase lamp and ushered Uncle Billy to a rocker, patted his shoulder, and smiled down at him. An uncommon smile for her, Dude judged. 'Make yourself comfortable — I'll be right back,' she said and went to the kitchen.

Silently forming the words, Dude leaned toward Uncle Billy and said, 'The horse — sell — her — the — horse,' at the same time jabbing a forefinger in the direction of the kitchen to emphasize his meaning.

The old man nodded.

When she rejoined them, she had a

bottle of whiskey and glasses, which she sat on a side table. 'My late husband, Dewitt, would drink this whenever he had a cough, which seemed pretty often to me. You gentlemen help yourselves.'

Dude poured the drinks. On his manners, the old man sipped at his instead of tossing it down. 'Your husband was a good judge of whiskey,' he said.

After some moments, she coughed and said, 'There's a chill in the evening air. I believe I would like a small glass of dandelion wine — which a neighbor brought over when I had a cold,' she quickly clarified.

'I think you should have a glass of wine,' Uncle Billy assured her. 'Not only would it be proper, but needfully medicinal after the trying evening in which your poorly speaker failed you. I'm mighty sorry.'

'I understand. My late husband was often poorly.' She went to the kitchen and back.

Dude blinked at the size of the 'small glass of dandelion wine.'

They all sipped in silence. When Uncle Billy finished his drink, Dude refilled it.

'I am beginning to feel much better,' the old man said after an interval. 'Believe I can make it back to camp on my own. Go ahead, Dude, if you want to see that fella at the Jayhawk.'

'You're sure you're all right?' Dude asked, taking the hint.

A smile split the seraphic features. 'Thanks to Mrs. Wheeler.'

Dude finished his drink, thanked her, and took his departure.

★ ★ ★

As a young cowboy on long trail drives from Texas across Indian Territory to the Kansas railheads, roused out at any hour of the night, especially when springtime storms threatened, Dude McQuinn had become a light sleeper through training and necessity, waking at faint sounds or a light touch. This night something broke his sleep. He sat up on his bedroll, fully awake, his instilled sense of time telling him that it was past midnight.

The sounds reached him again: the scrape of boot steps approaching unsteadily. They would come on, pause, seem to hesitate, then come on again. The walker was whistling a meaningless tune until it grew louder and more distinct. He knew instantly who it was when he recognized that annoying Yankee song, 'The Battle Hymn of the Republic.'

He rolled out and stood by the wagon, mouth set, arms folded, waiting.

The whistling ended suddenly as the figure, weaving out of the darkness, headed straight for the water barrel. The tin drinking cup that hung on the side of the barrel rattled. A hurried scooping followed, and a thirsty gulping and spluttering and finally a grateful 'Ahhh.' Bourbon fumes rode the air.

'Dad-blamed if you haven't come home roostered,' Dude said, his tone severe.

'That Ah may be, Dude, pardner . . . but Maude . . . Ah mean th' widow Wheeler . . . filled my ear with th' goin's-on around here. Number one — don't match this G.L. fella. He's never lost anything. Horse racin' or business.'

'That's old news. But neither has Old Dominion been up against a true runnin' horse like the Judge. Besides, we could use the money.'

'Been other fast horses brought in here. Remember what Van and Cy told us.'

'Why would the widow Wheeler tell you all this?'

The old man was holding on to a wagon wheel spoke for support. He gave a bleating, Billy goat laugh, 'Heee — heee. You've overlooked the Plymouth Colony ante — ante — '

'Antecedents — that fancy word for ancestors. Did she tell you anything we *don't* know?'

'Maude's late husband . . . Ah mean th' widow Wheeler's . . . was a pardner in th' bank, y'see. . . . But when he passed away, there wasn't much left for poor

Maude. . . . She hired an out-of-town lawyer t'look into matters. He couldn't dig up one little thing. Nothin' wrong showed on th' books. Ever'thing in apple-pie order. Y'see . . . that G.L. fella also keeps th' books — two sets of books.'

'What's all this got to do with matchin' a race?'

'Roundabout — plenty. Ah don' want you t'match this race, Dude. Too chancy. . . . Friends o' th' widow back in Missouri told her that good mare never raced again. Y'see somebody might slip in here an' fix th' Judge an' ruin him for life.'

'Not if there's one of us on guard all the time.'

'Dude' — and all at once the old man's voice had the ring of near sobriety — 'Ah see Ah haven't schooled you enough. There's as many ways to fix a man's horse as there's to cheat a poor widow woman out of her heritage.' He had another scoop of water from the barrel and was setting an erratic course for his bedroll under the wagon, when Dude asked, 'Well, did you sell her Amos?'

'Didn't tell you about that, did Ah? Oh . . . we visited awhile about our ante — ante — '

'Antecedents — can't you remember that'

'An' pretty soon . . . she had some more dandelion wine . . . an' at her insistence Ah had another little toddy or two.'

'Just two?'

'Does a gentleman count?'

'Well — ' Dude prodded, 'did you sell her Amos?'

'Ah told her what a fine hoss Amos is. Y'bet Ah did . . . '

Dude felt a thrust of alarm. 'Did you say Amos or Avalanche when you told her?'

'Have Ah ever made a false move in a hoss deal?' The old man was most indignant.

'Well — no. What then?'

'She had some more wine. . . . Ah had another toddy . . . a light one, o' course . . . when she insisted. But somehow Ah seemed to get off th' subject o'

212

Amos. Ah mean Avalanche. Next thing I knew . . . '

'Well — ?'

To his surprise, Uncle Billy was scrambling under the wagon to his bedroll.

'Uncle, you didn't finish your story. Then what happened?'

No answer came. Moments more and Dude caught the steady chuffing of the old man's snoring. Little by little, understanding seeped into Dude's mind. What had Uncle Billy said? Yes: 'The next thing I knew.'

Dude was shocked. *Why, the old hoot owl! And her a poor widow woman!*

8

The Tipster

A chipper, white-whiskered pixy yelling, 'Rise and shine, you hoot owls!' choused Dude and Coyote out at dawn. Crawling from under the wagon, Dude saw the fire going and the coffee pot on.

'How come so early?' he complained. 'This is no trail drive.'

'A true horseman eats breakfast with his horses.' If Uncle Billy felt any unpleasant physical effects from last night, Dude guessed he concealed them as assertions of independence and refutations of old age.

During the meal, Dude asked him, 'Did you sell Amos to the widow Wheeler? You didn't say last night.'

'That's right, I didn't.'

'I would take it then that you didn't?'

'That's the way I would take it if I were you.' Dude turned his face to the sky and shook his head.

The morning dragged, settling into the uneventful courseof past days. Coyote was exercising Texas Jack for public view on the east road. Uncle Billy was behind the wagon, giving Judge Blair his 'weekly tonic' mixed in a bucket of water. Toward the square, Lightfoot appeared to drowse, causing Dude to examine his doubts. Had Vinson's puffed-up newspaper story and the bragging ad scared off the game? Still, the other side had taken the bait about blowing out Texas Jack. That is, taken it to the extent of timing the speed work. Did that mean they had swallowed it? There was a difference. If nothing developed in a day or two, the outfit might as well punch the breeze for Texas.

While Dude watched the square, his thoughts wandering, a man took the street leading to the campground. A short, stocky man in western hat, varicolored shirt, vest, dark trousers and Wellington boots: Stub Tate, the Honorable G.L.'s Man Friday.

A quiver of anticipation ran through Dude, also a wariness.

Tate had reached the center of the camp before Dude, fussing with a bridle, pretended to discover him. 'Good morning,' he said, walking out.

'I was here the other day,' Tate said, releasing a dry smile, the first Dude had seen by the man, and introduced himself. Dude spoke his own name and shook hands. 'I remember. What can I do for you, Mr. Tate?'

'I bring word from the Honorable Gideon Lightfoot at the bank. Having seen your challenge in the paper, he would like to converse with you about a possible match race.'

'That's neighborly,' Dude said, thinking to himself, At last. 'However, I was thinking about breaking camp today.' Never show eagerness.

'I told him how smooth your horse is, Mr. McQuinn. Mr. Lightfoot won't run his horse at just any common racehorse.' He smiled the dry smile, conveying the impression of privately not favoring such a notion.

Dude shrugged his shoulders and

said, 'Won't hurt to talk to him,' aware that Uncle Billy stood listening at the wagon's tailgate.

'Mr. Lightfoot will be at the bank till four o'clock. You name the time.'

'Say two o'clock?'

'Fine.'

Tate was barely out of earshot when Dude found Uncle Billy at his shoulder, outright concern and disapproval warping his mouth and hardening his eyes. 'I don't like this,' the old man said flatly.

'They took the bait, didn't they?'

'Bait is not the race itself. You're going in against a stacked deck. There's a time to match a race and there's a time to ride on. This is the latter.'

'And not swap or sell Amos?'

'I might still do that and you not match this race.'

A crease furrowed Dude's forehead. He kicked at a pebble. He rubbed the underside of his nose with a forefinger. He said, 'I don't say you're not right, after the way you've schooled me to spot a bad lay and back off. And the Lord knows I'm no do-gooder. But the longer we stay here the more I think about the good horses that have come in here and been fixed somehow — that good Missouri mare forever. Overdosed her, I reckon. And I think about Cy and Abby Kirby. And there's the money we could use. But most of all, I guess it comes down to I can't stand some uppity bird that thinks his horse can outrun my horse. Uncle, I ache to match ol' G.L. I do.' And silently he thought, I want it for you, Uncle. I do most of all.

The old man made a motion of futility, of the young ignoring the sage advice of the old. 'I can see that rock head of yours is set,' he said. 'I've told you I want none of this, being poorly. But I see I'll have to. I can't stand by and see you and Coyote outslicked — or even worse — the Judge ruined as a running horse because of some Alamo Texan's ego.' He stepped abruptly to the wagon, and Dude heard the rickety doors of the medicine chest open, and, after a moment, the almost inaudible *thung* of the corncob stopper on the jug.

The old man walked back, showing reluctant though firm resolve. 'I'd better go along with you.'

'Don't feel that you have to,' Dude said deliberately to draw him on.

'He's going to ask you about Texas Jack's breeding. Have you thought about that?'

'Just now I am.'

'You'll have to put up more than tall Texas talk. Better let me handle that end of it.'

'If you think you're up to it — poorly as you are,' Dude needled him again, fashioning his face into mock solicitude.

The cold blue eyes closed upon Dude. 'Wait till I get back,' Uncle Billy said, and led Amos out and harnessed him to the buggy and climbed to the seat, saying, 'A true horseman never walks when he can ride,' and without explanation drove away, snapping the whip.

Twice around the square he drove.

Watching, Dude did not see him come out for a third time, and was left amused at the secrecy, which was nothing new, therefore not surprising today, and which could lead Dude to expect the unforeseen. Most important, Dude hoped it meant that one William Tecumseh Lockhart was rounding the turn toward being himself again, if he wasn't too poorly!

★ ★ ★

At one o'clock Uncle Billy drove back to camp. Dude waited him out, playing for a hint of what his old partner had in mind, but he said not a word; instead, he idled over a long toddy and then had a short nap. Rising, he said, 'It is my judgment that we should time our arrival at precisely ten minutes after two — no sooner, no later.' A kind of impish smile trickled across his face. 'Any earlier would throw us in an overhankering light. Any later would be gauche, as the French say.'

'Sounds just right,' Dude went along.

'There's one thing I want you and Coyote to understand before we go. I'm going along only as a consultant in setting up the conditions of the race. I'm not up to what I used to do. You understand that?'

'Oh, we understand, don't we, Coyote?' Dude said, and Coyote, deadpan, nodded behind a solemn Comanche wink.

At precisely ten minutes past two o'clock the two entered the bank. Dude's immediate impression was of a jail: bars on the massive door, bars across the broad glass windows, bars across the two tellers' cages, bars across an inner door marked: PRESIDENT. Beside it Stub Tate awaited them. He glanced at his pocket watch, frowned his rebuke at their tardiness, and inclined his head toward the inner door. He opened the door, closed it softly behind them, and posted himself there.

As they entered, a graying man of regal bearing rose behind his desk, glanced reprovingly at the clock on the wall, and came around the desk to meet them.

'I am Gideon Lightfoot,' he said formally, yet cordially, bowed his head and extended a pale hand.

Shaking hands, Dude gave his own name and said, 'This is Dr. William Tecumseh Lockhart of Kentucky.'

'Pleased to meet you gentlemen. Please be seated. As one gentleman to another, I am delighted that you have accepted my invitation to confer over the possibility of matching our horses.' Lightfoot waggled a linger and Tate brought whiskey and glasses.

'Pour your own, gentlemen.'

The whiskey was smooth to Dude's taste, with perhaps a touch of rye. Lightfoot next offered long, thin cigars, likewise smooth. He downed his whiskey neat and took short puffs on his cigar, holding it fastidiously between index and middle fingers while regarding his visitors through hooded hazel eyes that served to mask his thinking. His head was domelike and his mouth was cut like a slit in the ginger-bearded face. His brows were shaggy hedges, his nose beaked, his jaws pronounced, his voice soft-spoken, yet emitting a reedy quality. He wore a black broadcloth frock coat and a full cravat.

'Foremost,' he said, after a conventional pause, 'in a race of this nature is the question of registration. I race Old Dominion only against Thoroughbreds of certified breeding. My horse, for example, goes straight back to the celebrated English-bred Janus.'

'Ah, yes, the immortal Janus,' said Uncle Billy, joining the conversation for the first time. 'A chestnut horse of great bone and muscle . . . very compact, very swift. Fourteen hands, three quarters of an inch. Imported into Virginia early in the summer of 1752. Foaled in 1746. Got by Old Janus, he by the Godolphin Arabian, out of the Little Hartley Mare.'

Lightfoot blinked. 'You know the Janus line, I see.'

'Not only a progenitor of the Thoroughbred, but also of the short horse. Because he sired so many fast short horses out of ordinary mares, the misconception arose that his get had no bottom and couldn't go a distance of ground. When the fact was, when bred to quality mares, he had as many, if not more, stayers than any other stallion in the South.'

'Very true, Dr. Lockhart. Very true.' Lightfoot leaned across his desk, the hooded eyes kindling interest.

'Not overlooking,' Uncle Billy continued, 'when Janus daylighted the celebrated Valiant in a four-mile race.'

'Yes, Doctor. Yes.'

'In all, Janus was an exceptional individual. Not only a distance horse, but possessed of great early foot. He exemplifies those early Virginia runners of whom it was said, 'They could run four miles, or they could run a quarter of a mile, like an arrow from a bow.' No doubt those qualities have been passed on to Old Dominion.'

'That is very true. Again, I must say that your knowledge of the Janus line impresses me, sir.'

'Dr. Lockhart is on leave from the Cedar Crest Farm in Lexington,' Dude said, thinking he should throw in something. 'He is the resident veterinarian there.' The moment he spoke he cauht the warning Hick of his partner's eyes, and Lightfoot said at once, 'I know all the leading horse farms in Kentucky, and have never heard of Cedar Crest.'

'Mr. McQuinn means Crestwood Farm,' Uncle Billy said, at ease. 'The two are often confused. Cedar Crest is a much smaller farm, though at one time it stood a good stud of fast Kentucky whip blood.'

'I have heard of Crestwood Farm,' Lightfoot said. He leaned back and gazed off through a barred window. 'Before we proceed further, gentlemen,' he said, 'I should like to inquire as to the breeding of your horse Texas Jack,' and, turning, looked directly at Dude.

'Here is his certificate of registration,' said Uncle Billy and pulled a long envelope from the inside pocket of his frock coat and laid it on the desk before Lightfoot.

The banker's eyes rose from the envelope to Dude. 'Am I mistaken, sir? I thought you were the owner.'

'We are partners,' Dude improvised,

hardly hesitating, speaking casually. From the start of his association with Uncle Billy, he had learned to expect the unexpected, to think quickly, but stay relaxed and outwardly cool and to speak unhurriedly. 'Dr. Lockhart now owns half interest in Texas Jack. I do the matchmaking.'

Lightfoot opened the envelope, drew out a sheet of worn-looking paper that showed a printing of short, horizontal lines from top to bottom that graduated to a point on the left-hand side, and began reading.

Suddenly he bent forward. An eyebrow shot up. His heavy jaw fell slack. His head came up. 'Why, this shows Texas Jack going back to the great Sir Archy.'

'Ah, yes, the great Sir Archy,' Uncle Billy followed through. 'Foaled in Virginia in 1805. Got by the imported Diomed, out of the English speed mare Castianira. Diomed got by Florizel, he by King Herod, he by Tartar, he by Croft's Partner, he by —'

'I am quite familiar with Sir Archy's bloodlines, Lightfoot cut in, apparently piqued at being told what he already knew. He read on. 'I see this says Texas Jack was sired by Gone to Texas and out of Alamo Miss. Gone to Texas was sired by Ranger Boy, he by Copperbottom, he by Sir Archy. However, I do not place this Copperbottom on Virginia's early paths.'

'Doubtless,' Uncle Billy said, smiling, 'because although foaled in Virginia, he was brought to Texas as a juvenile by General Sam Houston. I believe that was in about 1839. Is that correct, Mr. McQuinn, according to your family recollections?'

'That year or soon thereafter,' Dude agreed. 'I remember hearing my mother recall what her pappy told her, he what his pappy told him.'

'Mr. McQuinn,' Uncle Billy added, 'is a direct descendant of Sam Houston on the maternal side.'

'I read about that,' the banker said, unimpressed. Finished reading, he sat a little straighter and turned the certificate over and back, as if doubting its authenticity, though finding no grounds not to. He said, 'I see this was issued by the Jockey Club.'

'Which, as you know,' Uncle Billy said easily, 'is the custodian of *The American Stud Book* and has the task of registering and maintaining the file of Thoroughbreds in the country.'

'Very well, gentlemen,' Lightfoot said, convinced, and returned the certificate.

'Now, as a further matter of mutual interest among us horsemen,' said Uncle Billy, as genial as a country peddler, 'may we see Old Dominion's certificate?'

Dude felt like jumping up and whooping, but kept his face straight.

Lightfoot looked startled for an instant, his cheeks flushing. 'Of course,' he said and opened a right-hand drawer and searched. Not finding it, he opened a lower drawer. Neither was it there. He stood and stepped to a wooden filing cabinet, his regal manner gone. He flipped and dug and, finally, took out a sheet of yellowed paper. By then he had regained his composure. He came back to the desk and handed the paper to Uncle Billy. 'Here it is, sir,' he said, visibly annoyed.

As Uncle Billy read, with Dude looking over his shoulder, he said, 'Mr. McQuinn, I would not doubt our valor, but I might our judgment, if we run against Old Dominion. Look! Straight up the ladder to Janus. Old Dominion by Old South, he by Cumberland, he by Roanoke, he by Twigg, he by Janus. And speed all the way on the distaff side.' He paused, seeming to reflect and doubt, then looked across at Lightfoot. 'I do not quite place Old South among Virginia Thoroughbreds. Could there be another Old South of Maryland breeding?'

'Old South,' Lightfoot replied, a firmness to his inflection, 'stands today in Richmond. He has impeccable Virginia breeding.'

'Cumberland also escapes my memory. I seem to recall a colt by that name who was said to be just fast enough to lose money.'

Lightfoot bristled. His lips bunched. His gaze became cool. He said, 'I can assure you, sir, that this Cumberland had more than a mere turn of speed. He was never beaten from a mile to four miles.'

'Where the confusion comes in is the number of horses bearing the same name. For instance, there were a number of horses named Janus.'

'But only one true Janus,' the other said, a small' edge to his voice.

'Ah, yes, the 'true' Janus blood,' agreed Uncle Billy, but not without a lingering skepticism. 'Some Januses won at all distances, some not at all.'

That caused a decided break in the conversation, a near deadlock. Lightfoot's mouth was set and his nostrils began to dilate. In another moment Uncle Billy, with his challenging, would have him shouting. Seeing this, Dude made his tone genial and said, 'Sir, would you like to look at our horse?'

'Mr. Tate, who serves as my jockey and trainer, has already done so.'

'That's jim-dandy, sure. In turn, we'd

like to take a gander at your horse.'

'I make it a rule never to show my horse until just before the race.'

Dude was silent. *Now, that's a new wrinkle.* He smiled from the teeth and said, 'We also have a rule never to match a race unless we see the other man's horse first.'

For a standoff moment his eyes met the hooded ones. And then, just when Dude decided the match was off, Lightfoot, back on his show of gentility, said, 'I can depart this once, since you gentlemen have publicly shown your horse. Will it be convenient for you to come to my farm this afternoon? It is five miles south of town.'

Dude shrugged indifferently, then nodded.

'Mr. Tate and I will meet you there shortly. You will see my sign by the road.'

They had tied Amos at the hitching rack in front of the hank. As they seated themselves in the buggy, Dude said, 'You really ruffied ol' G.L.'s tail feathers. For a second or two there I thought he would hack out.'

'Just the opposite, Dude, pardner. There are two main ways to make a man mad. One is to kick his dog around. The other is to run down his horse, question its breeding and speed. I wanted to make him mad enough to match us at our distance. I believe he will before long. Meantime, don't act eager. Put him off, like I've schooled you.'

'I know. Now you tell me how in the world you managed to come up with that certificate of registration?'

'Thank Van Vinson. It took some hand-iwork. One problem was making the paper look old enough. He smudged it and used some old fashioned type. As speed helps out bottom, so age helps out authenticity. Fresh-looking print on clean, white paper might have given us away.

'Why didn't you tell me?'

'I said I'd handle it, didn't I?'

Dude started to say more, his patience taxed, hut at that moment a handsome white horse pulling a fancy buggy with the top down sped from behind the bank to the square. Lightfoot was at the reins, Tate beside him. They took the south road out of town.

'A trotter,' Uncle Billy observed.

'Which tells me there's a better way to rub G.L.'s dander.'

'How's that?'

'Have Amos pass him on the road.'

'They're already out of sight.'

'It's worth the try.'

'Why, I believe it is. Sometimes you Alamo Texans come up with a fairly good idea. Let's go!' He snatched the reins from around the whip socket, hacked Amos away from the hitching rack, turned him and, snapping the reins, tore down the street. When they came out on the south road, Lightfoot had a lead of several hundred yards and the white trotter was going fast.

Instead of taking the whip to Amos, Uncle Billy chirruped to him, and the blue roan seemed to shift into another range of speed. Gradually, the other buggy grew nearer.

They stayed like that, spaced at that

distance, for about another quarter of a mile. 'I'm letting him warm up,' the old man told Dude.

Soon, Uncle Billy chirruped again, a series of insistent chirrups.

Dude could feel the wind whipping faster past his face as the big horse quickened. In a surprisingly short time they were within some hundred yards of the buggy. Dude saw Tate glance back and speak to Lightfoot, who looked over his shoulder and shook the reins and hunched his shoulders.

Amos continued to close the gap. Some fifty yards now, Dude judged. He glanced at Uncle Billy. The old man's face was a portrait of pure enjoyment. He looked younger, in his element of horse against horse.

It happened quickly, with a rush of gathering speed, when Uncle Billy chirruped once more. Amos, in his distinct, diagonally gaited motion of the trotter, appeared to lengthen stride, head out-thrust like a chaparral cock, that stance Dude remembered.

'Come on, Amos!' Dude heard himself yelling. 'Take him!'

He saw Lightfoot jerk and glance back, then reach for the whip and lay on the leather.

Amos was still gaining, while Uncle Billy chirruped. Watching, Dude became aware of a deepening insight, of the communication between blind horse and driver. Uncle Billy's voice was Amos's eyes.

Only a few yards separated the two buggies now.

Uncle Billy reined left to go around. When he did, Lightfoot stood up to use the whip to better effect. The white trotter was game, but he could move no faster. He was already giving all he had, Dude saw.

Amos's head drew even with the high rear wheels of Lightfoot's buggy. Lightfoot went to the whip again. For a space nothing changed until Uncle Billy chirruped again. Amos laid back his ears, moving faster, gaining with each long stride. Uncle Billy shifted the reins to his left hand, his head tilted back, and gave a perky little wave with his right forefinger as they passed.

Lightfoot's face was a study in frustration. His mouth like a crooked slash across his bearded face, his thick brows hanging like dark thunderclouds over his hooded eyes.

Amos took them by at a rapid clip, not easing off, though Uncle Billy clucked at him only now and then.

On down the road a piece, Dude said, 'If Lightfoot's not mad now, he never will be.'

'I'm not finished with the Honorable G.L.,' the old man said, but, peculiar to his enigmatic ways, did not elaborate.

'Next to the Judge,' Dude said, 'Amos is the doggonedest horse I've ever seen. Lordy, how he can move on out! And you . . . you want to get rid of him.'

'I keep telling you, it's a disgrace to keep a blind horse.'

'But Amos is no ordinary horse.'

Uncle Billy seemed not to hear.

A short distance on a bold wooden

sign stood by a side road that led to a large house. Uncle Billy pulled up. The sign read:

LIGHTFOOT FARM

Home of the Unbeaten Old Dominion

He will be let to registered Thoroughbred mares only at $50 the single leap, at $100 to ensure a mare in foal. The season starts mid-February and ends mid-June. Mares coming from a far distance will be provided pasture and feed at reasonable terms.

Description & Pedigree

Old Dominion is a beautiful dark chestnut, with a white stripe down the length of his face. He stands 16 hands, weighs 1,300 pounds, was got by the celebrated Old South, likewise never beaten, and traces back to the peerless Janus, greatest of imported sires. Old Dominion's dam, the swift Betsy Drake, holds numerous track records, being unbeaten from four furlongs to one mile. She was got by Pegasus, likewise unbeaten, who produced most excellent bottomed stock in Virginia.

Arrangements may be made with
The Honorable Gideon Lightfoot,
in the town of Lightfoot,
at the Lightfoot County Bank

'Everything's celebrated and unbeaten,' Dude said sarcastically. 'I still don't like this,' Uncle Billy said, driving on.

Seeing the house, Dude was reminded of old-time prints he had seen: a rambling two-story structure, white columns across the front. A graveled drive circled up to the wide porch. Another road, well traveled, led off to an immense barn and a maze of corrals and sheds. Below that spread a long straightaway that joined an oval track. White railings marked the entire course.

'We won't be invited in — that's a cinch,' Uncle Billy said, 'so we'll mosey on down to the barn.'

They had no more than stopped by the paddock when Dude saw a man, sitting in the runway of the barn, get up and come to the door, watching them.

'Just like Cy Kirby said,' Dude nodded. 'Keeps a guard around the clock.'

'A man whose main forte is skinning the other fella is always suspicious of others,' Uncle Billy mused.

Minutes passed before the other buggy arrived. Grim of face, Lightfoot got down, eyeing Amos in disbelief. 'I thought Jupiter was the fastest trotter around here. He traces straight back to Messenger through his male line.'

'All Standardbreds trace back to Messenger,' Uncle Billy drawled, his tone knowing. 'Some just move faster.'

Lightfoot, disgruntled, called to the man at the barn, 'Bring Old Dominion out and lead him around for these gentlemen to see.'

A short-lived unwillingness stood in the man's eyes before he entered the barn. There was a long pause. And then Dude heard the squeal of a stall door opening. Another pause. After which hooves rattled against stallboards and pounded the runway. Suddenly man and horse burst down the runway and outside, the man tugging on the halter rope.

'Take it easy with that horse — you fool!' Lightfoot yelled. He tore open the paddock gate and rushed inside to lend a hand on the halter rope, while the wall-eyed stallion swung around the two, jerking them like puppets. Lightfoot shortened his hold on the rope; after a minute or more the horse quieted down, though still moving nervously, powerfully.

Old Dominion, Dude saw, was all the sign had described — and more. A handsome, dark, glossy chestuut. Great bone and muscle. Straight legs. An excellent head, the white marking complementing his looks. Speed and power. In his eyes shone the bold look of a runner. For the first time, Dude had misgivings about pursuing the match.

Lightfoot was saying, 'What do you gentlemen think of him?' His tone implied that he anticipated glowing approval.

'He's a fine one,' Dude said, his admiration sincere, and went inside the paddock with Uncle Billy.

'He used to sweat a great deal when we took him to the saddling paddock before a race,' Lightfoot said reminiscently. 'To cure him, I would send him there after working him in the morning at the farm, and then again in the afternoon. I thought he was over it.' Lightfoot chuckled. 'The very next time I matched him and saddled him in the paddock with people around, he broke into the worst sweat ever.'

'It's easy to school a horse, but hard to fool him,' Uncle Billy said.

He started his usual walk-around examination, head bent, shoulders hunched, experienced eyes assessing details. He moved slowly around the prancing stud, slackened step, engrossed, and went around again and stopped. 'Mr. Lightfoot,' he said, 'I see characteristics that go back to the Darley Arabian in England. You are to be congratulated on your keen eye for outstanding horseflesh. Old Dominion is an exceptional individual, unequaled as to muscular form and action.'

The hooded eyes smiled, barely.

'However,' said Uncle Billy, hunching shoulders and squinting, 'in all honesty of judgment, I must say he's a mite thin in the withers.'

'Thin in the withers!' Lightfoot was dumbfounded.

'And a little straight in the shoulder,' Uncle Billy resumed, peering closer, left hand on hip.

'A little straight in the shoulder! Why, this horse has perfect conformation.'

'Every horse, no matter how imposing, has a defect or two. It was said even of Janus that he had a coarse head.'

'Not Janus! The perfect Janus!'

'Also,' said Uncle Billy, bending lower

to look, 'I would say that Old Dominion is just a trifle long in the barrel.'

'Long in the barrel!' stormed Lightfoot.

'You cannot expect a horse to be perfect in all departments.'

'Well, I'll show you what Old Dominion can do against the likes of this Texas Jack!' Lightfoot exploded, head held high. 'Though only recently treated for a swelling on his left thigh, I'll run him as he stands. Anytime, anywhere.'

'A swelling? I see none, only where the hair is white from treatment low on the thigh. I trust that indisposition would not hinder his speed?'

'Two weeks ago I'd have said yes, when he hurt himself in his stall. Today he's as fit as ever.'

'As a matter of medical interest, sir, may I ask what remedy you found efficacious?'

Lightfoot drove his words at Uncle Billy. 'Strong vinegar saturated with common salt — used warm. None of your shaman's concoctions.'

'Ah, very good,' replied Uncle Billy, ignoring the thrust. 'I also recommend one ounce of white vitriol, one ounce of green copperas, two teaspoonfuls of gunpowder, all pulverized together, dissolved in one quart of soft water — no more, no less — and used cold, rubbing it in thoroughly. I'll be glad to put that down for you.'

'Another concoction,' Lightfoot mocked. 'Well, gentlemen, I have made my challenge. Do you accept or not?' He split his gaze between Uncle Billy and Dude.

Dude let it settle between them. Almost by habit, he began to circle, to evade and stall, as his old mentor had schooled him, a tactic that the other side generally interpreted as fear of losing and, therefore, produced favorable odds more times than not.

'Neither accepted nor refused,' Dude said. 'After seein' your horse, I think we'd better study on this before we get down to taw.'

'I believe,' Lightfoot said, back on his

formal manner, 'you understand why, until today, I haven't shown my horse until shortly before the race. You would be surprised at the horsemen who've forfeited at the last minute rather than lose.' He turned to Tate and they appeared to share remembered amusements.

'We'll powwow with you before long,' Dude said, continuing the no-hurry show. 'If we don't shove off for Texas.'

'Very well.'

Driving off, Uncle Billy said, 'You played it about right. Just like I've schooled you.'

'You got his bristles up, the way you ran down his horse. Though I didn't see any of the faults you found.'

Uncle Billy smiled thinly. 'There were none. The horse has perfect conformation.'

'Did the great Janus have a coarse head?'

The old man smiled again. 'All the early accounts said his head was so noble it could have been sculptured.'

'Sore as ol' G.L. was, he surprised me

with the challenge.'

The old man thought on that for a time. He said then, 'For a fella who never takes chances, who studies every angle before he makes his move — that was too sudden. He was too eager. I don't like this, Dude. No part of it.' They had reached the main road, Amos striding strongly, as if he knew no other way, when Uncle Billy spoke again, 'This may be as far as I can go with you matching this race. At my age a man has to slow down when he's poorly. I hope you savvy that?'

'I savvy,' Dude said to humor him. 'Except you're not old.'

'You take the reins. I'm too played out to handle Amos on the way back.'

In camp, Uncle Billy took to his bed-roll under the wagon, and stayed there until Dude called him to supper. Yet, when Coyote filled a tin plate with beans and biscuits and bacon and stewed prunes and brought it to him, the old man, as cantankerous as of old, snapped at him, 'Next thing I know, you two hoot owls will halter me with a baby bib and serve me milk toast. By godlins, I can help myself!' He got up, as nimble as a barn cat, and poured himself a cup of black coffee and marched back to his cane-bottomed chair.

'Whatever you say, Grandfather Billy.'

'And don't call me Grandfather! Will I ever break you of that?'

He scooped up a mouthful of beans, chewed experimentally, sampling, and swallowed without complaint. He opened a biscuit, eyed it critically, broke it in quarters, examining each piece, ate it all, sampling again, and said, 'You must have made the biscuits, Coyote, pardner. Not bad. Just like I schooled you. Nice and light.'

Coyote nodded, pleased.

'I can always tell Dude's because they're loaded with baking powder and sometimes I find a cigarette butt or two.' He turned to his supper and ate in silence.

Dude caught Coyote's eye and a wordless understanding passed between them: Tetchiness was the best sign of all.

With coming of evening and the town square falling silent, the only sounds the gentle tinkle of a cowbell or a hallooing voice in the distance, Dude became restless and said, 'Let's two of us scout out the Jayhawk. I'll watch the horses if you and Coyote want to go.'

'Stay I will,' Coyote said. 'White man's poets I want to read.'

One thing about the Jayhawk, Dude found as he and Uncle Billy entered its smoky confines — weekdays or Saturdays made little difference as to the number of patrons, only in the groupings. There were more townsmen than farmers this Wednesday night.

Big Boy Brody spotted them the moment they put booted feet on the bar rail. 'Evening, gents. Where's your educated Indian friend?'

'In camp reading the classics so he can keep up with your quips,' Dude grinned.

Looldng immensely flattered, Brody said, 'As the bard quoth, 'That calls for drinks free — and I mean on me,'' and set out glasses and a dark-looking bottle bearing the uninviting label of Old Sagwa. One sip and Dude nodded approvingly. 'That, sir, is mighty good whiskey.'

'Glad you like it. The label is a fooler. I put that on there to keep the help out of it. It is private stock, ordered for my use only. Have another round.'

They did.

Afterward, Brody took the bottle away and set out some Old Green River.

A man squeezed in beside Dude, who recognized Lon, the droll hanger-on, and with him Mack, the squat, cocky member of the duo.

On the bar in front of Mack rested the limp remains of the saloon's free lunch, around which buzzed a bevy of flies: a bowl of baked beans, cheese and crackers and a jar of sausages. Mack was in the act of slyly fishing out a sausage when the alert Brody, spying the appropriation, leaned across the bar and seized Mack's hand and returned the sausage to the jar.

Brody leveled an admonishing finger.

'As the bard quoth, 'Do not help thyselfto the wurst — unless the house gets some trade first.' ' He focused his disgust on the pair. 'Do you birds have to come in here every night? Ain't there another place you can hang out — like the livery barn?'

Lon's eyebrows shot up with mock hurt. 'I understand a travelin' evangelist is comin' here to preach and baptize. Don't want to miss my chance to be saved.'

'Count your blessings. The last preacher in here stayed just long enough to clean out the free lunch, borrow ten bucks off me he claimed he needed to send his dear old mother on her deathbed in Philadelphia, steal another ten off a gambler durin' his baptism, then sneak out with a quart of my best whiskey.'

'And what did the bard quoth to them shenanigans?' Lon asked.

'To wit: 'Preacher, linger not here — or out you go on your ear,' which reminds me. It's time you two gave the house some trade.' Without waiting for their assent, he set out bottle and glasses. Each paid, though slow about it, and he left them.

Recalling that Lon's passed-on rumor had panned out to be true, and hoping there might be more, Dude, making his tone sociable, asked, 'Did you boys ever settle your argument about the Topeka mare versus the great Old Dominion?'

'No — but he knows she can outrun 'im.'

'She wouldn't have a chance,' Mack sneered.

'Let me buy you boys a drink?' Dude offered.

'Don't mind if we do,' Lon said, pretending shyness.

Dude signaled Brody, and the drinks were paid for and drunk before Dude ventured another approach. 'We went out to look at Old Dominion today. He's quite a chunk of horse, all right.'

'Looks ain't everything,' Lon said, sneering for Mack's benefit.

'We chinned with Gideon Lightfoot about a match race. Maybe we will, maybe we won't.'

Lon's face shaded off from its indolence. His brows contracted, and Dude saw a trace of bitterness. 'I used to work for Gideon Lightfoot,' Lon said. 'He let me go when I asked for a fair wage.'

'I'd like to get a better line on Old Dominion before I agree to run at him,' Dude said and laughed. 'That's just good horse sense.'

Lon scratched inside his greasy shirt, looked up and down the bar, and leaned toward Dude. 'In case you're interested, Lightfoot will be blowin' the horse out at daybreak tomorrow morning at the farm.'

'How far?'

'Five and a half furlongs.'

'How do you know?'

'See that fellow at the end of the bar? Friend of mine. On the day shift. Same one I used to have.'

Dude looked. It was the man he had seen at Lightfoot's barn. Dude turned to Lon. 'Be a little galloping ... that all?'

'No — a speed work. Old Dominion needs it to sharpen him.'

'I'll keep that in mind. Let's have another drink, you and your friend.'

A little later, when the saloon was behind them, Dude asked Uncle Billy, 'You heard what the man said?'

'I heard.'

'His tip was right about the swelling. He must be right about the speed work. I want to clock that horse, and I want you and Coyote to go with me. Will you?'

'I'll go. But I still don't like this,' the old man said.

9

Bait for Bait

When the sign pointing to the Lightfoot farm loomed out of the predawn darkness, Dude pulled rein and, keeping his voice down, said, 'Let's go on a way and tie our horses. There's no cover from the road to the track, and none near the track that I remember.'

'Nothing suits me better than walking and crawling through grass full of chiggers,' Uncle Billy grumbled. 'But if I hadn't come along, you'd both be as helpless as dogie calves in a snowstorm. Makes a body wonder what this generation of Alamo Texans and Comanches is coming to.'

Down the road they dismounted, tied the horses to fence posts, and eased through the strands of barbed wire.

Dude guessed they had gone three hundred yards or more when he sighted the high blur of the two-story house.

He angled away from it to his left until the barn materialized before him. Here they hunkered down in the sweet-smelling prairie grass about fifty yards from the paddock. Some fifteen minutes later Dude saw a light in the rear of the big house.

Before long the rattle of a gate being opened alerted Dude. Dimly, he could see a figure going to the barn. The sound also gave him a start, for he hadn't seen the man come to the paddock gate.

Voices became audible at the barn: the guard and the jockey, Stub Tate? A pause — after that the hoof racket of horses evidently being led from stalls. Then a man took a horse from the barn, followed by another man leading a fractious horse. Out of the thinning darkness a third man appeared at the paddock gate. A delay while the horses were saddled and the riders mounted. The man waiting at the paddock opened the gate and riders came through, the horses close together. They were ponying Old Dominion to the track, Dude saw, the rider forced to take a short hold on the lead shank, judging by the way the racehorse was behaving.

When the riders and the man afoot were well on their way, the three watchers rose and followed. Some distance on Dude stopped and they crouched down, watching the horses reach the track and move to· ward the head of the straightaway. The man on foot had taken position along the rail.

The horses, obscure forms bobbing beyond the white railings, trotted past where the oval entered the straightaway. Far down there, barely visible, they turned and started back.

Nervously, Dude gauged the sky. Dawn would break before long. He felt a touch on his shoulder and Uncle Billy whispered, 'Let's move back some. I can clock it from there. We can hear the start and they should finish where that fella's standing.'

They slipped back and watched on bent knees. Peering through the dingy light, Dude felt his concern subside.

The horses were moving faster, the pony rider apparently giving Old Dominion more slack. They trotted past the man at the rail, whom Dude guessed was Lightfoot, come to observe and time the speed outing. By now the horses were in the first turn. They rounded it and seemed to slow down. Since Old Dominion was going five and a half furlongs, if Lon's report was true, the start would be on the backstretch not far from the first turn.

'Right there,' Dude heard Uncle Billy mutter, and knew the old man was figuring where the starting line should be.

Scarcely had Uncle Billy spoken when Dude heard a distant shout and the rapid drumming of hooves. He could just make out the low blur of the running horse. He followed it with straining eyes the length of the backstretch and into the turn. Beside him, Uncle Billy held his stopwatch, squinting, concentrating, shoulders hunched.

The horse took the turn and on to the head of the stretch, running steadily, seeming to hold about the same speed in

Dude's judgment, and down the straight-away and past the solitary watcher at the rail.

Instantly, the three rose to go, but Uncle Billy held back, as if questioning something.

'Come on,' Dude whispered. 'It's fixin' to light up.'

Striding through the grass to the road, they mounted and walked their horses away. Broad daylight found the outfit within sight of town.

'Well, Uncle,' saia Dude, reining up, 'what did the celebrated Old Dominion run it in? Record time, no doubt?' As he spoke, he saw his partner's puzzlement.

'I don't have to look at my watch to tell you and Coyote that the time was slow,' the old man said. 'Frankly, I'm surprised after having seen Old Dominion.'

'What did he run it in?'

'That horse,' Uncle Billy said, holding the stopwatch farther and farther away from him, 'ran it in . . . one minute . . . and . . . .uh — '

'And you say you don't need glasses!

Here! Let me read it.'

'In one minute and fifteen seconds,' the old man concluded quickly. 'That slow? I don't believe it. You're not reading it right.'

Uncle Billy handed him the watch without argument. Dude's eyebrows flew up when he looked. 'You're right. One minute and fifteen seconds.' Abashed, he returned the watch.

'A good horse,' the old man reflected, 'will run five and a half furlongs in a minute and seven, eight or nine seconds. I remember one track record at a minute and five seconds.'

'Where was that?' Dude pried.

Pointedly ignoring him, Uncle Billy considered a moment and said, 'From what little I could tell at that distance in the poor light, it seemed to me, even though I can't read a stopwatch' — he measured Dude a put-down look — 'that Old Dominion is not a long-striding horse and runs with his head too high.' He shrugged. 'Anyway, Dude, you and Coyote got yourself a match race, and you know the Judge can daylight that stud at that speed. Just the same, I don't like this.'

'Why not?'

'Call it whatever you like. A premonition or hunch.'

'I happen to like it. I want the Judge to throw dust in the face of that uppity G.L.'s 'celebrated racehorse,' and I want some hard-luck friends like Cy Kirby and Van Vinson to win some money bettin' on our horse.' And, most of all, he said to himself, Coyote and I want it for you, old-timer.

Never, his old mentor had schooled Dude, never act eager to match a horse race, since eagerness could be interpreted one of three ways: that you possessed a horse that could outrun anything above ground, or you knew how to fix the other man's horse, or knew in advance that his jockey could be bought off.

On the Saturday morning following the nighthawking foray to the Lightfoot farm, Dude concluded that he had waited long enough.

'Pardner,' he said to Uncle Billy, stressing the equal status, 'it's time to go match this horse race. I want you to go along in case you see me about to ride off into a bog hole. A two-man front is better than one.'

The old man looked weary. 'Guess I know by now how a wet nurse feels. I'll trail along. Only you and Coyote will have to understand again I'll have nothing to do with the actual running of the race. I'll go merely as a — ' He groped tiredly.

'As a consultant, like you said before.'

'That and no more.'

'Good, that is, Grandfather,' Coyote nodded.

'Wait a minute and don't call me Grandfather,' Uncle Billy said and hurried to the wagon. Humoring him, Dude expected to hear the *thung* of the jug's stopper, but did not, even though the old man was delving into the innards of the medicine chest. Dude saw him close the doors of the chest, carefully keeping his back turned. The breast of his coat sagged when he walked back. He did not explain.

Again, the old gent drove to the bank in the buggy, and again Dude had the closed-in sensation when he saw the bars, and again Stub Tate was waiting by the inner door. Odd, Dude thought, how Tate seemed to be expecting them.

Wordlessly, Tate opened the door and escorted them inside, and the same obscure feeling touched Dude when Gideon Lightfoot, dressed the same, rose slowly behind his desk and came out to meet them, hand outstretched.

'Good afternoon, gentlemen. What can I do for you?' He shook hands formally, yet warmly. As inscrutable as the high-domed face was, it seemed to harbor an inner anticipation.

'Thought we might powwow about a little match race,' Dude opened the ball.

'Might,' said Lightfoot, smiling that smile that really wasn't a smile, and waving them to chairs. 'How far would you like to run?'

Lightfoot, Dude figured, would not

run his horse the classic shorthorse distance of 440 yards. Still, why not start there, then increase the distance as they dickered back and forth, since the Judge was conditioned up to seven furlongs? The longer the race, the more Lightfoot would think he had the advantage.

'How about going a quarter of a mile?' Dude fished.

Contempt rushed to the regal face. 'That's no distance for a Thoroughbred.'

'I thought Old Dominion could go any distance?' Dude mocked, equally contemptuous.

'Registered Thoroughbreds, Mr. McQuinn, do not deign to run so short a distance. Old Dominion is a stayer.'

'So is Texas Jack. I'll run you three furlongs on a dry track or mud.'

'You are beginning to get the point, Mr. McQuinn. However, you are still far too short.'

'So? Then you name the distance.'

'Delighted. One mile.'

'For a horse that got over the colic not long ago that would be asking too much of him, though normally he could. Takes time to bring a horse up to the longer routes. I'll run you six.'

'You are doing better, Mr. McQuinn. As a sporting gesture, taking into consideration that your horse is just over the colic, I'll even shave it half a furlong.'

Shorter the better, Dude thought, and said, 'Five and a half furlongs? That is sporting of you. We'll match at that distance, if it's agreeable with my pardner here?'

Uncle Billy nodded once, no more. Slumped, arms across his chest, eyes half shuttered, he appeared to doze, indifferent to the negotiations.

'If,' Lightfoot said, 'you gentlemen have the wherewithal?'

Dude smiled. 'We never bet more than we can afford to lose. By the same token, we like to see the shine of the other man's coin.'

'I assure you, sir, that should Old Dominion lose, the wager would be paid off immediately after the race.'

'Now that's the way I like to hear a

man talk.'

'Let's get down to taw, Mr. McQuinn,' Lightfoot said, becoming impatient. 'How much do you want to bet?'

'Five hundred dollars.'

Derision flecked the hooded eyes. 'Sir, I would not bring Old Dominion out of the barn for that paltry sum.'

'Would you for a thousand, and give us three-to-one odds?'

Llghtfoot sat suddenly upright. 'I never give odds. If so, three to one would be out of the question.'

'A heap of horse races are run on odds, if one man has the advantage — and you do. I don't like to admit it, but your horse is fancier bred than Texas Jack.'

'Even so, I never give odds.'

'In that case, it'll have to be five hundred even. If you want more money on the line, we'll have to have odds. Do you agree, Dr. Lockhart?'

Uncle Billy's chin rose and fell once.

'I haven't seen any of your wherewithal yet, Mr. McQuinn.'

Looking bored, Dude drew a worn

leather wallet from his hip pocket and counted out ten fifty-dollar greenbacks on the desk.

'I see only a mere five hundred,' Lightfoot said.

There was a rustling sound as Uncle Billy, sitting up, said, 'Take a look-see at this,' and from his coat took a leather poke and plopped it beside the greenbacks with a clink. Opening the drawstring, he spilled a glittering flood of fifty-dollar gold coins.

Lightfoot's eyes shone, and Dude's flew wide.

'Now, sir,' said Uncle Billy, 'may we see what you will lay on the line?'

The other was aghast. 'Surely, you don't think I am without funds? This is most unusual.'

'Want to see your wherewithal same as you wanted to see ours!'

Lightfoot called, 'Mr. Tate, bring me some money.'

Gone but a short time, Tate laid a thick stack of greenbacks tied with a string on the desk. Leaning across, Uncle Billy started thumbing through the currency note by note.

'Don't you accept the legal tender of our nation?' Lightfoot protested.

'Just a precaution I've taken ever since an old Johnny Reb, bless his unreconstructed heart, tried to pass off some Confederate money on us back in Missouri. This all looks genuine,' he said, turning to Dude. 'Not a bogus bill in the bunch.'

'Bogus!' Lightfoot roared. 'I want you to know, sir, that my bank is an upstanding institution of moral trust.'

'I said all the bills were good, didn't I?' Slowly, one by one, his care solicitous, the old man returned the coins to the poke while Lightfoot watched and Dude collected his money. 'But since you don't want to give odds,' Uncle Billy said, 'the race is off so far as I'm concerned.'

Lightfoot's eyes had not left the poke. His mouth hardened. 'I will give you two-to-one odds, gentlemen, if you will bet a thousand.'

He has an advantage we don't know

about or he wouldn't give odds, Dude thought. But odds were odds and the Judge could run. Dude nodded and Uncle Billy nodded.

'With half forfeit,' Lightfoot tacked on.

'Fair enough,' Dude said.

'With both jockeys weighing one hundred and thirty pounds, saddles excluded.'

Dude caught that one on the fly. One-thirty was Tate's weight, whereas Coyote's was around a hundred and five or eight. Dude grinned at Lightfoot. 'I believe your Open-to-the-World sign says catch weights, and catch weights it will be if we run you. Tate is heavier than our rider.'

'Can't blame a man for trying, can yon, Mr. McQuinni?'

'It's catch weights, then?'

'It is. And now for the starter. I suggest Mr. Big Boy Brody, proprietor of the Jayhawk Saloon. Although I personally do not approve of open saloons and their accruing evils, I find Mr. Brody a man of reputable character.'

Dude had to stille an outright guffaw. Why, the old hypocrite, and him the true owner. 'I won't accept Brody,' Dude said and sniffed, 'a saloonkeeper who allows gambling and pie and music and bawdy singin'. I've heard it said that he even waters the whiskey and the free lunches are loaded with salt to make the poor suckers buy more beer to quench their thirst.'

'Since I do not patronize the Jayhawk, I would not know about that, sir.'

'Instead,' said Dude, 'I propose Mr. Cy Kirby, a farmer of honest reputation hereabouts.'

Lightfoot scowled. 'I won't accept Kirby. He is not on good terms here at the bank and would be prejudiced against me in a close race. However, I am willing to flip for it.' He took a silver dollar from a pants pocket. 'You want to call it?'

'I will — in the air.'

Lightfoot flipped and as the coin neared its peak, Dude called, 'Tails.'

Lightfoot caught the downward spinning coin in the palm of his hand and held it out for Dude to see. It was 'heads.'

'So Brody is the starter,' Lightfoot said, flashing Dude his elation. 'Now for the finish judges. It is customary to have three. Each side picks one, then we negotiate for the third. You name yours first, Mr. McQuinn.'

'Mr. Van Vinson.'

Plainly, the Honorable G.L didn't like Vinson either. He said, 'Mine is Mr. Mordecai Fretwell, a longtime teller here at the bank, a deacon in the church, and, I am pleased to say, a teetotaler of the first water.'

At the word 'teetotaler,' Uncle Billy hooted, 'I have known teetotalers who would steal candy from an orphaned baby and sneak off with an old woman's last sack of flour. I hereby pick the widow Wheeler as our choice for the third judge.'

'I have another worthy person in mind. A man.'

'Let's flip for it,' the old man said.

Lightfoot nodded and when he reached for his pocket, Uncle Billy stopped him curtly, 'I'll flip this time and you call it.' He held out a silver half dollar and showed both sides and tossed it high. As the coin spun downward, Lightfoot called, 'Heads.'

Uncle Billy caught it deftly in his palm and everybody stared. 'Tails,' he said and cut his blue eyes at Lightfoot. 'It's against the law of averages for heads to come up twice in succession.'

Lightfoot shrugged it off, saying, 'Now, where and when do you want to run? We can use the track at my farm or the Lightfoot Paths west of town, which is the town's track.'

Uncle Billy was silent, so Dude, like an actor on cue, took up the dickering. He knew from experience there would be less opportunity for skulduggery at a public track; therefore, he said, 'The Paths are closer to town and more convenient. We prefer to run there.'

'That is agreeable with me. Now, when shall we run?'

The Judge, trained for short races in Missouri, could use more time to prepare for this longer race. On that reasoning, Dude, jockeying for time, said, 'Today is Saturday. What say we run two weeks from today at three o'clock?'

'Whatever you gentlemen say. Saturday is trade day and the race will draw folks from miles around. In fact, when the word gets about, I'm predicting that people will come from all over eastern and south eastern Kansas. Old Dominion has quite a reputation, you know.' He was smiling while he talked, more obliging, Dude sensed, than his character allowed. 'By the way, we've forgotten one more condition. Shall the start be lap-and-tap or from chutes?'

'Lap-and-tap,' Dude said. 'A horse can get hurt in a wooden chute.'

'How right you are, Mr. McQuinn. Valuable horses like our Thoroughbreds. I still can't place Copperbottom in the records I have, but since he goes back to Sir Archy that is quality enough for me.'

Dude had never matched a race on a

more obliging note, which warned him that Lightfoot had that unknown advantage. As the uneasy thought occurred to him, Lightfoot was saying, 'This calls for a drink. Mr. Tate!'

They drank, shook hands, Lightfoot bowed, and the partners walked out to the buggy. There, Dude asked curiously, 'Where'd you get all that gold?'

'You rocked back and forth with him just right on the conditions, Dude, pardner,' the old man said, as if he hadn't heard; in a rare show of affection, he slapped Dude's shoulder. 'The only piece of bad luck we had was losing the toss on that loudmouth Brody. He'll do his damnedest to give the other horse the edge at the break. Too, we haven't looked at Lightfoot Paths, which can't be much. And since we haven't run the Judge around a turn in alongtime — believe Fort Smith was the last time, when we cleaned out those cagey Arkansaw-yers — I want to see if he still changes to the left lead the way he should when he comes off the backstretch into the turn, then makes a flying change back to his right lead when he hits the homestretch into the straight-away . . . You see, Dude, the Judge will break in the right lead — that's natural for him. He runs in the right lead on the straightaway. That inability to use both leads loses races for many Thorough-breds in a close go. Also, when a horse changes leads, he has to reach a little far-ther with that front foot he's changing to. When he does, he gains ground. Chang-ing leads also gives the other front leg needed rest. No other leg has to take the strain that the lead leg does.'

'Yeah,' Dude said. He knew that. Uncle Billy had schooled him on the line points of lead-changing before, but it was encouraging to see the old man taking an interest in the race despite his hands-off claims. 'But what about the gold you came up with?'

'Oh, that. Just a new wrinkle was all.'

'But I didn't know . . . .'

'Let's go out and take a look at the Paths,' Uncle Billy cut him off, and Dude knew he would hear no more about the gold, if ever.

The Lightfoot Paths were about as Dude had expected for a small town, a straightaway and an oval laid out on the level Kansas prairie. No railings. Stakes marked the common distances and the turns. Flanking the finish-line posts was an open grandstand of modest dimensions, and near it, toward the homestretch turn, was a saddling paddock which opened on the track.

The partners, driving down the track in the buggy and around the turn to the approximate starting point for a five-and-a-half-furlong race, found the lanes overgrown with bluestem grass.

'Both lanes look the same,' the old man observed. He got out and tossed a small rock off the track. 'No advantage either way, unless Old Dominion takes the lead and we're on the outside and Tate pulls some rough stuff when Coyote starts to pass.'

He took his seat and when he chirruped sharply and slapped the reins, the big horse broke like a shot, quickly in full stride. Down the backstretch he moved, ears laid back, that head extended. The old man guided him through the turn.

When they raced into the straight-away, Amos stepped faster and Dude exclaimed, 'Look at him fly! He senses he's in the homestretch, headin' for the finish! Let 'im go!'

Uncle Billy did so, not easing Amos off until they rushed past the finish line.

'I tell you, he's a horse!' Dude said admiringly. 'You ought to keep him.'

Again, the old man might not have heard. 'There is a problem,' he said presently, driving Amos along at a cooling-down walk. 'The Judge will have to be worked around that one turn. How do we do it and not get spied on? I want to check his leads. If he's making the right changes, fine; if not, back to school for him and Coyote too. The ground the Judge makes up on the changes may mean the difference. I'm speaking of inches, not daylight.'

'Guess you've heard me speak of Grandpa McQuinn, when he rode with

Nathan Bedford Forrest in the War Between the States?'

'How could I forget when I've got both ears bent? Of course, you mean the Great Rebellion.'

'I mean the War Between the States and what Grandpa called a diversionary maneuver when he was out lickin' Yankees.'

'A diversionary maneuver?'

'You bet. In military strategy, that's a maneuver that draws the attention of the enemy away from a planned point of attack. In match racin', that means you make a move here for everybody to see to cover up a move you're makin' somewhere else.'

'Meaning exactly what?'

'Meanin' Monday morning, after the stores and the bank are open, the Honorable Coyote Walking and the Honorable Dude McQuinn will take smooth-lookin' Texas Jack and show him off around the square. The Honorable Mr. McQuinn will pony the impressive-lookin' Texas Jack on his rockin'-chair saddler, Blue

Grass. A likely crowd will gather, it is hoped. At such time Mr. McQuinn will announce the big horse race. From there he will hold a public gallop by the dangerous Texas Jack — he by Gone to Texas, he by Ranger Boy, he by Copperbottom, he by Sir Archy — just east of town — so folks can walk there and admire him.'

'All right, Dude, what are you up to this time?'

'While all this is goin' on, one William Tecumseh Lockhart will ride the Judge to the track and work him on that turn for the changes. See?' Dude asked, pleased with himself.

'Me? Now, Dude, I've gone as far as I can. This is my limit.'

'You can still ride a horse, can't you? Or has this soft buggy seat got you where you can't hoist yourself to the saddle?' When the old man didn't answer, Dude laid on the sickening-sweet sympathy. 'If you're too poorly to help out a little bit . . . ?'

'I'll swear, if you and that Comanche

don't get more helpless every day,' the old man replied, wearing a pained expression. 'Next thing I know I'll have to ride the Judge in the race, poorly or not.' Where upon, he headed Amos for town at a lively trot.

Dude smiled inwardly. Sometimes it was all a body could do to get ahead of the old gent and keep him interested.

★   ★   ★

A light rain fell during the night, and the outfit rolled out to a sparkling-bright Sunday morning. They fed and watered the horses and cooked a leisurely breakfast. Afterward, Uncle Billy examined each horse and told Dude that Blue Grass, although in good condition, had 'a peaked look around the eyes' and needed 'a brightener.' Forthwith, the old man got out one of his heavy 'tomes.' Holding it near, then at arm's length, then near, then far, he perused it and directly mixed something in a can and set it back to be added to the saddler's evening feed. Meanwhile, Dude and Coyote went over the harness and saddles. Church bells were ringing by the time they had finished.

At noon Cy and Abby Kirby, dressed in their Sunday best, drove up in a light buggy and were invited in.

'You can start hauling us some hay and grain,' Dude told him. 'We're matched a week from Saturday against Old Dominion at Lightfoot Paths.' Noting Kirby's lack of enthusiasm, he asked, 'Something the matter, Cy?'

'Every good horse that's come in here has either been way outrun or something has happened.'

'We clocked Old Dominion early one morning on the sly and he ran in slow time.'

'Slow time?' Kirby's gray-stubbled face reflected a mixture of surprise and doubt.

'Took him a minute and fifteen seconds to go five and a half furlongs. It was a speed work.'

'Don't fit Old Dominion.'

'We were tipped off he was goin' to run.'

'You sure it was Old Dominion?'

Dude stared at him, puzzled. 'No reason not to. Why?'

Kirby looked down before answering. 'Lightfoot has another dark chestnut. Not that you could tell much about the color that early in the morning.'

A sickening feeling began to stir within Dude as he looked at Uncle Billy and their eyes locked for a moment. The old man turned to Kirby. 'Is this chestnut a rangy Thoroughbred?'

'He is. Some years older than Old Dominion. A horse called Or . . . Or . . . .' He stopped.

'Orestes,' Abby said for him, smiling. 'From Greek mythology. But that doesn't make him run any faster.'

'Lightfoot bought this horse back East before he got Old Dominion,' her husband explained. 'When he ran him out here a few times and got him beat, he retired him.'

'You have seen Orestes run?' Uncle Billy asked.

'Every time he ran here.'

'Is he a long-striding horse?'

Kirby frowned, recalling. 'No, he is not.'

'Does he run with his head high?'

'As I remember, he does. Too high. That was one of his problems.'

'That was the horse we clocked,' the old man nodded. 'On the basis of that slow work, we matched the race.' He smiled as a mandoes when he knows he's been taken, a wry smile. 'They took our bait and we took theirs. That was clever the way they pulled it. Their first tip jibed with what Gideon Lightfoot told us at the barn about the swelling — so we believed the second one. Dude, we're up against the slickest outfit we've run into yet.'

'Tell me this,' Dude asked, 'why did Lightfoot say he didn't show his horse till just before a race?'

'That was just more come-on bait.'

'Watch your horse day and night,' Kirby warned. 'Never leave him. I'll start hauling in feed tomorrow morning.'

After the Kirbys left, Uncle Billy said,

'I knew this was an extra slick lay from the start. But now that we're in it, let's make that Lightfoot fella eat the Judge's dust.'

At his words, Coyote broke into a stomp dance and Dude marked time with him, clapping his hands and tapping with his right foot.

At last, Uncle Billy was back. Poorly as he was!

10

Skulduggery Before Dawn

Beneath the great copper eye of the Monday morning sun, the town of Lightfoot appeared to be rousing itself by degrees for another day of outward propriety. Buggies and wagons moved, a few horsemen. A man crossed the broad street between the square and the post office. For more than an hour an incessant hammering had sounded from the blacksmith shop. Dude looked at his watch, which read nine twenty-one.

'You ready, Coyote?'

Coyote nodded. He was dressed for the track: naked above the waist, clad only in breechcloth and long-fringed moccasins, an eagle feather in his blue-black hair, cropped at his neck. For added effect, streaks of vermilion slanted from his high cheekbones to his ears.

'I won't take up slack on the lead shank till we start around the square,' Dude said. 'Believe we'd better go around once before we make any moves. Want to get their attention first.'

They mounted and rode out on the street, Coyote aboard Texas Jack, curried and brushed till he looked unbeatable, truly a walking picture of the speedy running horse, Dude on Blue Grass, ponying Texas Jack.

Heading into the square, Dude shortened his hold and pulled the gelding's head higher. They jogged slowly down one side of the square and made the turn, Coyote riding with his head high and haughty, looking straight ahead, disdainful of this mere white man's town.

Marshal Epps, in front of the Lightfoot Drug Emporium, gave them a careful stare. Two young women paused before the Lightfoot Ladies' Wear and one oohed, 'My, what a beautiful horse! And that's a real Indian, I know! Isn't he fearsome!'

'You ain't seen nothin' yet,' Dude wanted to shout at her.

They rode to the next turn. Texas

Jack tossed his head, resenting the short lead. The early spitters and whittlers and horseshoe and checker players under the courthouse elms stopped their games to watch. Some people left the stores to look. Dude saw all this from the corner of his eye.

They rode to the end of the block, coming out on the broad street leading into town, and jogged on to where they had entered the square. Glancing down the long street toward the campground, Dude spied Uncle Billy loping Judge Blair for the Paths.

'All right, Coyote,' Dude said, low, when they were halfway down the block. 'Anytime now. There's the bank.'

Of a sudden Coyote let go a screeching whoop, causing Texas Jack to jump, and Dude yanked on the lead shank and hollered, 'Watch out! He's tryin' to run away!' And around they went, and again, apparently struggling to control the racehorse. The reliable Blue Grass even threw up his head in excitement. Straightening out, Dude noticed heads at the main window of the bank. A man opened the bank door and came out to watch. It was Stub Tate. Dude felt an immediate relief, for Tate accounted for one of the pair who might be bird dogging the camp.

A straggle of courthouse-lawn loafers left their games and strolled out to the street. Dude drew the lead shank shorter, making Texas Jack dance and swerve.

They were approaching the Jayhawk Saloon. Dude, who rode on Coyote's left, nodded and Coyote screeched and with the heel of his left moccasin jabbed the bay gelding's flank, a move hidden from sight of the watchers. Instantly, the startled Texas Jack humped his back and started pitching, scattering the watchers like quail. He would have quieted down after a few jumps, for there was no gentler horse than Texas Jack, but Dude didn't pull his head up and the gelding went on bucking. Duae yelled, 'Hold 'im, Injun! He's tryin' to bolt!' and took horse and jockey around and around, in a taut, dust-raising circle that had viewers lining the boardwalk in front of the stores. Dude then pulled Texas Jack's head up and he settled down to prancing.

Glancing toward the saloon, Dude found what he had hoped for: Big Boy Brody watching outside the bat-wing doors. His presence took care of the other half of the morning's worry.

Out of the Pioneer Courier, note pad and pencil in hand, sleeves rolled up, derby at that jaunty angle, Van Vinson rushed on the scent for news.

Dude slowed Texas Jack to a walk and called loudly, 'I've got a story for you. We're matched against Old Dominion a week from Saturday.'

Vinson's mouth flew open. He thumped the brim of his derby. 'That'll give me something to write about besides how many pounds of butter sell in town that day. When can I get the details for Thursday's paper?'

'I'll talk to you back at camp. We're headed for the east edge of town to work Texas Jack' — Dude scowled at the gelding — 'if he'll simmer down. He's a wild one today.' He turned to the crowd. 'You're all welcome to watch Texas Jack. Be no secrets about the way we train our horse.'

They jogged on, slowly to allow the spectators to follow at a walk, Dude careful to set Texas Jack to dancing now and then.

At the edge of town, Dude halted and, waving his arms, said, 'Now, folks, don't get too close. Give Texas Jack plenty of room. As high-strung as he is, he might bust loose. Mr. Coyote Walking will start the horse when I drop my hat. Stand back, everybody!' He reined out of the way. 'Keep him headed straight, Coyote. You know how spooky he is. You folks get back there!'

That was when he glimpsed Tate and Brody, both looking somewhat amused.

Dude raised his hat high. To his chagrin, however, Texas Jack looked bored instead of keyed to run. *Wake 'im up, Coyote. Make 'im look spirited.*

Coyote, at that moment catching Dude's eye, heeled the gelding even with Dude, who continued to hold his hat high for another moment, thereby fixing the crowd's attention. Then, with a flourish, he brought the hat down and Coyote whooped and the surprised Texas Jack took off faster than usual.

For the first fifty or seventy-five yards, he looked like a running horse, moving fairly fast, and then he commenced to fade as it was his wont to lose speed after a short distance. Watching, Dude wondered how so smooth-looking a horse could be so slow and he thought of what Uncle Billy had said:

'Texas Jack is a cold-blooded horse — that's why he can't run. However, I've seen some well-bred horses that couldn't run a lick. Breeding isn't everything. Kings and queens can have some mighty ugly offspring. When you come right down to it, maybe it's heart that makes a runner. Combine that with breeding speed to speed and you have a scorpion.'

Minutes passed before Coyote brought the lathered horse back at a walk. With most of the crowd still there, Dude said, for public benefit, 'Glad you eased him off after the break. Don't want to take any chances with him, since he just got over the colic.' He had spoken mainly for the ears of Tate and Brody, but when he looked arouud they were gone. Dude and Coyote turned for camp.

Uncle Billy was waiting, seated in his cane-bottomed chair, his mien that of one who had accomplished his mission. 'The Judge,' he told them; with a trace of his old sparkle, 'changed leads like the dancing master at Monsieur's Academy of Dance. I worked him out twice around the turn. He went into his left lead, then back to his right on the straightaway, and he didn't bear out.'

'Did you let him run?' Dude asked.

A puckish smile, then, 'As the Honorable Dude McQuinn would say, 'I'll put it this way. I didn't let the grass grow under 'im.' He sighed, and for a moment Dude feared he was about to go poorly again. Instead, he said, 'Believe I'll have me a little toddy,' and headed for the wagon.

Coyote and Dude, their eyes meeting, nodded ever so slowly. So far all signs were good. Wherefore, Coyote pointed to the Four Great Directions, a Comanche's petition for power and good luck.

* ★ ★ ★

Thereafter, Uncle Billy went to the post office each afternoon, guarded as usual about what he had in mind, a silence that Dude dared not intrude upon, and on Thursday, Van Vinson, in a rush, brought copies of the *Pioneer Courier*.

'This race will be the biggest event in the history of Lightfoot,' he predicted breezily and slapped his derby for emphasis. 'I exchange papers with other publishers all over the state, and I've run off extra copies for distribution in nearby towns. Wait'll you read my story! Even jarred loose a few ads. A lot of people will be coming in here, hoping to see Old Dominion get beat. The Honorable G.L. is about as popular as a skunk in the bunkhouse during a snowstorm, the way he takes hair and hide in business deals.'

He left in a hurry.

Dude whistled when he saw the banner headline set in huge black capitals across the top of page one. 'Listen to this,' he chortled.

Uncle Billy, who had been napping under the wagon, sat up and yawned. 'More Plymouth Colony folderol, I suppose?'

'Just listen and don't interrupt. Here's the main headline: TEXAS CHAMPION CHALLENGES UNBEATEN OLD DOMINION. Under that's another headline: RACE TO BE STAGED IN LIGHTFOOT. THRONGS TO JAM OUR FAIR CITY. Here's Van's story:

'The greatest horse race in the colorful history of Kansas, if not the entire West, will be staged at Lightfoot Paths, May 16, when Texas Jack, the fastest Thoroughbred in Texas, meets the unbeaten Old Dominion, the fastest Thoroughbred in Kansas and probably the entire Middle West.

'The two nonpareils of the turf will

race 5½ furlongs. Local devotees of the sport of kings see a close race down to the wire, since both horses are bred for distance. The amount at stake was not disclosed, but is thought to be considerable. The race is expected to draw hundreds of racegoers from over the state.

'Old Dominion, a five-year-old stallion sired by Old South, is owned by the Honorable Gideon Lightfoot, president of the Lightfoot County Bank and widely known in Thoroughbred racing circles from Kansas to New York.

'Trainer and discoverer of the famed Texas Jack, a six-year-old gelding sired by Gone to Texas, is the Honorable Dude McQuinn, a direct descendant of the redoubtable General Sam Houston. The eminent Mr. McQuinn, a scion of pioneers, hails from Live Oak, Texas, on the Salt Fork of the Brazos. Modest by nature, the affable Texan opines that Texas Jack 'has been known to run a little when the wind is with him and his feet don't hurt.'

'On the other hand, Mr. Lightfoot predicts victory. 'Old Dominion has never been headed after the first furlong,' he says. 'I see no reason to expect otherwise.'

'Also taking a prominent role in Texas Jack's training is the estimable Dr. William Tecumseh Lockhart, a true horseman of the old school who recently acquired half ownership of the Hashy gelding. A veterinarian, scientist and author from whom success did not long withhold her hand, Dr. Lockhart has made a host of friends in the short time he has enlightened our community with his uncanny alleviation of equine ills. The good doctor's sage advice is simple: 'Remember that he who buys a horse needs a thousand eyes. Furthermore, do not think of using a common stallion because he is cheap. His get will be cheap to sell and dear to keep.'

'How does that sound to you, Uncle?' Dude asked, pleased.

'Much better, even if I didn't say it.' Dude went on reading:

'The speedy Old Dominion is being trained at Mr. Lightfoot's spacious farm south oftown by Mr. Stub Tate, who also will ride the horse in the forthcoming spectacle. Mr. Tate, formerly a leading jockey on Eastern tracks, is regarded as a keen judge of pace.'

Uncle Billy interrupted with a wave of his hand. 'There's something about this fella Tate that sticks in my craw somewhere. But I can't place him. Sign of old age, I guess, when a man can't remember.'

'Maybe you saw him ride on one of the big tracks?' Dude pried. 'Maybe Sarntoga or Pimlico?'

'Now, did I say?' the old man huffed, crawling out from under the wagon.

'Quit interrupting and listen,' Dude said. 'In the irons for Texas Jack will be Mr. Coyote Walking, truly the epitome of the Noble Red Mao, whom loyal readers of the *Pioneer Courier* will recall having heen introduced to previously in our newsy columns as the son of the chief of all Comanches. As a mere boy, Mr. Walking rode buffalo-running horses on the Great Plains and was soon recognized as the greatest buffalo slayer of all Comaoches.'

Dude paused, head cocked. 'What do you think of them words, Coyote?'

'That white man who writes talking paper constructive imagination has.'

'What comes next is mighty important,' Dude told them. 'It will help us tiain the Judge on the sly. I had Van put this in:

'As the *Pioneer Courier* was going to press, the obliging Mr. McQuinn announced Texas Jack's training schedule. Starting Friday, he will be worked every other morning at nine o'clock on the road east of town. Local residents are welcome to watch, which is in contrast to the usual secrecy prior to a race of this importance.'

Dude lowered the paper and rubbed hard on his forehead. 'I thought by announcing that schedule we could work the Judge at daybreak the same days on the Paths or the north road. What do you think?'

Both partners nodded agreement, aod Dude read on:

'Of high interest is the selection of Mr. Big Boy Brody, cordial proprietor of the genteel Jayhawk Saloon, as official starter for the big race. A walk-up, lap-and-tap start has been agreed on by both principals instead of wooden chutes.

'Finish-line judges include the widow Maude Wheeler, of whom no more be said regarding unquestioned integrity and dedicated service to our growing community; Mr. Mordecai Fretwell, associated with the Lightfoot County Bank for many years in positions of trust; and your humble editor of the *Pioneer Courier*.'

Finished, Dude awaited his partners' reaction.

'That's all very well the way you and Vinson have laid it out,' the old man said thoughtfully. 'But there's one detail lacking: We don't know what the other side is up to. Neither have we seen the true Old Dominion on the track.'

He drew out his watch, looked at it,

and little by little, held it farther from him until his arm was outstretched, and said, 'About time for the mail,' and took his punctual walk to the post office.

In the days that followed, the outfit settled down to the every-other-day routine of working the Judge at dawn on the Paths and Texas Jack at midmorning for the townsmen to see, limiting the latter to gallops or easy breezes, which gave no hint to his lack of racing speed. In the afternoons the courthouse-square loafers helped pass the time; sometimes a farmer would bring by a lame or sick animal and Uncle Billy would examine and prescribe and, in between, lecture on the diseases and injuries common to *Equus caballus:* bruises, abrasions, bucked shins, bowed tendons, strained ligaments, wobbles, periodic ophthalmia or 'moon blindness,' the common cold and colic.

★ ★ ★

On Wednesday afternoon before the race, the widow Wheeler and Mrs. Haley drove up behind the old gray horse, and when Dude went out to them, the widow asked, 'Is Billy — I mean Dr. Lockhart — here?' She blushed as she hastily corrected herself and gave, what was for her, a coquettish lowering of her eyes.

'There he is now, coming back from the post office.'

Dude left them as Uncle Billy approached, his step becoming more lively when he neared the buggy. An intimate, animated conversation ensued between him and the widow Wheeler, after which the ladies drove off waving wee handkerchiefs, Uncle Billy, strolling to the wagon, took a tug on his coat. 'Don't wait supper for me, boys. I'm invited to Maude's — I mean the widow Wheeler's — for the evening.'

'Don't forget your sales pitch on Amos,' Dude reminded him.

'I won't.'

'Why not drive Amos over there and tie him in front of her house so she can

300

get a good look-see? Remember what the good Dr. William Tecumseh Lockhart says, 'A true horseman never walks when he can ride."

'Oh, all right, if you insist.'

The hour was late and a sickle moon shed bleary light when Dude, waking, heard the clop-clop of a horse coming slowly down the street from town, sounds that mixed with the light crunch of buggy wheels. At the entrance to the camp the horse slowed and seemed to hesitate in doubt, then take a few tentative steps, then hesitate again. After a brief wait and much stamping of hooves, it walked straight into camp and halted near the wagon, stamping and shaking its bridle.

Dude rose from his bedroll, pulled on his boots and stood by the wagon in his long underwear, waiting for Uncle Billy to get out.

But nothing happened.

Going to the buggy, Dude heard the soft chuffing of unbroken snoring. He reached in and shook a booted leg, at the same time catching a whiff of sour Bourbon fumes.

'Wake up, Uncle, you're home. And durned if you're not roostered again!'

'No such thing,' a slurred voice answered. Scrambling noises followed as the old man got out and down and stood unsteadily but defiantly erect.

'Not only roostered,' Dude scolded, 'but you went to sleep on the way back and Amos had to bring you home. Pretty remarkable, I'd say, for a blind horse!'

'What happened was . . . Ah sorta dozed off when Ah saw we'd reached camp . . . was all.'

'Well, did you sell Amos to the widow Wheeler or not?'

'Ah tried. Oh, Ah tried, Dude, padnuh. But ever' time Ah broached th' subject, Maude — Ah mean th' widow Wheeler — got off on that cussed Plymouth Colony or — '

'Or what?'

'Or brought me another toddy, an' she had some more dandelion wine, an' finally . . . Well, it's kinda personal.'

'An' finally what?' Dude asked, his disgust mounting. Uncle Billy was already past him, moving wraithlike to the wagon and quickly under it to his bedroll.

'An' finally what?' Dude called after him.

More silence. Shortly, a steady chuffing drifted out to Dude. At the same time a belated inkling came to him, growing and growing. He was jolted.

Again! Why, the old hoot owl!

* * *

Thursday's issue of the *Pioneer Courier* carried another banner headline: OLD DOMINION FAVORED SATURDAY, and rehashed the previous week's facts, with emphasis on the large crowd expected to swell the local economy.

'That suits me fine,' Dude told his partners. 'So G.L.'s people will bet their money. I aim to have the rest of our bankroll bet by Saturday morning.'

'Don't bet it all,' the old man cautioned. 'If these were ordinary horsemen trying to get the advantage, I wouldn't mind. But the other side is too quiet. Also, we'd better agree on a rendezvous after the race in case we need it.'

'Cy Kirby says there's a nice spring about fifteen miles west. Keep on going on the road past the Paths. Was a camping place for freighters in the early days.'

Uncle Billy and Coyote nodded to that, and after a moment of reflection, the old man said, 'Think I'll harness Amos and keep him handy for the getaway.'

'If,' Dude amended, 'you haven't peddled him to the widow Wheeler or Rufus Hubbard.'

The old man drew back, feigning aversion. 'Peddling, you say? A blind horse to a poor widow woman? Even a horse trader has his scruples. As for friend Rufus, if he had the money he'd been to see me by now.'

'If you drive Amos, who takes the wagon?'

'You or Coyote.'

'Not Coyote. He'd better fade out

down the road right after the race — rain or shine. Somebody might want to wash the Judge's face. I'll drive the wagon. Tie Blue Grass and Texas Jack on behind.'

Come to think of it, Dude mused later, it was a little unusual for Uncle to switch. He'd always driven the wagon after a race as they hurried separately to their distant rendezvous. Sometimes he left early, like the last time. Did the fact that Amos was faster than the sorrels mean anything? Dude wondered.

★ ★ ★

Most trainers would have worked their horse hard three or four days before the race, and then rested him, save for moderate galloping and walking, but because Judge Blair was a heavy eater, Dude decided on a stiff blowout at dawn Friday morning to keep him sharp.

At breakfast Dude could tell that his old mentor was feeling the usual prerace tensions, and not once did he mention being poorly. He was restless and bristly and also preoccupied. Twice during the morning he went behind the wagon to look at Judge Blair.

'I want to make certain there's no heat or puffiness in his ankles and legs after that hard work you and Coyote put him to,' he said, his voice gathering disapproval. 'There is such a thing as riding a good horse down. Or maybe you Alamo Texans never heard of that?'

Dude smiled. 'I just want him quick and full of himself. Be a light feed in the morning and only a few sips of water at noon. When do you plan to switch the markings?'

'Late. Just before dawn. In case the Honorable G.L.' — he actually sneered — 'figures he can slip some lightfooted hombre in here during the night to fix our horse. How do you want to set the night watches?'

'You the first one, then Coyote, then me. That all right?'

A nod. 'I'll tell you and Coyote one thing for certain. If I catch some hombre sneaking in, don't bother to run for the

306

doctor — just get the undertaker.'

Dude and Coyote beamed.

Now, that was the real Uncle Billy!

★ ★ ★

Friday afternoon the old man looked at his watch and made his daily trek to the post office. He was soon back, wearing a troubled face when he walked into camp, shaking a letter at his partners.

'Finally got an answer to the letter I sent back East to an old friend.' He crossed his arms and his eyes revealed the keenness of an old-time horseman up against odds and the determination to outslick the other side and defend his horse, hell or high water. 'First thing is this Stub Tate. It all comes back to me now. I read it somewhere and don't ask me where, Dude. . . . Tate was a leading jockey and later a leading trainer under the name of Mick Tate. A few years ago he was ruled off the New York tracks for doping horses. A lifetime suspension. Must've been after that when he and this

G.L. fella got together.' He smiled dryly. 'Now more good news. This Old Dominion is everything he's said to be — and more. He holds the record for five and a half furlongs at Saratoga in 1:04. Boys, we've matched a stakes champion at his best distance.' He moved to the wagon and back, head bent, thinking, projecting, and regarded Coyote as gently as he might if instructing a boy. 'Coyote, pardner, you'll have to take the break. Use the swinging start this time.' Turning, 'Dude, you'll have to tell Brody ahead of time the way we start our horse or sure as shootin' he'll call the horses back and say no go. Just remember that a man can start his horse any way he chooses so long as he doesn't hinder the other horse.'

That said, he went to the wagon and presently Dude heard the doors of the medicine chest being opened, and then the *thung* of the stopper on the jug.

By midafternoon Editor Vinson's prediction took form as visitors streamed into town for the race. Wagons and buggies and saddle horses jammed the streets around the square and crowds milled on the boardwalk and in and out of the stores, creating a festive air. A banner proclaiming post time at Lightfoot Paths was draped across the face of the Lightfoot Mercantile. Two foot-tapping fiddlers took turns entertaining outside the hotel, and young folk danced on the porch. The square soon overflowed and the campground was filling up a short distance down the street from the outfit, a congestion that worried Uncle Billy. To please him, Dude and Coyote stretched a rope corral around the horses. Fortunately, Dude pointed out, there were no campers behind the wagon where the horses were haltered, since the camp was backed up to a fenced pasture.

Around four o'clock Dude went alone to the Jayhawk Saloon for a drink and 'to listen around,' as he put it, when Uncle Billy declined, since he was taking the first watch.

Dude literally had to elbow a path to the bar. The busy Brody sighted him at once. 'Another Old Green River, my friend?' Dude nodded and as Brody slapped down bottle and glass, he asked genially, 'How's the great Texas Jack?'

'All primed to take the slack out of anything this side of Kansas City. How's the unbeaten Old Dominion?'

A shade of Brody's civility vanished 'how would I know? As the bard quoth, 'All I do is start the race — fear not for the pace.' '

'Glad you mentioned that. I'd better tell you we have a slightly different way of startin' our horse. It's a peculiarity of Texas Jack's.'

'This is gonna be lap-and-tap. No chutes.'

'Yes, we agreed on that. In addition, we use the swingin' break.'

Brody frowned. 'Wouldn't be tryin' to get the edge, would you?'

'As the bard quoth, 'It's all simple an' fair — an' won't ruffle anybody's hair,' ' Dude said, and fed him a sly smile that was deliberately provocative. 'Our jockey turns the horse a little before he breaks, that's all there is to it.' What Dude didn't explain was that turning gave the Judge extra momentum at the break, that the Judge pushed off and swung into his get-away. A short step to pull on — then a jump and he was off.

'Sounds all right,' Brody said agreeably. 'Just so the horses don't bump and are evenly lapped.'

'How will you tap 'em off?'

'I will be holding my hat high in my right hand. I will bring the hat down and holler 'Go!' at the same time.'

'The old-time way — good. By the way,' Dude asked, thinking of the bait that he had swallowed so readily here, 'where are Lon and Mack? I sorta like those boys. I'd like to buy 'em a drink.'

'Probably in jail where they belong,' Brody burst out, guffawing explosively, and at that moment seemed to spot a needy customer far down the bar.

As Dude worked his way out of the noisy crowd, a farmer said, 'Good luck tomorrow. Hope Texas Jack is ready.'

Dude thanked him and said, 'I believe

he'll win it,' a confidence he didn't fully feel. Brody had been too agreeable, a sure sign the other side had a wrinkle the little outfit didn't know about.

From the saloon Dude walked along the crowded boardwalk toward the Lightfoot Hotel, where a stage drawn by four horses was pulling in. A watching boy ran out and opened the stage's door and a man descended and assisted a woman passenger. Another man stepped down, and another.

Dude froze in midstep, staring.

The last man, chunky and as alert as a watchdog, was observing his surroundings, blinking rapidly against the sunlight. A gold watch chain shone across the vest of his black suit. Gazing down the street, he tipped back his black bowler, providing Dude a clear view of his hawkish features, and all at once Dude remembered. It was the bowler-hatted man he and Coyote had seen in Roseville, where the race had ended in the rain and near disaster.

While Dude watched, the bowler man

spoke to the driver, who tossed down a carpetbag from the railed top of the stage, and the man, catching it deftly, turned and faced to the hotel, blinking constantly, his aggressive walk remindful of a trailing hound dog on scent, watching about as he went.

Dude's thoughts were spinning as he walked on, letting his mind run over possibilities. None made sense. He said nothing at camp, and tonight's watches and the concerns of tomorrow's race soon occupied his thinking.

Evening light faded and the supper fire turned to cherry-red coals. Coyote read by lantern light, while Uncle Billy rested in his chair. Dude just sat, thinking of the race. In the distance, the murmur of campers' voices and the low, plaintive strains of a harmonica pulsed through the camp. Gradually, even those sounds ceased and Dude, after looking at the horses, went to his bedroll. When he did, Uncle Billy moved his chair to the end of the wagon where he could watch the horses without getting up. The two sorrels were tied side by side, then Blue Grass, Judge Blair, Texas Jack and Amos. Later, Dude heard the old man wake Coyote for the second watch.

At three o'clock Coyote touched Dude awake and he rose for the last vigil. Uncle Billy also stirred and Dude knew that the old man, who never slept soundly before a race, was only catnapping. Dude strolled quietly around the horses and sat down in the chair. A late moon had risen, bathing the campground in a luminous wash. Almost like daylight, he thought. Now and then he heard a horse stamp. After a while, catching himself on the verge of dozing, he stood and moved away from the wagon. A cloud was drifting across the face of the corn-yellow moon, curtaining the light.

Observing that change, he heard a buggy coming slowly from the square and before long he saw its dark, upright bulk. Slower it came, until the driver halted across from camp. Voices rose — a woman's and a man's.

Dude grinned. Lovers this time of

night in Lightfoot, where, as the worn joke went about small towns, the sidewalks were rolled up at sundown? He stiffened as the woman's voice shrilled, 'Let me alone.' The masculine muttered something muffled. Dude grinned again. That fellow would catch it, bringing a girl home this late. Behind him Dude could hear Uncle Billy and Coyote stirring. Soon Dude caught what sounded like blows and grunts coming from the buggy. He moved to the edge of the camp, feeling his first concern, seeing two dim figures in the buggy who appeared to be struggling.

'Let me alone!' the woman cried again.

Still, Dude hesitated, not wanting to interfere in a lovers' quarrel. Possibly fifteen seconds of silence followed. Then:

'Help! Help! Somebody help me — please!'

Dude held back no longer. Behind him Uncle Billy and Coyote were coming on the double. As Dude reached the street, the buggy moved off. When he hesitated, it stopped and he heard the woman's cries again. He ran forward, and again the buggy moved on. Simultaneously came the pounding footsteps of his partners behind him.

It was then that he became aware of the outbreak of sounds from the camp, the stamping and snorting and halter pulling of a frightened horse. Dude swung around, meeting Uncle Billy and Coyote running up.

'Back there — the camp!' the old man yelled, and Dude and Coyote wheeled with him. Some inner sense of wrongness prompted Dude to glance back. The buggy was gone, disappearing rapidly down the cloud-darkened street. There were no more shrieks of distress.

They sprinted to the wagon and behind it, and found the horses still haltered, but Amos, tied at one end, next to Texas Jack, continued to rear and pull on his halter rope.

'There's something wrong here,' Uncle Billy said, and Dude, hurrying, lit a lantern, and brought it around.

Immediately, Uncle Billy went straight

to Judge Blair, stroking him, talking to him. Even he, normally a quiet horse, was moving nervously. Texas Jack was not. Beside him, Uncle Billy looked down and picked up something. A rag, which he held to his nose.

'Chloroform!' he gritted. He put his face to the gelding's nostrils and took a deep breath, drew back, and, swiping a hand across his nose, gritted again, 'They drugged him!' Moving swiftly to Judge Blair, he went through the same inspection. 'No. . . .' he said, audibly relieved.

'A good thing you didn't switch the markings last night,' Dude said. 'And a good thing Amos gave the alarm,' the old man said, looking up and down the line of horses. His face, outlined in the lantern light, had taken on the acute alertness Dude remembered from other times when the outfit was threatened: the other Uncle Billy, the mysterious one with the guarded past, whose story Dude and Coyote likely would never know. 'You see,' Uncle Billy said, fingering his beard, 'I think that, they figured we might have a look-alike horse.'

'If they did,' Dude said, 'why didn't they also drug the Judge?'

'Didn't have time, because Amos started making a fuss and they heard us coming back. A blind horse is like a blind person in that his senses are extra keen. He could smell that stuff. It was foreign to him. It troubled him. He knew it was wrong. Anyway, if the doper wasn't sure which was the real running horse, why not drug both horses? Amos prevented that.' Uncle Billy shook his head in self-reproach. 'I'll never tie the two horses side by side again — that was a mistake.'

Coyote walked to the pasture fence behind the wagon. He came back showing a piece of torn cloth. 'Mean white man ripped shirt going through barbed wire fence he did,' he said. 'Same way he came in.'

'That was a slick damsel-in-distress wrinkle they pulled to give the doper time to slip through the fence to the wagon,' the old man said.

'Did I ever fall for that,' Dude groaned.

'One of my own diversionary maneuvers.'

'We all did,' Uncle Billy said, his tone dismissing Dude's self-blame. 'Let's make some coffee, then I'll change the markings.'He turned to go around the wagon and stopped short by Amos, as if suddenly remembering. 'I didn't even bother to look at you, did I, old hoss?' he said earnestly, apologetic about it, and stroked the big horse's face and neck and talked nonsense to him before going on.

11

Lightning Power

Race day.

When the sun bulged like a huge golden ornament shining down on the outfit, CoyoteWalking stood in the center of camp and, gazing up at the sky, made signs to the Four Great Directions, came back and announced solemnly, 'No rain there will be on the race today, Grandfather. Last night the Owl Person told me. Today, Grandfather the Sun tells me. This thing has been promised.'

Uncle Billy looked stooped and tired this morning, yet his eyes had the pre-race glitter of old. A half grin moved across his face. He said, 'I ought to get after you for calling me Grandfather, but since Comanche medicine is bringing us clear weather, I won't, His smile fell away and his eyes took in both partners. 'Let's keep both the Judge and Texas Jack behind the wagon. If the other side sees a droopy bay with a blaze, they'll know they doped the wrong horse. Texas Jack is still sluggish — looks drowsy. Let 'em think they got the right one as long as we can.'

Coyote said, 'My father the chief has old Comanche way of painting warhorses to impart speed and power. Do that I would like.'

Dude nodded slowly, Uncle Billy nodded slowly, both weighing the idea, and then both nodded faster, their grins widening.

'Good,' the old man said. 'A new wrinkle. That will give them something to ponder on, besides looking surprised when our horse shows up to run. Keep the Judge out of sight till we go to the track.'

Coyote took his parfleche bag from the wagon, removed some objects, put the bag back, and stepped behind the wagon. He was there a long, long time.

'Judge Blair ready is,' he said, coming out.

A quiet morning set in, unbroken until

racegoers started passing to the square, there to mill and wait, renewing the holiday air of yesterday.

Cy and Abby Kirby arrived at the camp, bursting with overnight news.

'Lightfoot had Old Dominion walked in from the farm late yesterday,' Kirby reported. 'He's in the barn behind Lightfoot's house, guarded by four men.'

Dude's laughter pealed out. 'My, my, the Honorable G.L. is afraid somebody will slip in and fix his horse.' He was about to tell them about the doping, but refrained, seeing Uncle Billy shake his head.

'We've bet all we can scrape up and so have our friends,' Kirby went on. 'Got three-to-one money at the Jayhawk. If we win, the farm will be ours again. Brody's gamblers are covering everything in sight.' Doubt entered his voice. 'They act mighty confident.'

'Cy,' Dude said, 'would you place some money for me at three to one? If I do it, they might get cold feet.'

'Glad to.'

Dude peeled off most of what the outfit had left and handed it to him. Coyote dug into the parfleche bag, betting most of the money he had put back to send to his father the chief, and Uncle Billy wagered a large portion of his place-by-the-f'ar savings.

'That's something when the jockey bets on the horse he's riding and the trainer bets on the horse he's training,' Kirby said, encouraged.

At noontime the outfit packed the wagon and Dude gave the Judge a few sips from a water bucket and sat down to wait, while Uncle Billy napped and Coyote read. Time seemed to crawl.

By two o'clock the vanguard of the crowd was heading for the track. At two-thirty Mrs. Haley and the widow Wheeler drew up in the buggy. 'We came to wish you luck,' Maude Wheeler said when Dude and the old man greeted them. 'The best thing that could happen to this town would be for Old Dominion to get beat. Gideon Lightfoot needs to be taken down a notch. We've put our money on Texas Jack.'

'I hope you didn't bet a lot,' Uncle Billy said.

'Why, Billy, isn't Texas Jack a fast horse?'

'He is. But any horse race is a gamble.'

'He'd better win. Just about my whole future depends on him. I even put up my house with one of Brody's gamblers.'

'You what!' The old man was truly concerned.

'Oh, I didn't go to the Jayhawk in person,' she said, on her dignity. 'I placed the bet through Fannie's husband, Levi. And then I bet my bank savings when that tightwad Gideon Lightfoot offered me two-to-one odds. How I'd like to skin him good after the way he treated Dewitt at the bank.'

Uncle Billy just shook his head.

'Texas Jack will run his best,' Dude assured her, likewise wishing she hadn't gone so far.

The two drove on, waving blithely.

'I wish we'd never got into this,' Uncle Billy said, hanging his head. 'There's too much at stake. People are betting with

324

their emotions instead of their common sense.'

'Isn't that the way most people bet?' Dude said. 'Anyhow,the Judge is ready to run.'

'That's not all. We've got to see that he gets every chance to run his race. I keep asking myself what Stub Tate will try. Coyote will have his hands full.' He seemed to pull himself together for whatever might come. 'We won't pony our horse to the track till that G.L. fella passes with his horse,' he said, and took himself to his cane-bottomed chair.

Soon after, Big Boy Brody rode by on a buckskin saddler. He waved, as genial as a lightning-rod salesman, and hallooed, 'Good luck. How's ol' Texas Jack?'

'Tol'able,' Dude replied. 'Tol'able.' *Let him chew on that. Let him and the Honorable G.L. expect a sluggish horse.*

At two forty-five an entourage appeared: a jackbooted Gideon Lightfoot in the lead on a high-stepping bay saddler, even on horseback Lightfoot wearing stovepipe hat and frock coat, and Stub Tate on a pony horse leading a skittish Old Dominion. Dude's hopes took a dive when he saw how smooth and powerful the chestnut looked. Four men carrying sidearms flanked the Thoroughbred racehorse, two on each side. Dude stared. Two of the guards were Lon and Mack.

For the devilment of it, Dude waved and hollered, 'Hey, Lon! How's your friend on the day shift at the barn?'

Lon flung him a sullen glare.

'Don't forget to bet on the Topeka mare,' Dude needled him. Lon looked straight ahead.

When they had passed out of sight, Uncle Billy stood and said, 'Let's go, but take our time. I'll drive Amos. In a race like this with a big crowd, we'll be expected to take our horse to the paddock so everybody can have a look-see.'

'Where's Coyote?' Dude asked.

'Behind the wagon getting himself ready. Come on, Coyote. We're ready.'

'Coming, Grandfather.'

Leading Judge Blair, Coyote was naked

to the waist, wearing his customary jockey's attire: breechcloth, moccasins and a single eagle feather in his hair. In addition, a small buckskin medicine bag hung on a rawhide cord around his neck, and he wore three stripes of white painted down each side of his face below his eyes to his jaw.

Coyote was hideous enough, but when Dude saw Judge Blair his mouth fell ajar. Wide bands of white paint encircled each dark brown eye, and two horizontal stripes of white lay across his nose. Beginning at both ears, white lightning streaks zigzagged down his neck to the muscled shoulder and down his legs to his ankles, and more lightning streaks raced downward from the high point of his rump to his muscle-packed hindquarters to his feet. A hand, also white, the fingers spaced, was painted in the center of the Judge's wide chest. Three golden eagle feathers fluttered in his black mane. A rawhide thong was tied to his lower jaw to provide double reins.

'He looks fast and fearsome,' Dude

said, impressed.

'Mean white men who doped my friend Texas Jack, lightning power will feel today,' Coyote swore and raised his right fist high and shook it. 'My Comanche blood boils, it does.' He pointed to the rawhide reins. 'War bridle,' he intoned. 'Today is war.' He drew the reins over the Judge's head and leaped to the saddle, a pad of buckskin with quilled fringes secured to the horse by a hide strap passed over the pad and under the horse's belly.

Dude had never seen Coyote look so determined and fierce, a warrior of the Great Plains ready to ride his war-horse against tribal enemies.

Uncle Billy stepped to the buggy seat and drove Amos out and Dude mounted the saddled Blue Grass to ride beside Coyote.

The noise of the crowd, sounding like bees swarming, was audible long before they jogged to the track. The crowd lined both sides of the track from the home-stretch turn to the stands and more eager railbirds jammed the fencing of the saddling paddock. Old Dominion was there in an open stall, surrounded by guards, held by Tate, while Lightfoot fussed over his racehorse.

Uncle Billy halted near the paddock, hopped down nimbly, tied Amos to a paddock post, and Dude tethered Blue Grass to the buggy. Then the partners, one on each side of Judge Blair, escorted their runner to a stall amid a rising chorus of oohs and ahs as the crowd stared at horse and jockey.

'A real live Injun!' a boy shouted.

Lightfoot and Tate and the guards literally gaped, as if seeing a lively apparition, Dude thought with satisfaction. In the stall, Coyote dismounted and stood impassively beside the Judge, haughtily ignoring the noisy railbirds, while Dude and Uncle Billy inspected the hide strap and settled the light buckskin pad, which had the crinkly feel of being packed with grass. Everything was secure.

At that instant Old Dominion, apparently unstrung by the chattering crowd, lunged to the paddock's open area, dragging a muttering Tate yanking on the reins.

'Hold him — you fool!' Lightfoot yelled.

Around and around the chestnut and Tate went, until he shortened his grip on the reins and grabbed the bit and brought the stud under control and back to the stall, there to flounce and turn and rear, finally settling enough for Lightfoot to lay on blanket and saddle and fix the leather cinch.

Judge Blair stood calmly, head bent, possibly dozing, but Dude knew when he moved to the starting line and Coyote turned him for the swinging break, the spectators would see a different horse: head up, alert, muscles tight as fiddle strings, ready to tear down the straightaway. Now, however, he seemed not unlike an old saddle horse, resting between the demands of his rider. If there was one dominant quality Judge Blair possessed besides speed and soundness, it was the most vital of elements for a running horse taking on all comers, short or long, from the Mexican border into Missouri — and that was heart. This mystery horse out of the hot flatlands of Texas whose breeding the outfit would never know.

Lightfoot kept eyeballing the Judge.

To Dude's surprise, Lightfoot strolled over to the stall, his manner patronizing. 'Would you care to forfeit, Mr. McQuinn? I do believe your horse looks off his feed.'

Dude smiled from the teeth. 'True, he looks a little droopy. But I never won a race by forfeiting. Who knows what will happen in a race? Maybe the other man's horse will fall down or jump the track?' He looked across at Tate, letting an appraising smirk work across his face. 'Or maybe the other man's jockey has been paid to pull the horse, unbeknownst to the owner?'

Lightfoot spun on his heels back to his horse. A bugler was sounding the clear notes of 'Boots and Saddles.' Lightfoot gave Tate a leg up on Old Dominion, mounted his saddler, and took the high-strung chestnut to the track on a short lead shank to begin the post parade.

'Remind Brody again about the swinging break,' Uncle Billy told Dude. 'Coyote, I figure Brody will try to give Tate the advantage at the break, so stick close to the other horse. I also figure Tate will try something on the turn.'

'Watch I will, Grandfather.'

The old man raised an eyebrow at the persistent address, but let it pass today, and his mouth curled in a cagey grin. 'One more thing. Break early a time or two like you did against that rank stud at Sedalia the time the other side had the starter bought off. That will make Old Dominion break. High-strung as he is, he'll run a piece before Tate can pull 'im up.' His grin disappeared. He sobered. 'Be careful, Coyote, pardner.' He left them to go to the finish line.

In moments Dude, on Blue Grass, took a light hold on the rawhide bridle to pony Judge Blair past the stands. As they moved by at a slow, prancing walk, there burst a spontaneous swell of applause. At first Dude supposed it was for Old Dominion, as it generally was for the local horse, but when the applause continued, he realized that it was meant for his horse and rider. For all of them, in fact. He waved his hat and flashed his rodeo arena smile, and Coyote smiled at the crowd and gave his high Comanche salute.

Dude spotted Uncle Billy, arms folded, and a serious-faced Cy Kirby standing behind the three finish-line judges. Kirby's future, Dude realized, rode on the outcome of the race. Both men waved. Uncle Billy's upturned face at that moment had the appealing concern of an elder for his tutored charges.

Now the widow Wheeler waved excitedly, displaying an open hopefulness of victory for the dark bay gelding that somehow softened her sharp features. Why, Dude thought, she looks younger. Almost comely. Beside her Van Vinson smiled and vigorously thumped his derby. Beside him stood Lightfoot's man, Mordecai Fretwell, a thin, seedy man, whose glasses sat far down on his blade of a nose.

Riding on, warmed by the crowd's liking, Dude felt an inexpressible gratitude. He glanced back. A man was getting down from a buggy such as one might rent at the local livery. A chunky, watchful man, blinking rapidly against the afternoon glare. Dude's mind switched back: the bowler-hatted man again, the Roseville man, the man entering the Lightfoot Hotel.

He rode thoughtfully on, and as they rounded the turn and he saw Brody standing at the starting place, a mere line drawn across the track, Dude forgot all but the race. Lightfoot was fussily inspecting his horse's bridle; finished, he gave final instructions to Tate, jabbing with forefinger to punctuate his orders.

Dude rode over to Brody and said, 'Thought I'd better remind you again our jockey will swing his horse a little at the break. Are we clear on that?'

'We are,' Brody replied genially. He

looked very official and formidable today, even larger than he had in the Jayhawk: broad western hat, a purple scarf knotted at the neck of his checkered shirt, tight across his bouncer's beefy shoulders, tan riding trousers and cowboy boots.

Just then Lightfoot turned to Brody and said, 'We'll take the inside lane.'

As quickly, Dude countered with, 'We'll flip for the lanes, gentlemen,' Uncle Billy's warning about rough riding on the turn jumping to his mind.

'Flip?' Lightfoot bristled, instantly on the prod. 'There was no question about that when we matched the race.'

'There is no question now, sir. We'll simply flip for it. That's fair. Will you oblige us, Mr. Brody?'

Brody, after a glance Lightfoot's way, dug for coin and held up a silver dollar.

'May I look at it?' Dude asked politely.

Pained, Brody held it out for Dude to see. Dude turned the coin over and nodded, remarking lightly, 'Thought maybe somebody might have slipped a phony one by you at the Jayhawk.'

'Nobody slips anything by on me,' Brody growled. 'Call it in the air, McQuinn,' and Dude called, 'Heads,' The coin dropped and Brody caught it in his palm.

Dude looked. It was 'tails.'

'Mr. Lightfoot's horse gets the inside lane,' Brody said, temperish. 'If everybody is ready, the jockeys will walk their horses ten yards back and approach the starting line. When the horses are evenly lapped, I'll drop my hat and holler, 'Go.' Not until.' He stepped to the edge of the tack.

The jockeys walked the horses back, turned and came forward. A few feet from the line, Dude saw Coyote turn the Judge and nudge him with his left heel, unseen by Brody or Lightfoot. The Judge broke only at moderate speed. Before Tate could restrain the chestnut, the eager stud took off, breaking fast. Within a short distance, Coyote reined in his horse. Old Dominion sprinted on, Tate sawing on the reins, cursing like a mule skinner. A good piece down the track, he expertly fought the stallion under control and forcibly turned him and headed him back, leaping, lunging, fighting the bit.

Lightfoot was furious. 'Damn it to hell, man, control the horse!'

Once more the jockeys walked the horses back and turned, approaching the line, and once more Coyote heeled his horse off prematurely and Old Dominion broke.

'Your jockey is deliberately breaking your horse first to draw my horse off!' Lightfoot shouted at Dude.

'Why, Texas Jack is just beginnin' to wake up — that's all. He's been droopy all morning' But Dude looked at Coyote and the message was clear between them: two false starts were enough.

Coyote rode to the rear again, where Tate was holding the fractious Old Dominion. Together, the two horses moved toward the starting line, Brody posted there, hat in upraised hand.

Now the horses were quite near the line. As Coyote started to turn his horse for the swinging getaway, Tate suddenly rushed ahead to the line and Brody brought his hat down and shouted, 'Go!'

Dude gasped as the chestnut broke ahead by a length. Coyote whooped and Judge Blair, though caught late, took off running, the swinging step giving him momentum.

'Damn you, Brody!' Dude yelled. 'You gave Tate the advantage.'

'The Injun was turnin' for the break, wasn't he?' Brody retorted, and strode away for the other side of the track. Lightfoot turned his horse, galloping across toward the finish line.

Dude stayed put, watching the race, thankful for today's longer distance. In a shorter race, loss of the break would have meant defeat.

Coyote had Judge Blair stretching out and moving up on the chestnut as they sprinted down the backstretch. Dude caught the Judge's change to the left lead as they entered the turn and saw him suddenly close half a length to Old Dominion's saddle girth.

Dude was shouting encouragement, fists clenched. He stared when Tate, seeing Judge Blair making up ground, began forcing the gelding to the outside. Coyote had to give way or take a bumping. He gave, the Judge almost breaking stride. At that, Tate straightened his horse back on course and hugged the inside lane, holding a length's lead again.

Dude spurred across the infield of the track to be near the finish line, watching the race as he rode. He reined up as the horses headed into the homestretch, Old Dominion still maintaining that lead. Dude bit his lip. *Get him going, Coyote. Come on.*

Then Dude heard what he sensed he had been waiting for: Coyote's whoop. At last it came, sounding far away, muted by distance and the noise of the crowd. Not just one whoop — but a series of whoops, primitive and stirring, a born rider calling for more speed from his horse. And the horse, answering with heart, beginning to make up ground.

Judge Blair raced to the chestnut's

girth again. Coyote whooped once more and the dark bay gelding moved to Old Dominion's shoulder, to his neck, to his head. Now the horses ran locked as a team. They rushed past the one-eighth pole. The crowd was shouting and screaming.

Coyote's whoop rose to a screech. Tate went to the whip. Even so, Judge Blair began to pass the chestnut.

He was a head in front and slowly increasing his lead when Tate switched the whip to his left hand and made a frantic grab for Coyote's saddle pad. He caught and yanked — and Dude saw his hand jerk loose with a fistful of quilled fringes as Judge Blair drew away. Coyote so low all Dude could see of him was a blur of coppery legs and arms and the dark head against the mane of whipping eagle feathers. And the zigzagging lightning streaks on Judge Blair's neck and shoulders and legs seemed to vibrate, powerfully alive.

Scarcely a hundred yards to go now.

Furiously, Tate laid on the leather and

Old Dominion gamely picked up speed. He surged to Judge Blair's hindquarters. There he seemed to hang.

Coyote glanced back. He whooped once and daylight appeared between the horses.

They finished like that, Tate still pounding his horse. Dude whooped and shook his right fist. *Lightning power!*

The crowd pushed to the finish line. The widow Wheeler and Van Vinson and Cy Kirby were waving and congratulating each other and jumping up and down. Mordecai Fretwell disappeared in the direction of the stands. Uncle Billy stood quietly by, on his face a mixture of pure relief and the joy of a hard-won victory.

Down the track Coyote was easing Judge Blair into the turn, preparatory to bringing him back so the crowd could feast eyes on the first horse to beat Old Dominion. Dude felt a crinkling grin come to his face. You could do that when you had a Comanche jockey and Comanche weather and a horse with great heart.

Stub Tate was jogging on around the track, no doubt dreading what his boss would have to say to him.

On that insight, Dude sought Lightfoot in the crowd, remembering that he hadn't seen the man since the finish. He still didn't see him. Then, glancing up, he sighted Lightfoot beyond the track, tearing for town on the bay saddler.

Dude rode through the jostling crowd to Uncle Billy and called down, 'Lightfoot's runnin' out on us! I'm goin' after 'im!' '

'I'll follow you.'

'We'll all follow you,' Maude Wheeler said. 'He owes me, too. Come on, folks! Where's Fannie?'

Dude reined out of there and, reaching open ground, bogged the spurs and Blue Grass shot away running. As Dude cleared the track area, he spotted Lightfoot far ahead. By the time Dude passed the camp, Lightfoot was no longer in sight. Dude galloped to the square, turned the corner and saw Lightfoot's saddler standing with grounded reins in front of the bank. Marshal Epps stood by the door.

Dude rode to the hitching rack, swung down, tied his horse and charged to the door. Epps stepped in front of him. 'You can't go in. Bank's closed.'

'The hell it is. I'll bust down the door. Lightfoot owes me two thousand dollars.'

Epps rested his right hand on the butt of his six-shooter. 'You'll stand for bank robbery if you try it.'

'Whoa, now. The agreement was the loser would pay off right after the race. He's tryin' to welch out of it. I want my money an' I'm gonna get it.'

'Bank stays closed till Monday. Besides, Mr. Lightfoot told me your jockey cheated. So he don't have to pay off.'

'It was the other way around,' Dude fumed, his face so close to Epps's he could smell Brody's cheap whiskey on him.

They were locked in that stalemate when two buggies raced up, and out piled Uncle Billy, Vinson and Kirby, the widow Wheeler and Fannie Haley.

'Lightfoot's holed up in there an' won't come out,' Dude told them. 'I'm goin' in, hell or high water.'

'You'll go to jail for bank robbery,' Epps warned, his voice deepening.

The widow Wheeler stared a momeot, as if sizing up the situation, and turned her eyes to the doorway that led upstairs to the town hall. She tugged on Dude's arm and pulled him away, the others following. She said, 'Don't try to break in — just come with me,' and marched for the doorway.

Epps was there before her, blocking her way. 'Town hall's closed Saturday same as the bank.'

'Why, you pompous windbag!' she raged, hands on hips, jaw set.

'Get out of my way!'

Epps put forth a hand to check her.

'How dare you lay hands on a poor widow woman!' She clutched a pocket-book the size of a saddlebag, which she whapped against the side of his head.

344

Epps's big hat flew off as he flinched from the blow, too astonished to stop her. 'Door's locked,' he mumbled. 'You'll be charged with breaking and entering public property. Don't say I didn't tell you.'

'I,' she said, glaring him down, 'am president of the Lightfoot County Historical Society, and we're going upstairs to hold a meeting.' She dug inside her pocketbook for a key and unlocked the door. When Dude and the rest were inside, she locked the door behind them and pounded up the strairs to the landing. There, after hesitating, she went slowly past the meeting room and down the long hall, lips and brows pursed in thought. She stopped at the last door, started to open it, then retraced steps to the third one from the end, opened it and entered a dingy room smelling of dust and old furniture.

'I think this is the room Dewitt once told me about,' she said, scanning the place. 'In the early days, this was the office of a lawyer who got in a lot of shooting scrapes. Sometimes he needed an escape route.' She went to the cluttered center of the room and back, eyes searching. 'Will you gentlemen move that wooden wardrobe away from the wall?' Dude and Kirby quickly obliged. She looked down and shook her head, puzzled. 'But this has to be the room. I know it is.'

'Maude,' Mrs. Haley spoke up, 'could that little writing desk farther down the wall be over the place? It would have to be something the lawyer could move in a hurry.'

'Fannie, you're thinking!'

Dude lifted the table aside, exposing a worn rose-patterned rug underneath. He pulled it back and saw a hinged trapdoor.

'There!' Maude Wheeler breathed. 'It used to lead to the rear of a general store before old Gideon foreclosed on it and made it into his bank. It should open on a sort of storeroom. Open it, Mr. McQuinn. Quiet everybody.'

The hinge squealed as Dude carefully lifted the door. A ladder led to the dim room below. He listened and heard no sounds. He stepped to the top rung and soon let himself down into a small room stacked with thick ledgers and boxes. There was a single door. Kirby followed, next Uncle Billy and Vinson. Dude heard the widow Wheeler whisper after them, 'We're coming down. Don't you men look.'

When the women were down, Dude grasped the doorknob and twisted. Nothing turned. It was locked. 'I'll have to kick it in,' he told the others. Stepping back, he raised his booted right foot and kicked. The door jarred but held. He kicked again, making a racket. Still, it held. 'Cy — Van,' he said, 'let's ram it together with our shoulders.'

They all slammed against it at the same time and the door flew open. Dude found himself looking down a row of two tellers' cages at an empty bank. Lightfoot wasn't there; however, his office door was closed. Dude motioned that way and ran to the door and flung it open.

Gideon Lightfoot was standing behind

his desk, alarm frozen on his bearded face. 'How'd you get in here?'

'Never mind,' Dude said. 'We've come for our money. Divvy up.'

'After you pulled that ringer on us?' Lightfoot said scornfully, trying to assume an injured role. 'The horse you ran today wasn't the horse we clocked on the north road.'

'He was — he just ran faster. But he wasn't the horse your man doped last night. Neither was the horse we clocked Old Dominion. All's fair in love an' war an' horse racin'. You took our bait an' we took yours. We beat you fair an' square, despite Tate's dirty tactics. Now you come across with our money or I'll tear this place apart an' you with it.'

Lightfoot paled. 'You'd be robbing my bank, sir. You'd go to jail.'

'Just hold on here,' Maude Wheeler said, striding past Dude to confront Lightfoot. 'You owe me, too, Gideon. I bet my savings at two to one. You owe me eight hundred dollars.'

'I refuse to pay a bet made in passing

jest.'

'Gideon, you will pay us every cent or I'll see that your name is ruined forever in this town. I'll tell how you left me with a mere pittance after Dewitt passed away, you claiming losses on bad loans.'

'You can't prove a thing.' His reedy voice had changed to a squeak.

She strode around the desk and looked him in the eye, her resolute face within inches of his face. 'I know enough to bring in the bank examiners and send you to the state pen. I could tell 'em all about the two sets of books you keep. I've kept quiet for years out of respect for my Dewitt, not wanting his name involved. But this is the last straw. You pay up or I'll spill the beans.'

Lightfoot seemed to wilt all at once. Without a word, he turned to a filing cabinet, opened it with a key on a chain, and took out a fat roll of greenbacks.

'Pay Maude first,' Dude said.

Reluctantly, in visible pain, Lightfoot began peeling off hundred dollar bills.

'Whoa, there,' Uncle Billy stopped him.

'You took that last bill off the bottom. I want a look-see.' He picked up the greenback, eyed it, turned it over and laid it aside. 'The Honorable Gideon Lightfoot never gives up, does he? This is as bogus as your claim to Virginia gentility. Take the rest off the top.'

Glowering, Lightfoot complied.

'Now, our two thousand,' Dude told him.

When Lightfoot had finished, Uncle Billy examined each bill on both sides and, satisfied, passed the money to Dude.

The scene ended there, in silence. No more was said until they reached the door of the bank, when Kirby handed Dude a wad of greenbacks. 'I collected this at the track on that three-to-one money you had me bet.'

'Much obliged. I'd forgotten. Hope you won enough to pay off the mortgage?'

'And then some, though I tell you I was sweatin' it out there for a while.'

'Oh, Maude,' Mrs. Haley bubbled, 'I must tell Levi to go to the Jayhawk right away and get your winnings.'

Dude opened the door and they all trooped outside. A crowd was gathering. Epps wasn't around.

'Did you get your money?' a farmer asked Dude. 'We all saw of Lightfoot hightailing it after the race. Him gettin' beat is the best thing that's happened around here since we hung the Blake gang.'

'No trouble. Just had to make a little call and sort of remind him.' *Why say more? They had won and collected the bets, thanks to the widow Wheeler. Now was the time to fade out. Fetch the wagon and horses and take a slow an' easy ride to the rendezvous.*

Dude spent the next minutes answering questions about details of the race. Evidently many farmers had bet on 'Texas Jack.'

Rufus Hubbard moved through the crowd to Dude. 'Where's Dr. Lockhart? I won me enough money today to buy Avalanche.'

'He's here.' At last, Dude thought, Uncle can get rid of blind Amos, and discovered that he didn't like it.

'I don't see him anywhere,' the young man said.

'Yes . . . where is Billy?' the widow Wheeler asked, her voice very close to a lost wail. 'I must talk to him.'

'I don't see him either,' Fannie Haley said.

In sudden concern, Dude looked about and was surprised not to see the old man. Aware of a vague uneasiness, he faced the street and was startled to see Amos and the buggy missing. Uncle Billy had gone. Something was wrong.

Another searching moment and Dude turned and stared hard, struck motionless. There was the bowler-hatted man again, intent on the milling crowd coming and going, blinking against the lowering western sun as he watched.

Unobtrusively, then, Dude slipped through the crowd to his horse. The wrongness smote him again as he mounted and rode for camp, trying not to hurry. What was it?

12

Painted Rock

Twilight was weaving a hazy webbing over the shaggy hills above the spring when Dude drove up to the rendezvous, with Texas Jack and Blue Grass trailing the wagon on halter ropes. A ruddy campfire glowed. The partners waved and hurried out. Coyote had donned his white man's cotton shirt and Levis and boots and his face was free of war paint: a reservation Indian again. Dude could not but feel a stab of regret at his regression.

'Anybody follow you?' Uncle Billy asked.

'No — why should they?' Dude replied, regarding the old man curiously, but decided not to broach the matter of his abrupt fade-out in town until later.

After supper, while they sat around the fire and listened to the steady cropping of the horses filling up on good prairie bluestem, Dude divided the winnings, and as he passed Uncle Billy his share, he said, 'You sure lit a fast shuck out of town, Uncle. How come?'

'You know the old rule for a racehorse outfit, Dude, pardner: Make far apart tracks as soon as you've collected the bets.'

'Sure. But there was no call to hit the breeze this time. You did an' missed sellin' Amos. That sodbuster Rufus came up with the money. Said he'd won big.'

'How did I know he'd won?'

'Would, if you'd stayed around another minute or two. Furthermore, the widow Wheeler just about cried when she looked for her 'Billy' and he had vamoosed,' Dude went on, making a mournful face.

'No woman throws a bigger loop than a widow on the prowl for some poor devil with a few dollars in his jeans. One more reason to take to the tules.'

'Just when we were the toast of the town for once, instead of on the dodge.'

'Never rest on your laurels,' the old man said. His purposeful walk to his medicine chest ended further talk, and Dude whispered to Coyote, 'The man in the black bowler who blinks. I saw him again, in town and at the track. That's what it was.'

And Coyote nodded gravely.

At breakfast Dude looked at his partners and asked, 'Well, gents, where do we go from here?'

The old man hawked in his throat and tapped his chest. 'I might feel better if we went on southwest.'

'You poorly again?' Dude came back, surprised. 'Coyote and I figured when we took the slack out of the celebrated Old Dominion, he by Old South, he by Cumberland, he by Roanoke, he by Twigg, he by — '

'All right, now, Dude,' Uncle Billy protested.

' — would put you back on your feet.'

'Do I sound like a well man? Besides, I'm still afflicted with a blind horse.'

'Which is your fault for hightailin' out of town. What's your notion, Coyote?'

'Southwest, white father.'

Dude gave him a lopsided grin. 'More we head that way, closer we get to Comanche country, eh?'

'Wise you are, white father, like Grandfather Billy.' Once more the established understanding passed between them: Was the challenge of another match race with unscrupulous horsemen needed to keep their old partner going? It looked that way. And why was he running?

★ ★ ★

On this evening a lone horseman called out as he drummed up to camp, and as was the custom, Dude invited him to light and eat. The rider was soon stowing away great helpings of hot bread and bacon and potatoes, which he covered with lakes of gravy, and when the gravy was gone he poured molasses on biscuits.

He was wiry and of indeterminate age, and his quick eyes, set in an enterprising face, indicated a bold nature. A dark beard fringed his chin. He was dirtier than need be and twice Dude got whiffs of the man — he actually smelled. While he wolfed down plateful after plateful, he would run his tongue around his mouth and over his lips and make annoying hissing sounds between broken teeth.

The last to finish eating, the rider poured himself a fourth cup of coffee from the blackened pot, leaned back and said, 'Them two dark bays look like runnin' horses. I like the one with the blazed face. He's got the eyes of an eagle.'

'That's just an ol' cow horse we call Judge Blair. Sometimes we hitch 'im to the wagon. He can do about anything.'

'What about the other horse?'

'He can run a little when the spirit moves 'im.'

'What's his handle?'

A warning flashed through Dude. What if this rider had heard of the so-called Texas Jack's victory over the unbeaten Old Dominion, and what if this rider passed word on down the way that he had seen the great Texas Jack? Could make it difficult to match a race under that name. Like Uncle said, news traveled fast when a horse had won a big race. Better play it cagey. So Dude replied, 'That's Hoot Owl.'

'Hoot Owl?' The man appeared to roll the name around on his tongue. 'Sounds like a Texas horse.'

'He is. Range bred. Nothing fancy.'

The man took a noisy pull at his coffee, leaned back, made that irritating hissing again, and asked, 'Anybody got the makin's?'

Dude handed him a sack of Bull Durham and a packet of brown cigarette papers. To refuse him would be an insult.

The man rolled a deft cigarette, seemed to consider sticking the makin's in his shirt pocket before returning them, struck a match on his left thumbnail and lit up expansively. 'In case you're on the lookout for a match race,' he said, 'you can find one in Painted Rock.'

'Painted Rock?'

'That's the next county seat the way you're headed and where I'm goin'. N. A. Hathaway has a stud called Flying Tom that's not only dusted everything in southwestern Kansas and half of Colorado, but clean down into central Texas. It's got so he can't be matched anymore.'

'Flying Tom? Don't believe I've heard of him!'

'You will, mister. You will.'

To Dude's gratification, the man rose and ambled to his horse, stepped to the saddle and rode off without even a 'much obliged.'

'There goes a mean white man,' Coyote said. 'Look how he spurs his poor horse. He also ate all of Grandfather's biscuits and stewed prunes.'

'A cheap price to get rid of him,' Dude said. 'For a while I was afraid he'd stay all night.' He thoughtfully regarded his partners. 'But, you know, that Flying Tom interests me. We might take us a little sashay on to Painted Rock. It's a right pretty name, too.'

'Is, white father.'

The old man let out a low groan. 'Now don't you two tumbleweeds get any more match-race notions for a while. That last go-round with that G.L. fella just about did me in, poorly as I am. Believe I'll have me a little toddy and turn in early.'

After Uncle Billy had gone to bed, Dude said, 'As much as we hate to, Coyote, we'll have to help him sell Amos or Uncle will never be the same again.'

'Sad this Comanche will be when big horse leaves us. Same time and other match race against mean white men more good medicine for Grandfather Billy will be.'

Painted Rock.

Dude guessed the pioneers had so named the town from the sticklike figures, some black, some copper-colored, inscribed by ancients on the eroded cliff where the wagon road passed a few miles to the east. Seeing the high shape of the stone courthouse, he was reminded of another in Lightfoot, and frowned, but when he heard the toot of a train whistle and saw the loading pens, he knew Painted Rock was more cow town than sodbuster.

As they came to the railroad crossing,

the sorrels put their heads down and stared wall-eyed at the strange tracks and shied sideways. When Coyote spoke to them, they straightened and moved ahead, but something, likely the sound of their hooves clicking on the rails or the series of shrieks from the train's whistle, spooked them and away they tore.

Amos, pulling the buggy behind the wagon, likewise took alarm, and jerked a lolling Uncle Billy upright. And even the steady Blue Grass, as if wanting to join the fun, humped and crow-hopped a stretch before Dude could settle him. The sorrels rushed on while Coyote struggled to hold the runaways, Judge Blair and Texas Jack, haltered to the wagon, trailing in flight.

Dude spurred after the wagon.

Ahead, pedestrians scattered like quail and shouted warnings to others. Men ran out of the stores to find the cause of the commotion.

About then, as suddenly, Coyote had the sorrels under control and Uncle Billy, after Amos's short tear, had the trotter in hand.

'It never fails,' Dude said, laughing as he caught up. 'Country horses are like country boys when they come to town. They both get into trouble. Leastwise, this attracts as much attention as a parade around the square.'

The wagonyard looked well kept and spacious, with plenty of wood, water and shade, and so the outfit unhitched there after buying oats and hay, always a wise beginning in a strange town. The proprietor said his name was Hap Gary, and he shook hands and wanted to know their names. He was a round, ruddy-faced man whose handlebar mus- tache showed tobacco stains, and whose nasal voice had the slow drawl of the Southwest. Garrulous and obliging, he said the outfit could use the 'horse trap' behind the yard, and, 'If you boys need anything, just give me a holler.' He hung around while they were setting up camp. His experienced eyes kept returning to the horses; finally, with a grin, he asked, 'Wouldn't be carryin' a racehorse, would you?'

'That dark bay gelding there can run a little sometimes, sometimes not,' Dude said, grinning back. 'And we carry a trotter that can get down the road. None other than Avalanche, the Missouri champion, now retired from the track. He's the big blue roan there. Know anyody who needs a sure-enough drivin' horse? Dr. Lockhart might listen to a fair offer.'

Gary mused on that and said, 'There's Lige Swink, the preacher man. He needs a means of conveyance when he calls on folks out in the country and shows up at mealtime. His ridin' mule just flat disappeared two weeks ago.'

'A preacher?' Dude said doubtfully. 'I've yet to hear of a sky pilot that wasn't short on *dinero*.'

'There's always an exception to every rule, and Lige is. He's got the ladies in this town behind him because of his stand on morals. One of his stunts is to stand outside the Elkhorn — that's the only public water hole left since he came in here last year — is to stand there and take down the names of every man that goes in for a drink. Then announce the names from the pulpit the next Sunday. Are the womenfolks for that! Saturday is his big jot-'em-down day. Lige means well. He's just so durn straitlaced.'

'I have never sold a horse to a teetotaler,' Uncle Billy stated, 'and do not intend to begin here. A teetotaler is narrow-minded and lacks the necessary understanding of our equine friends.'

'Now, Uncle, you know Avalanche is too much horse for you with your arthritis and catarrh,' Dude said, letting drop the reason, and turned to Gary. 'Is this Lige Swink also against horse racin'?'

'Is he! Anything that's fun. Includes dancin', kissin', huggin', tobacco in any form. Even novel-readin'. He's got the whole town buffaloed. I tell you somebody stole that mule.'

'Then how has N.A. Hathaway managed to stage all those big races I've been told about?'

'They used to run the races down Main Street and finish in front of the

Drovers' House. No more. When Lige came, he stopped that. Said it was sinful. Bad influence on young people, with gamblers and whiskey around, though I never heard of a boy who took the wrong path because he watched a horse race. Anyway, when that happened, Boots Kell, Hathaway's ranch foreman and trruner, moved the races outside town on the prairie.'

'I hear tell Flying Tom has dusted everything in this part of the country?'

'He's never lost a race.'

'Hathaway must be quite a horseman. What's he like?'

An odd reticence and evasion, suggestive of amusement, seemed to come over Gary, unusual for so talkative a man, and he said, 'That's hard to say.'

'I mean how is he to deal with about a match race?'

'Since I don't have a racehorse, I can't say. Besides, Kell is the one you'd have to dicker with first.'

★ ★ ★

Next morning, after the stores were open and the early tipplers had time to wet their whistles at the Elkhorn, Dude hitched Amos to the buggy and drove to the square. There he reined the eager blue roan to a walk until sighting some early shoppers, when he flipped the whip over Amos's hindquarters and off they moved in the rhythmic beat of the trotter, taking the first corner smartly, and past the Drovers' House, and past the Elkhorn, where Dude noticed a tall, ungainly man dressed in black posted at a corner of the saloon, intent on the swinging doors. The man looked up and his eyes followed the trotter. Other heads also were turning.

Entering the square for the second time, Dude let Amos out to full stride. His one-two cadence quickened, his powerful rear legs driving. My, how the old horse cottoned to going! This time around people were watching from store windows, others paused on the board-walk. The watching figure at the Elkhorn quit his vigil to observe the trotter's swift passage.

His audience's attention gained, Dude drove to the wagonyard, tied Amos by the entrance, still harnessed, and sat on a bench to await the first wave of interested lookers.

They came strolling up before long, singly and by twos, mostly idle oldsters. They nodded and one elderly gentleman with a cane, who volunteered that his name was Shug Neely, said, 'That's a fine drivin' horse there. Is he for sale?'

'Only with regret. He belongs to a gentleman back there who is getting on in years and feels he has to sell. This horse is Avalanche, the famed Missouri trotting champion.'

Eyebrows flew up at that.

'How much does the gentleman want for his horse?'

'You'll have to ask him.'

'Not that I'm interested in buying,' Shug Neely said. 'I just admire a good horse.'

'Would any of you gentlemen like to drive Avalanche around the square?'

Dude asked. 'He's as gentle as a kid pony and will obey in every way.'

None of the oldsters answered, only the ungainly man seen outside the saloon, now standing at the rear of the gathering, who waggled an arm and said, 'I'd like to.'

'Come on,' Dude invited, and waved him to the buggy.

This prospect had a fascinating face — lugubrious and earnest, and the deep-pooled eyes were as crucibles of an inner fervor, the nose beaked, the cheeks sunken, the mustache scraggly, the bushy eyebrows like porcupine quills. His voice hoarse and as mournful as his features. A slab-bodied man, a near scarecrow of a man, his black coat and trousers hanging loosely on his gaunt frame, the sleeves lapping over his bony hands and the brim of his black hat flapping. He moved with a sort of shuffling gait, his arms swinging like blades on the wheel of a windmill.

Taking the reins, he said, 'Thank you, brother,' and a knowing ran through

368

Dude. It was Lige Swink the preacher.

Afterward, Dude watched Swink drive around the square, watched as Swink went around again, at a faster clip the second time. When he drove back to the wagonyard, Uncle Billy and Coyote had come outside.

'A right nice trotter,' Swink said. 'Where is the gentleman who owns him?'

'Over there,' Dude said, pointing. 'Dr. William Tecumseh Lockhart.'

'Brother Lockhart,' Swink said, shuffling over and extending a skeletal hand, 'I am the Reverend Lige Swink of the Good Tidings Church. I like your trotter and I'd like to know your askin' price?'

Uncle Billy withdrew his hand as if he had touched a hot poker. He said, 'My trotter is not for sale.'

Swink, surprised, glanced at Dude, who said, 'What Dr. Lockhart means is the horse, being a champion, comes high.'

'How high?' Swink persisted, turning to Uncle Billy.

'Four hundred dollars,' the old man

said, blunt about it. 'Harness comes to another fifty.'

Dude saw through that. Uncle was jacking the price so high the preacher would back off.

'Sounds reasonable,' Swink said, instead. 'I think that can be arranged in time through my congregation. Not as a personal indulgence, you understand, but as another arm of my ministry, to help us bring the good tidings to folks in the country.'

Uncle Billy merely looked pained.

'Sin is all around us these evil days,' Swink went on, waving his arms, his voice rising hoarsely. 'It's right here in Painted Rock, you bet'cher boots. But I've got it on the run. I've got a holt of the old devil and I'm a-shakin' him' — he shook his fists together — 'and I'll throw him to the ground before long — like this.' He made a slamming motion and stomped his feet. Calming himself, he swept his deep-socketed gaze over Dude and Coyote and Uncle Billy. 'We're havin' a revival this week, starts tonight at seven-thirty. There'll be healin' services and dynamic readin's. Tonight also kicks off our campaign to raise funds for a Sunday school room for our little ones. I invite you all. You are welcome. Brother Lockhart, I hope you will come and stand up and be counted tonight?'

'I'm too poorly to attend,' the old man said flatly.

'All the more reason for you to join us at the healin' services.'

Uncle Billy did not reply, and Swink's attention shifted to Coyote. 'You, brother, look like an Indian to me.'

'I am. A Comanche. My name is Coyote Walking.'

'Heathens are especially welcome.'

Coyote stood quite straight. 'A heathen,' he said, 'is one who does not acknowledge existence of the Great Spirit. Although Comanches have been called the skeptics of the plains, heathens we are not. About the Great Spirit, we know. There is a place beyond where Grandfather the Sun sets. A beautiful valley covered with streams, cool timber and meadows. There is no rain, no wind, no darkness there. Only the sun. All the warriors are young. All the horses are fleet. They are plenty buffalo, elk, deer and antelope and there is corn. There is no suffering or sorrow, because the Great Spirit is everywhere. It is His place. We also know about the Evil Spirit, which is the antithesis of the Great Spirit, and which you call the devil. Heathens, we are not.'

Swink was dumbfounded and impressed. His face changed, losing some of its moroseness. 'Well spoken, young man,' he said 'I invite you to speak to our young people tonight after the main meetin'.'

Of a sudden Coyote clutched his midsection and bugged his eyes. 'Me feel sick. Got Evil Spirit in belly.' And he dashed behind the wagon.

'Maybe some other time, Reverend,' Dude said in a smoothing-over tone, thinking of the horse sale. 'We'll be here awhile, though not long.'

'I will see you again about the trotter,

Dr. Lockhart, after I have talked to the Good Tidings ladies. Good day.' He went shuffling away, drawing the oldsters after him.

'He really wants Amos,' Dude said, 'and I believe he'll raise the money.'

'He didn't even blink when I said four hundred. Well, if he raises it, he can have the horse.'

Dude felt a twinge of guilt for pushing the sale. 'I'd hate to see you sell Amos. So would Coyote.'

'It's a disgrace for a man to be fooled into buying or trading for a blind horse, and it's even more of a disgrace to keep a blind horse. That's how I feel.' Uncle Billy walked back into the wagonyard.

13

Big Horse in a Dark Stall

When the days began to waste and no more than a dribble of visitors came to look at the horses and still no prospects for a match race and Amos unsold, Dude, growing restless and thinking ever more of Texas, told his partners he would drive Amos to the square 'to visit around and try to kick something loose.'

He stopped first at GROCERIES (C. B. Peabody, prop.), where he purchased a gunnysack of supplies, and after introductions and handshakes, he let fall that his horse outfit was camped at the wagonyard.

'You have a racehorse?' Peabody asked, interested. He was broad-faced and affable and obviously enjoyed small talk with his customers, particularly one who had just paid cash.

Dude let a slow grin play across his face before he responded. 'I call him a racehorse when he wins. When he loses, he's just a horse.'

Peabody chuckled richly, laughter being uncommon in a grocery where the bulk of the business was conducted on long-term credit. 'Mr. McQuinn,' he said, casting a look around the empty store, 'step inside my office and let's raise a glass to your racehorse or horse, whatever he is.'

'Why, thank you, sir. That is hospitable of you.'

Inside, Peabody darted another look at the doorway, reached behind a rolltop desk, pulled out a bottle of Sam Thompson, drew the cork with his teeth, foraged for a shot glass, and handed the essentials to Dude, who poured his own.

'I can see that you are a gentleman,' the merchant said. 'Not one drop over the brim.'

'Towels are for taking spring baths,' Dude said, grinning.

Peabody found a second glass and poured, held it high and, an eye on the doorway, took his drink with Dude, who smacked his lips in appreciation. 'You're a good judge of good whiskey, Mr. Peabody.'

'Better at whiskey than I am at judging character. See that stack of ledgers? It's full of creditors who've moved off without paying me, or who are slow to pay, or who may never pay. My father ran a livery barn back in Iowa. I should have followed the family line.'

'This is a chancy game too. I've seen cowboys bet everything, down to their shirt, pants and boots — and lose it all.'

'Yet you are looking for another match race?' Peabody asked, passing the Sam Thompson.

'I'm in no hurry. If nothing shows up in a few days, we'll mosey on to Texas. Any runnin' horses in these parts?' Dude inquired, pretending ignorance.

'There's one of note. The Hathaway Ranch's Flying Tom. Never lost a race. A big Thoroughbred.'

'A Thoroughbred? Probably out of our class. Too much distance.'

'Maybe not. I'd like to see another big

race staged here. Helps business — cash business — with folks coming to town in a holiday mood. Been some time since we've had one.'

Dude assumed a thoughtful mien. 'You said the Hathaway Ranch owns Flying Tom. A big cow outfit, I suppose?'

'A horse ranch. N. A. Hathaway buys and sells horses as far away as Missouri and Illinois.'

'Mind telling me what Hathaway is like? I'm just an ol' Texas country boy from down on the Salt Fork of the Brazos, not much on fancy palaver.'

'I wouldn't want to speak for another person,' Peabody said tactfully, though genially, and for a moment or so Dude caught the equivocal expression on the merchant's face that he had noticed on Hap Gary's. 'The ranch trades here with me,' Peabody continued. 'Pays its bills every month. That should tell you something.'

They visited until a customer came in, and Dude took his purchases and left. From there he stopped at BOOTS &

SADDLES (Dink Simpson, prop.) and bought a new bridle for Judge Blair.

Simpson was a stooped, spindly man whose spectacles sat perched precariously far down on his nose. His white mustache was neatly trimmed and bushy, set in an open, friendly face. When Simpson learned that Dude was from Texas and had a running horse, he volunteered proudly that he too was from the Lone Star State; furthermore, that Steel Dust and Shiloh, those legendary Texas sires, were the greatest running horses ever.

'My Hoot Owl horse is a Steel Dust-Shiloh cross comin' down the ladder on his mammy's side,' Dude made up.

'A Steel Dust-Shiloh cross' Simpson was saying. 'If you match a race, I'll put some *dinero* on Hoot Owl's nose. You bet I will.'

'I understand that N. A. Hathaway has a fast horse called Flying Tom. Is that so?'

'True. On the other hand, there's no competition around Painted Rock, and folks from far off are kind of leery about bringing in a good horse after what happened to Smoky Joe.'

'Smoky Joe?'

'A real scorpion out of Colorado. I tell you he knew where the finish line was. They matched him at four furlongs.' Simpson frowned and rolled a brown-paper cigarette with leather-stained fingers. A core of anger flared behind his mild brown eyes.

'What happened?' Dude asked, aware that he could just about call it.

'He broke like a plow horse and never got untracked. The owner, a stove-up old cowboy I used to know in Texas, had the vet go over Smoky Joe. The horse wasn't sore-legged or hurt anywhere. He was rarin' to run the next day. Trouble was, he didn't run that day.'

'Or couldn't. He was fixed some way.'

'I wouldn't want to say that in public and have Boots Kell hear me. He's as high-strung as his racehorse. Mighty tetchy.'

'Boots Kell?' Dude repeated, playing dumb.

'The Hathaway outfit's *segundo* and trainer. Been here a couple of years. Brought Flying Tom with him.'

'What's Flying Tom's best distance?'

'Well, he likes to go long. You'd have to match him short, unless your horse can go a distance of ground.'

'I might listen to four furlongs, maybe five.'

'Flying Tom has never been headed around here.'

'If Kell is tetchy, maybe I'd better powwow with Hathaway?'

Again, like a cue, Dude caught the odd expression akin to amusement on a man's face when he mentioned Hathaway.

Dude visited around the square some more, doing more listening than talking, not forgetting to buy several rounds of drinks at the Elkhorn. All this while a conclusion continued to form in his mind: Nobody wanted to throw light on N. A Hathaway. It was as if the ranch owner were a mysterious and powerful person. Yet, there was no fear of Hathaway.

Kell was a different matter. He wasn't liked. Dude had the impression of a quarrelsome, taciturn man, sly at matching races.

'Where you been so long?' Uncle Billy grumbled when Dude returned. 'We've had company, such as it was.'

'Mean white man who ate all of Grandfather Billy's biscuits and stewed prunes saw Texas Jack and came to pow-wow,' Coyote said, pausing for Uncle Billy to finish, and the old man said, 'He wanted to know if we'd matched a race, and when I told him no, he said Boots Kell might be interested. He rides for Kell. Strange species. Acted friendly this time. Even had some manners. Said his name was Hoodoo Roup. Almost shook our hands off. Slapped Coyote on the back and called him 'Chief.''

'And Grandfather 'Mr. Lockhart,'' Coyote said.

'Which is better than Grandfather,' the old man replied, crusty about it.

'Good,' Dude said. 'I didn't want to make the first move. But I've decided one thing. I'm all wore out pullin' the switch. This time the Judge runs under his own true name or not at all.'

The old man eyed him. 'What if they've heard of the Judge?'

'If they back out, so what? If they don't, everything's gonna be on the up and up for once . . . though I might do just a little touch-up on the Judge here and there.'

'You'll be the death of me yet,' Uncle Billy groaned. 'Believe I'll rest a bit before you boys fix supper.' He trudged to his bedroll and lay down.

Coyote looked concerned. 'Grandfather still poorly is.'

'Don't worry,' Dude said. 'If we match Flying Tom, he won't be able to stay out of it.'

★ ★ ★

Another day slipped by without prospects. But early the second morning two horsemen came dashing through the wagonyard to the camp. Dude recognized the biscuit eater, who looked even dirtier than the first time, and waved to the partners as if they were old friends. The other man, astride a long-coupled gelding of apparent stylish breeding, said curtly, 'I'm Boots Kell.' His tone implied that Dude should know who he was.

'I'm Dude McQuinn.'

'Understand you have a racehorse?'

'A short racehorse,' Dude said, eyes crinkling. 'Where is he?'

'The dark bay there tied in the shade. Name's Hoot Owl.'

They dismounted and were striding that way when Dude added, 'I'd like to match him, but he's off his feed and turned colicky.'

Kell swung around, a slim, well-groomed man of hidden years: leather vest, string tie, dove-gray hat, tailored riding pants and polished boots. His face was sharply cast and he wore a neat brown beard. His slate-gray eyes, as cool as any Dude had seen during his extensive ramblings, showed a driving, businesslike intensity. In all, he was something of a dandy. He said, 'So it's no go?'

'Oh, I might run that ol' cow horse there tied to the wagon, if you're hurtin' for a match,' Dude drawled. 'The ol' horse we call Judge Blair.'

As Kell turned to look, a scoffing grin split his face. 'That nag?' he all but jeered.

Dude wondered if he had overdone his handiwork. Cockleburs knotted the Judge's uncurried mane and tail, sand rubbed into his hair made it look rough and irregular, the smears of peroxide gave him the worn appearance of a much-used harness horse, and he stood with hanging head.

'Just because he's got harness marks, don't think he can't run a little,' Dude said, sounding hurt. 'He's dusted a heap of cow horses in Texas.'

Kell and Roup slowly circled Judge Blair. 'Can your horse go a distance of ground?' Kell asked, making no attempt to cover his amusement.

'He'll try. He's got heart.'

'It will take more than mere heart to test my Thoroughbred. No doubt you've heard of Flying Tom?'

'I have and it scares me no little.'

'Boss,' Roup interrupted, 'that name Judge Blair sticks in my mind from somewhere. Does it you?'

'Hardly in Thoroughbred circles.'

Dude said, 'He was named after an ol' family friend back home on the Salt Fork of the Brazos.'

'It wasn't no judge I'm thinkin' about,' Roup said, puzzled. 'It was some race or other, but I can't recollect it.' He turned to Kell. 'Boss, did you notice how he's muscled up in his front and hindquarters?'

'Short muscle.'

'Did you notice his look? He's got the eyes of an eagle.'

'With his head drooping? Hoodoo, you're imagining things.' Roup shrugged and stepped back.

'Mr. McQuinn,' Kell said, coming at once to the point, 'I might listen to a match race. Our horse is at the Hathaway Ranch, six miles west of town, if you care to look at him?'

'I'm not itchin' to run you, but I will look at your horse,' Dude said, wishing Uncle Billy were here instead of visiting with Hap Gary in the office on the other side of the wagonyard.

'Early this afternoon agreeable?'

Dude nodded.

They left as they had come, riding fast out of town.

'What's all the commotion?' Uncle Billy asked, hurrying up, his step lively for one claiming a poorly state of health.

'Kell wants to match us and I told him I'd look at Flying Tom this afternoon.'

'Uh-huh. And you want me to go with you, poorly as I feel?'

'I do. Boots Kell is as slick as Gideon Lightfoot — only tougher.'

'What can I do?'

'You can back me up.'

The old man's sigh was drawn-out. 'Won't know till I've had my noon toddy and nap.'

Dude let him be. But Uncle would back him up. He always had.

Painted on the wooden archway over the wire gate were the foot-high letters: HATHAWAY RANCH, and above that the metal figure of a running horse.

Dude opened the gate and Uncle Billy drove Amos through. They went on. Mares with spring foals dotted the bluestem pastures on both sides of the road. At its termination rose a sprawling, one-story ranch house. Beyond, Dude saw a cluster of corrals and a long, low horse barn with paddocks, and looming over this extensive layout stood the massive main barn, painted a bright red.

'Now, Dude, pardner,' the old man said, his voice almost plaintive, 'you'll have to carry the load today. Don't expect me to get in the big middle of the dickering. I don't feel like it.'

'Just glad to have you along, Uncle, in case I'm about to step into a bog hole.'

Hoodoo Roup sat slouched on the long porch. He got upand greeted them with a broken-toothed grin as they walked up. 'Boss is waitin' in there,' he said, and hooked a thumb in the direction of a comer room over the door of which hung a sign marked: OFFICE.

Dude went in first.

Kell, facing the door, appeared older without his hat. His salt-and-pepper hair was thin and receding and there was a washed-out flatness to the cool eyes.

'Who's this?' he demanded bluntly upon seeing Uncle Billy.

Dude said, 'Meet my pardner, Dr. William Tecumseh Lockhart, of the Kentucky Academy of Science,' spieling the high-sounding affiliation he had decided on as they drove up to the ranch.

'An unusual connection,' Kell said, curious, and shook hands.

'Dr. Lockhart happens to be my uncle,' Dude went on, heavy on the doctor title, 'traveling with me to learn about the great Southwest.'

'Well,' Kell said, jerking his head, 'shall we go see Flying Tom? I'm not hurrying you, but a neighbor is bringing a mare over to the court of our Thoroughbred remount stallion.'

Uncle Billy, passive until then, came alive at the words. 'Isn't it a little late in the season for breeding, Mr. Kell? A late foal is always behind older youngsters in development.'

Kell flushed. 'I'm fully cognizant of that, Doctor. This ranch is likewise in the horse business to make money.' He motioned to the door.

With Roup opening the numerous gates, Kell escorted them to the main barn and down the long alleyway to a dark stall at the far end.

'It's good for Flying Tom's hair to keep him in a dark stall,' Kell told them.

The old man was silent, busy sizing up the stallion.

Flying Tom, untied, wheeled a couple of times and stood aloof, head up, eyes walling, blowing his suspicion through quivering nostrils. A beautiful dark bay, Dude saw, as big as Amos. Not a white mark on him. The commanding head. The well-arched neck. The long, sloping shoulder, the splendid muscling, long and solid, and the strong back and withers.

'If I saw this horse on the darkest night, I would know him to be a class Thoroughbred,' Uncle Billy said at last. 'I've never seen a better shoulder, Mr. Kell. Overall, I discern blinding speed and distance as well.'

'Obviously, Doctor, you recognize a superior horse when you see one,' Kell said, his voice less clipped than before.

'I would suggest, however, that those good black feet of his will remain sounder longer if you allow him to run free, instead of standing in a stall with shoes on.'

'Yes, for circulation and conformation of the feet,' Kell said, not to be topped in the exchange of equine savvy. 'I let him run out in the morning and stall him afternoon and night.'

'As a matter of interest, may I ask his breeding?'

'Glad you asked. Flying Tom is by Flying Truxton, out of Maid of Mine by Early Times.'

'Ah, the Truxton line made famous by Andy Jackson at the Hermitage. Truxton weighed thirteen hundred pounds, stood fifteen, three and had white hind feet.' The years seemed to fall away as Uncle Billy talked. 'As fast as Old Hickory's horses were — Truxton, Rifleman and Pacolet — none could ever beat Haynie's Maria, one of the last of the great Diomed's get.'

'I'm not sure that Truxton was ever beaten,' Kell said, clipped again.

'Greyhound did, before the general owned Truxton. Haynie's Maria beat Decatur, one of Truxton's best colts. Let's see . . . I believe that race was run on the Gover Bottom track in Nashville at the 1811 fall meeting. But enough of history, Mr. Kell. I am very much impressed with Flying Tom. May I ask his best distance?' He smiled a sly smile. 'That is, if you care to divulge it?'

'Anywhere from the quarter mile to the mile and up.'

'Ah, a sprinter and a stayer.'

Dude, coming in on the cue, said,

'Dr. Lockhart is internationally known as a horseman. Last year he was invited as a steward at England's famous long-distance race, the Ascot Gold Cup, which calls for a run of two and a half miles.'

'Yes,' Uncle Billy snapped, 'I happen to prefer a stayer, a horse with heart and muscle that can go more than a few jumps before throwing up his tail.' He chuckled scoffingly. 'These short-winded western horses make me laugh.'

Dude fashioned a reproving face. 'Uncle, you l know the Judge is an honest horse.' *Let Kell think short, then we'll match him long.*

'I daresay that honesty has little to do with winning a horse race,' the old man said, cackling. He moved to the stall and peered through at the stallion, ignoring the two men. 'I also like this horse's color for durability of use and appeal to the eye,' he said after some moments.

'Brown happens to be my favorite color in a racehorse,' Kell said.

Uncle Billy stared at him. 'Mr. Kell, I'm surprised at you, a veteran breeder and trainer and ardent devotee of the turf, confusing brown with dark bay.'

'But Flying Tom is brown,' Kell argued, scowling.

'Brown, yes, to the untrained eye . . . brown over the back and shoulders and rump. If you look closely, however, you'll find the true bay cast inside the hind legs, and along the muzzle and flanks and underbelly. Looking closer, you will detect a reddish tint in the dark areas you call brown. It's all a matter of distribution of pigment. Flying Tom, sir, is a true dark bay, and the next gradation is the lighter mahogany bay.'

'So,' said Kell.

'I hope this horse wasn't registered as a brown Thoroughbred?'

'So,' Kell shrugged.

Uncle Billy's tone became forgiving. 'Don't feel offended, Mr. Kell. It's a fine distinction, one that escapes many horsemen.'

Patently bored by the lecture, Kell cocked an eyebrow at the partners, flung up an impatient hand and said, 'Now that you've seen the horse, do you want to talk about a match race?'

'It won't hurt to talk,' Dude said, playing noncommittal.

Uncle Billy was the last to go, his attention lingering once more over the dark bay before following the others along the alleyway.

When the partners were seated in the office, Kell said, 'You may wonder why I would match a Thoroughbred of Flying Tom's class against any itinerant outfit's horse? Fact is, I've matched a race at Mobeetie a month from now. Some cowmen are backing a horse they're bringing in from south Texas. There will be bets at every furlong, with five thousand to the winner.'

Dude whistled at the stakes.

'Our horse needs a stiff conditioning race,' Kell said. 'He hasn't had an out in six months and there's nothing in this section of the state that can test him even a little bit. He's unbeaten, you know.'

Dude asked, 'At what distance is your match?'

'Seven furlongs.'

'So want to match us at that distance?'

Kell's face smoothed. 'That's logical, isn't it?'

'For you — not us. Judge Blair can't run that far.'

'How far can he run?'

'Depends whether the wind's with him or against him.'

'Aw, come on now, McQuinn.'

'Tell you what,' Dude said, slapping his leg, 'we'll run you half a mile,' knowing Kell wouldn't go that short. Meanwhile, he was thinking fast, sorting things out. Above all, he wanted this race for Uncle Billy's sake, to keep the old gent on his feet and going. The Judge was now trained for five-and-a-half furlongs. He could run under that or a little over without further conditioning.

Kell said, 'Not me, you won't. I'll match you six furlongs, take it or leave it.'

Dude stood suddenly. 'We're burnin' daylight, Uncle. It's time to go.' Uncle Billy, knowing the play as of old, headed for the door.

'Hold on!' Kell barked, snapping his head in that characteristic gesture of instant decision. 'You name me a fair distance.'

'Five furlongs,' Dude answered.

'It's a match. When do you want to run?'

'I always like to run on Saturday. Gives more folks a chance to bet.' Dude was thinking, Today is Monday. Time for two stiff works before the race. Just right.

'Agreed. Next Saturday, if the track is dry. Frankly, our horse is not a mudder.'

'Neither is the Judge. He was foaled in a dry year and I don't think the poor little cuss knew what rain was till he was a yearlin'.'

'How much do you want to bet?'

Dude hemmed and hawed and chewed on his lower lip and gazed out the window and scratched his ear and dug at a knot in the wooden floor with the toe of his right boot. And then, pinning Uncle Billy a look, he asked, 'What do you think, Uncle?'

'Although I prefer stayers, I guess I can put in a little.'

As if emboldened, Dude said to Kell, 'We'll bet three hundred.'

Kell curled one corner of his upper lip. 'Back East where I come from they feed that to chickens.'

'Maybe so on them big eastern tracks, but out here that kind of money feeds people and horses.'

'You'll have to raise the ante,' Kell said bluntly.

Dude glanced again at Uncle Billy, who dipped his chin in support, and Dude took a swipe at his ear and said, 'We might go five hundred.'

'That's a bare start.'

'I mean with four-to-one odds, if my ol' cow horse takes on the Thoroughbred likes of Flying Tom.'

'I would never give four to one, and that's not enough money to bring Flying Tom out of the barn.'

Dude took a hitch at his britches. 'Eight hundred — and that's my limit — and I mean with you givin' odds.'

'I told you four to one is out of the question.'

Dude took another hitch. 'I'm just an' ol' Texas country boy from down on the Salt Fork of the Brazos where the hoot owls holler, with an ol' range-bred horse that can run a lick when the ground's dry an' his feet don't hurt ... and you — you're a big come-here horseman from back East with a high-bred Thoroughbred. We get odds or we don't run.'

Kell cut his eyes at Dude. A considering moment and he snapped his head that way he had and said, 'You'll get some odds, McQuinn. Put up fifteen hundred dollars and I'll give you three to one.'

Dude slanted an eye back at him. Was Kell joking? He was not. 'All right,' Dude said, 'it's a go.' As he spoke, the old man's eyes seemed to jump at him.

Kell, exhibiting the first cordial expression Dude had seen from him, stepped across and shook hands. 'It's set, then,' he said. 'Let's work out the minor details.'

Dude had never dickered with a more obliging horseman. Any suggestion he made, Kell approved. The race was to be run at two o'clock with catch weights, Hap Gary the starter. 'A fine man, Hap. As honest as a schoolmarm,' Kell said. The finish judges: Dink Simpson, C. B. Peabody and Shug Neely. Kell said he was certain all would agree to officiate; nevertheless, Dude said he would make courtesy calls to inform them in advance. Both agreed a stakeholder wasn't necessary, since the loser would pay off right after the race. No forfeit money would be posted. If a horse was injured in training or fell ill, the race would be postponed or cancelled. A lap-and-tap start was agreed on.

'And now, gentlemen,' said Kell, his accommodating manner altering to one that Dude could not define, 'it's time to meet the boss of this horse ranch. Follow me.' He led them through a door that opened into a hallway, and down it turned into a handsome parlor of rose-colored carpet, cloth-covered sofas and oil-burning lamps. 'Wait here,' he told them and went out, closing the hall door behind him.

After a short time, Dude could hear a faint undertone of voices.

About then Kell opened the door and stood aside, that obscure look on his face.

At the same moment Dude heard light footsteps and then, to his amazement, an attractive woman entered the room, Both men heaved to their feet.

'I'm N. A. Hathaway,' she said, smiling graciously, and held out a slim, brown hand, first to Uncle Billy, who made a gallant bow and took her hand and kissed it.

'How nice,' she said, surprised and delighted, and turned to Dude, who was too flustered other than to bow and lightly take her hand and gulp, 'Pleased to meet you, ma'am. I'm Dude McQuinn. This is my uncle, Dr. William Tecumseh Lockhart.'

Stepping back, she regarded them warmly through wide hazel eyes. Dude admired her at once — a trim woman in her fifties, he guessed, standing about five feet five, clad in a white shirtwaist and long skirt. Her hair, which she wore shoulder length, was a lustrous, wavy auburn beginning to turn gray. Her face was tanned to an olive tint. Her cheekbones were set high and her lips were full, and when she smiled, as she did now, a man wanted to please her.

'Please sit down,' she said. Before she could seat herself, Kell was there before her, placing a chair opposite the partners.

She said, 'Mr. Kell tells me that we've matched Flying Tom against Judge Blair next Saturday.' Dude nodded and she continued, her voice clear and pleasant, with a note of apology. 'I know you're surprised to find N. A. Hathaway is a woman. Well, long ago I learned this is a man's world. Women's rights aren't recognized in any business I know of, and buying and selling horses is no exception, face to face or dealing through correspondence. . . . Some horsemen just won't sell to a woman. A breeder in Illinois wrote back that he wouldn't sell a stallion to a woman — said it was immoral. But when I started using my initials, the deals would go through most times.' She smiled again. 'My name is Nancy Ann. It's a kind of joke to my friends in town. They often call me N.A.' She turned appreciative eyes in Kell's direction. 'Yet, I had no trouble buying Flying Tom face to face with Mr. Kell when he came to Painted Rock two years ago.'

'Why, Nancy Ann,' Kell said, chiding her gently, 'how could any man turn you down on a horse deal, or for that matter on anything you set your heart on?'

She looked away, and a perception came to Dude. Kell was not only attentive to his boss, but he also deferred to her to the point of fawning. Another insight, less evident, also registered: Nancy Ann Hathaway, though a strong woman, was a lonely one.

'Flying Tom is beautifully formed,' Uncle Billy said. 'I've never seen a better balanced horse.'

She leaned toward him, her hands

clasped. 'That makes me feel my judgment was sound in buying him. Mr. McQuinn addressed you as 'doctor.' Are you a veterinarian, perhaps?'

'I am.'

'Uncle is with the Kentucky Academy of Science on a get-acquainted tour of the Southwest,' Dude chimed in. 'I'm glad he's along to doctor Hoot Owl, the colicky gelding we first wanted to run against Flying Tom.'

'Hoot Owl?' She clapped her hands. 'What a wonderful short-horse name. I'm particularly fond of the Peter McCue and Traveler lines. Do you happen to know Peter McCue's color? I've heard he's brown, he's bay, he's sorrel.'

Uncle Billy closed his eyes and tilted his head backward in a recalling attitude. 'I have never seen the great Peter McCue, who was by the great Dan Tucker and out of the very fast Nora M, by the Thoroughbred Voltigeur; but it is my understanding that Peter is a standard bay, which means he's a uniform clear bay all over. Of course, dear lady, you know that all bay horses have black legs just above the knee to the hoof, and the hooves should also be black. We call these horses 'bays with black points.' Remember?'

'I do. Yes, I do, Doctor,' she said, becoming as animated as a child. 'My father told me and my late husband Will used to say that. Does that mean Peter McCue has no white markings?'

'That is correct. Keep in mind, however, that all colors, regardless of breed, may show white markings on the head, legs and feet. I saw no white markings on your fine Flying Tom. He is a pure dark bay, a handsome one to boot.'

She glanced at Kell. 'Haven't we always called him brown?'

A tiny sliver of annoyance worked across his face before he managed a grin and said, 'We have. He is brown in places and bay in places. The doctor says he is dark bay, if you want to nit-pick about it.'

She frowned. 'Boots, you are being ungentlemanly.'

'Do horsemen ever agree?' He passed it off, forcing another grin.

Something hitherto hidden surfaced in her eyes, and vaoished as quickly, controlled, and she turned back to Uncle Billy. 'Please tell me about Traveler. I love those horses.'

'Traveler is a mystery horse,' the old man began. 'Would you believe that the first trace of him was found in Eastland County, Texas, when he was working on the Texas and Pacific Railway, moving dirt, pulling a scrapper? Imagine that — a workhorse! Some authorities believe that he was shipped in there with a bunch of horses from back East. He made his reputation when he beat Bob Wilson, the fastest quarter horse in central Texas. Nothing is known about his breeding — nothing.'

'Doctor, do you have a principle for breeding racehorses?'

An instant appreciation for her overspread his saintly face that he held for so long that color flushed her cheeks. Little by little a puckish grin crinkled his clear blue eyes. 'Why, yes,' he said. 'It's simple. Breed speed to speed, then pray for a dry track and an honest jockey. '

Her lips curved into a slow smile. 'What about breeding for conformation?' she asked next.

'Speed will take care of conformation. But conformation alone doesn't always produce speed and stamina and heart.'

They chatted on and on like that, Dude and Kell largely left out of the conversation, she asking question after question — veterinary treatments and medications? Feeding and training? Equine genetics? Foaling and foal development? Inbreeding? Outbreeding? Line breeding? — the old man hardly pausing when he replied.

Now and then Kell passed a preening hand over his thinning, meticulously combed hair.

When there was a lull, Dude said, 'Uncle, I believe we'd better make tracks for camp. Got horses to feed.'

'Can you come to dinner Wednesday evening?' she asked. Her smile alone was invitation enough.

Dude looked at Uncle Billy, and the response he saw prompted him to say, 'Thank you, ma'am. We'd be honored.'

Kell said, 'Nancy Ann, don't you have the Thomases coming over that evening?'

'Does that matter?' she said, shutting him off. 'We'll expect you gentlemen around six o'clock.'

Each thanked her and Uncle Billy dallied to chat another moment. While driving away from the house, Dude said, 'You didn't seem a bit poorly back there.'

'It's not how a man feels, it's how he has to act when he backs up a pardner who's always getting himself into tight places.'

'Mrs. Hathaway is quite a lady.'

'That she is. A lovely western lady.'

The way he said it made Dude turn his head. The old man seemed to be musing.

'Believe she took a shine to you,' Dude said.

Uncle had no reply.

'And you took a shine to her,' Dude drawled.

The old man was silent for a long time, staring straight ahead. His voice grew husky. 'It's hell to get old, Dude. It's worse when you meet a woman like her and wish you could peel back a few years.'

'You're not that old, pardner,' Dude said and meant it.

When Uncle Billy spoke again, after a run of silence, his tone said any further insight into his private world was out of the question. 'Dude,' he said, in an entire change of voice, 'I don't like to say this, because I've schooled you how to rock back and forth and hem and haw when matching a race, and when you with your Texas gab could match an elephant against a hop toad. But —'

'But what?'

'You bet too much when you went to fifteen hundred.'

'Didn't Kell offer three-to-one odds?'

'Think back. No man offers three to one unless he's got a cinch advantage.'

'I did kinda leap for the bait, didn't I? We'll have to be careful.'

Amos took them down the road a piece before Uncle Billy found voice again, his tone strangely questioning. 'I keep seeing that Flying Tom horse in that dark stall.'

'You mean there's something about him that puzzles you?'

'There is. I think I've seen that horse somewhere before, but I can't place him. I may forget a man's name . . . call him Hank when his name's Jake . . . but I never forget a man's face or a fast horse's particular markings or conformation. I've seen that big horse somewhere, Dude. I know I have.'

14

Calico Fever

Before daylight Tuesday, Dude and Coyote circled Painted Rock and breezed the Judge on the road south of town and had him back in camp soon after dawn.

When Hap Gary showed up for coffee with the outfit, Dude told him, 'We've matched a race with Flying Tom at two o'clock Saturday afternoon, and Kell and I agreed on you as the official starter. Lap-and-tap. Five furlongs. Hope you can tap us off?'

'Glad to. Only . . . '

'Only what?'

'I'd like to see a contest for once. No horse has come close to Flying Tom. All his races have been walkaways.'

'Judge Blair will make him hump.'

'You fellows have matched a tough one. I wish you luck.'

Later that morning Dude called on C. B. Peabody, who said he would be

410

pleased to be a finish-line judge just to get out of the store.

'Why didn't you tell me N. A. Hathaway is a woman?' Dude chided him. 'A fine-lookin' one at that.'

'It's a long story. Goes back to the early days. Nancy Ann's father, Giles Colter, was an old buffalo hunter. Made his first camp out by that painted rock. There's a nice spring there. When the hide business played out, he stayed and started the town, and planted wheat and ranched. But he was a horseman first, a farmer second. N.A. is the daughter of her father. After Giles passed on, she decided to improve the breeding of the ranch horses. You know the rest. How in her correspondence she started signing N. A. Hathaway, like a man, and it worked.'

'She's a smart lady.'

'Nancy Ann's done a lot for Painted Rock. Contributes to everything. So when a horseman comes to town and inquires about N. A. Hathaway, we don't spill the beans. Let him find out on his own.'

'Kell introduced us *after* we matched the race.'

'Kell . . . ' Peabody let the name drag. He hesitated and bunched his lips. 'Nancy Ann's husband, Will, passed away three years ago, a year before Kell showed up. Losing Will took a great deal out of her. Folks around town think Kell would like to marry her and take over the ranch. Sometimes a younger man can fool an older woman who's lost her husband. Kell's a fast talker and dresses fancy. For her own good, I hope she stays clear of him.' Peabody eyed the store's doorway. 'It's about time we paid Sam Thompson an early morning visit.'

At BOOTS & SADDLES, Dude found Dink Simpson at his workbench. 'Be glad to,' he said. 'You understand I'll have to call it like they finish — no favors.'

'That's the only way I want you to call it, you and Mr. Peabody and Mr. Neely. I haven't seen Mr. Neely yet.'

'Try the courthouse square where the shade's the deepest,' Simpson said, wearing a possum grin. 'When yon do

412

find him, better pull on your hip boots and head for high ground if Shug starts reminiscin'.' He stood to roll a cigarette. 'Besides Flying Tom, you'll have to worry about Cat Curry.'

'Cat Curry?'

'Kell's jockey. Came here with Kell and that polecat-smellin' Hoodoo Roup.' Simpson made a face.

'What about Cat Curry?'

Simpson stared down the long slope of his nose over the gold rims of his insecure spectacles. 'He's a slick one. Been on the big tracks? Chicago and St. Louis. Won some big stakes races, they say.'

'If he's a top rider, what's he doing way out here?'

'Good question.'

'Any little wrinkles of his I can pass on to our Comanche jockey?'

'Yeah. Tell him to expect anything.'

'Why, Dink, you sound like C. B. Peabody, when he said he hoped Nancy Ann won't marry Boots Kell.'

'He spoke for the whole town there.'

'Meantime, I'd better shake out the

tuies for Shug Neely. I'm sure much obliged to you.'

Dude found Shug Neely pitching horseshoes, supporting himself with a cane. He would hold a shoe before him and cock an eye, sighting through the lower part of the U, then bring the shoe to his side and forward, releasing it with a smooth motion.

Dude watched until the game was finished. Would Mr. Neely serve as a finish-line judge?

'Will I? Son, you are talking to one of the original short-horse men in these parts,' he said, drawing Dude to a bench. 'Used to have a little mare called Sweet Alice. She was honest an' she always ran straight, short or long, wet or dry track. Rode her myself. Before long she had taken the slack out of everything around here an' it was gettin' hard to match her even far away, she was that well-known.' He looked straight at Dude. 'Hope I'm not borin' you?'

'Oh, no. Go right ahead.'

'Well, I cleaned up so much money

that relatives moved in on us, two of my own distant uncles an' my wife's four strappin' brothers. All big eaters an' slow to chop wood an' help around the farm.'

One of Neely's contemporaries leaned in and confided to Dude, 'Hope you're in no hurry, stranger. Last time Shug told this the fellow was so late gettin' back to camp his wife accused him of runnin' around with another woman.'

'Go on,' Dude said. 'I want to hear all about Sweet Alice.'

A long, loose-jointed man, Shug Neely had a whimsical mouth and eyes to match. He was up in years, as the saying went, yet no telling how old; time seemed to have marked him gently and passed on. He settled himself and commenced. 'A loud-talkin' horse trader drifted in here with a string of work stock an' one racehorse. Could this trader stretch the blanket! Claimed he had the fastest horse in the West, an' he was the best poker player in the West. . . . Now his horse was called Big Jake, an' I tell you he filled out the name: seventeen hands an' over fourteen hundred pounds. All muscle an' bone. An' mean! Ever' time you looked at 'im, he'd wall his eyes an' bare his teeth. After one eyeful of Big Jake, I knew I'd better match him short. You see, Sweet Alice was a fast breaker but couldn't run over a quarter. We used to call that long. But once she got ahead there was no catchin' her.' He leaned back to let that sink in, waiting.

'What distance did you go?' Dude asked courteously.

'Three hundred yards.'

'How much did you bet?'

'All I had.'

'Did Sweet Alice take the break?'

A sheepish admittance. 'I got fooled. The other jock let one foot hang from the stirrup, like he wasn't ready to run — but he was. He jumped his horse out to a length lead right off the bat.'

'Then what?'

'I got Sweet Alice settled an' she caught Big Jake in the first hundred yards. But just as we started by, the other jock grabbed my saddlecloth.'

'What'd you do?' Dude asked.

'I couldn't pass. Sweet Alice fell back. But I squalled at her an' started by again.' Shug Neely paused — a portentous pause.

'And then?'

'The jock locked me with his leg.'

'The dirty so-and-so. So you fell back again?'

'Had to. Sweet Alice broke stride. But she came at Big Jake again. I tell you she had a world of heart, that little mare.'

'And that time,' Dude cut in, anticipating, 'you passed Big Jake like a slow freight and won by daylight?'

Shug Neely took a twist of black tobacco, broke off a piece, crumbled it in the palm of his left hand and filled his pipe, borrowed a match, struck it on the thigh of his trousers and lit up, puffed awhile and said reminiscently, 'I'd like to say so. But I reckon Sweet Alice was a little tired by then, charging at that big horse.' His gurgling pipe went out and he borrowed another match, lit up and resumed. 'I couldn't have throwed a rock an' touched Big Jake's dust, he was so far ahead at the finish.'

Dude's jaw fell. 'Hate to hear that.'

'But, you know,' the old gentleman said, brightening, 'one good thing did come out of that.'

'How could that be when you'd lost the race?'

'My two distant uncles an' my wife's four strappin' brothers moved out before dark. They knew the gravy was all gone.'

'And then some,' Dude sympathized.

'That wasn't all.' Shug Neely delayed to knock out his pipe, waiting' Dude knew, for him to take the story another lap with a question.

'What in the world happened next?' Dude asked.

'That evening there was a poker game goin' in the Elkhorn. I borrowed ten dollars from C. B. Peabody an' sat in.' He seemed to call back his thoughts, waiting.

'Well — ?' Dude prompted.

'When daylight came I'd won back everything I'd lost from that windy horse trader an'....' He opened his pocket-knife and started cleaning out his pipe.

'And what?' Dude asked, going along.

'An' Big Jake.'

Dude slapped his leg and guffawed heartily. 'That's a good one, Mr. Neely. Is there a moral to the story?'

'Happens there is. If you can't win on the track, you'd better be a good poker player.'

$\star$ $\star$ $\star$

An afternoon visitor was the Reverend Lige Swink, who was overjoyed when he saw Amos. He hastened step. 'I was afraid you'd sold Avalanche,' he said.

'He's the same as sold,' Uncle Billy said, without welcome. 'A farmer whose name I don't know came by here, tried him out, and said he would raise the money from his boys.'

'He'd better hurry,' Swink said, waving his windmill arms. 'I've cast my bread upon the waters and have found it again, thanks to the Good Tidings ladies. They're holdin' a string of pie suppers and the money is comin' in. Right now, I calculate we're only two hundred dollars short. I know the bountiful waters will soon bring in the rest. Could you hold Avalanche for me, Brother Lockhart?' An appealing, pleading smile broke through the mournful cloud of his gaunt face. Dude thought of a small boy longing for his first pony.

Even Uncle Billy looked sympathetic. He said, 'I'd like for you to have Avalanche, Parson, but it's first come, first served,' and looked the other way.

'Well, thank you kindly just the same,' Swink said, mournful again. 'Good day, Brother Lockhart.'

'Lyin' to a preacher!' Dude let fly, when Swink had gone. 'You ought to be ashamed.'

'It's not because he's a preacher. I've known some ex-preachers who swapped the cloth for the bar rag. It's because he's a teetotaler. You know my stand on teetotalers.'

'Mark my words, he'll raise the money. You'll have to sell him Amos.'

*　　*　　*

In the parlor Wednesday evening, Nancy Ann Hathaway introduced the partners and Branch and Hester Thomas. She was an easy-to-meet ranch woman near the age of her hostess, her smile quick, her tanned face oval and pleasant. Her husband was tall and angular, his beardless face the hue of a saddle seat, a quiet, soft-spoken man.

Kell was handsome in a gray suit of rakish cut, a double-breasted vest of light blue, a maroon cravat, tied bow-tie fashion, under the turned-down tips of his collar.

During the small talk that followed, Branch Thomas, aside, soon told Dude that he had been a longtime friend of Will Hathaway's, had grown up with him and Nancy Ann. His eyes became troubled when he saw Kell making over to her, reaching across to pat her hand, hanging on every word she spoke.

When a serving woman announced dinner, Kell took his boss's arm, his manner possessive, and escorted her to the lamplit dining room. She sat at the head of the long table, Kell at the other end, the Thomases on her right, Uncle Billy and Dude on her left.

'Dr. Lockhart,' she said, 'will you give the blessing, please?'

Uncle Billy was speechless so long that Dude nudged him, whereupon the old man cleared his throat and began, haltingly at first, 'Bless, O Lord ... this food to our use ... and us to thy service ... and .... keep us ever mindful of the needs of others — for Christ's sake. Amen. And, if I may be excused for mentioning Saturday's race at this time, may we not be as the poet wrote, 'Beggars mounted run their horse to death,' instead, riders who go by the gentle word and need no rein.'

Dude was surprised and proud, and their hostess, eyes warmly approving, said, 'Thank you, Doctor. That was well-said by a Christian gentleman and very apropos.'

As the dinner progressed, Kell waxed

at length about the importance of a good sire such as Flying Tom, and Uncle Billy, after keeping silent, said, 'That is true, Mr. Kell. But do not overlook that every foal inherits powerful influences from his dam. The foal's period of contact with his dam goes on for a long time, continuing until he is weaned.'

'How much influence?' Kell asked, his voice low but challenging.

'Sixty per cent, maybe more. Some authorities go so far as to state that more female lines are in existence today than male lines. That there are fewer outstanding stallions than outstanding mares.'

'You're in deep water there, Doctor,' Kell said, running a hand over his slicked-down hair.

'I agree, because our knowledge of genetics is meager indeed. In a way, the mare's role is comparable to women's rights, which are universally denied. It's the sire who gets the public acclaim when a great horse is produced, the mare who is overlooked. It is bias and ignorance toward the distaff side.'

Both women applauded. 'That's the first time I've heard a man admit a woman's worth,' Hester Thomas said, giving her husband a teasing look.

'It's merely a matter of being fair,' Uncle Billy said, affecting modesty.

'I think it's more than fairness where horses are concerned,' Mrs. Hathaway said. 'It's your knowledge of horses.'

'More emphasis is placed on the sire rather than the dam, and always will be,' Uncle Billy continued, now in his full lecturing stride, 'simply because the sire has so many sons and daughters around to enhance his name. From that many an estimate can be drawn of his ability as a sire. A stallion may serve fifty or more mares a year, whereas a mare will be mated only once a year.'

'To my way of thinking, pedigree is everything,' Kell kept on. 'Do you pick racehorses by the nick?'

'I'd want to check a horse's conformation first: straight legs, muscle, balance. Any mating is subject to chance, no matter how many kings and queens are represented, because there is one element that cannot be measured.'

'What's that?'

'Heart, my friend. Or call it desire. Some of your best-bred racehorses won't run a lick because they don't want to. They're not competitive. Yet some obscure horse will come up that is thunder and lightning.'

'Judge Blair, for instance?' Kell was fishing, Dude sensed.

Uncle Billy smiled. 'We'll find out when he runs Saturday.'

Kell not one to muffle his opinions, said, 'I favor inbreeding to duplicate the best characteristics.'

'True. You also run the risk of reproducing the undesirable characteristics as well as the good ones. Take faulty front legs, for example. They can be passed on with devastating effect, though otherwise a horse may have outstanding conformation, speed and heart.'

After dinner, as the ladies strolled to the parlor and the men trailed after them out of the dining room to Kell's office, Dude whispered to Uncle Billy, 'Where'd you get that stuff about the poet? That was *bueno*.'

The old man fixed him a high-flown look. 'Since when does an Alamo Texan, who hardly knows sic 'em, question a Christian gentleman's savvy of the classics? That was no less than the Bard of Avon, Dude, pardner. From . . . uh . . . *King Henry* . . . something or other. Ask no more.' His step was jaunty as he went on.

'I know. You been listenin' to Coyote.'

In Kell's office, the men chatted over smooth sour-mash whiskey and long cigars. Kell did most of the talking, still, Dude saw, determined to force his views. When they rejoined the ladies, Kell took a chair beside Mrs. Hathaway. To Dude, the move was ostentatious. Branch Thomas's face tightened at the clear claim of ownership.

Presently, the hostess, turning to Dude, asked, 'Do you know Judge Blair's breeding, Mr. McQuinn?'

'No, ma'am, we do not. He's range-bred

and cowboys first matched him in neighborhood races. I think he's got a good deal of mustang or *mesteño* blood.'

'And has heart, as Dr. Lockhart would say,' she concluded, bringing her eyes across Uncle Billy. 'That makes our race even more interesting. A Thoroughbred against a horse of wild blood. I hope we have a good race. I realize that Flying Tom is a heavy favorite,' she said, her voice somewhat apologetic.

'Well, ma'am, we could hardly pass up three-to-one odds.'

'Three to one?' She stared accusingly at Kell. 'I didn't know that. I assumed the bet was even money.'

Kell tried to shrug it off. 'What are odds when you have the top horse, Nancy Ann?'

She passed over the matter and, ignoring Kell, turned to chat with Hester Thomas, but the exchange had put a detectable damper on the evening, and before long Dude and Uncle Billy rose to leave, thanked their hostess and nodded to the Thomases and Kell.

Mrs. Hathaway followed them out to the porch. A pale moon cast a glow as soft as parlor light.

'I didn't mean to upset you about the odds, ma'am,' Dude apologized. 'I thought you knew.'

'That's all right, Mr. McQuinn. Boots spoke for the ranch and the match was made. I will honor the odds. I was brought up to keep my word.'

Murmuring a 'good-night,' Dude stepped off the porch to go to the buggy. Behind him Uncle Billy and Mrs. Hathaway tarried and Dude heard him say, 'I think you're a very lovely lady, Nancy Ann. I want you to know that.' His voice was utterly gentle and sincere.

'Oh . . . ' She sounded startled and confused. 'That is nice of you to say so. I'm not used to hearing things like that.'

'True things from the heart ought not to be left unsaid, dear lady.' She gave a little gasp. 'I don't know what to say.'

Their voices, thou low, still carried to Dude:

'Even though we've matched the race,

I don't feel like an adversary,' Uncle Billy said.

'Neither do I.'

'I hope you will pardon an old man for speaking his feelings?'

'It is wonderful to hear truth and sweet gentleness again. And . . . I don't think of you as old at all, because you aren't. You never will be.'

Walking on, Dude heard no more. When he came to the buggy and glanced back, the two figures on the porch stood quite close together. In the dusky dimness, they seemed to be holding hands.

Whoa, there, pardner! Dude thought. You're gettin' calico fever. After some time, Uncle Billy left her and walked out to the buggy.

She was still there on the porch when they drove away.

'This is one race I wished we'd never matched, Dude, pardner,' the old man said. 'But it could be the most important.'

15

A Horse of a Different Color

After checking Judge Blair following his final breezing Thursday morning, Uncle Billy ate breakfast and kept to himself, lost in thought, apart from the daily visitation of courthouse loafers.

Noting his old partner's continued abstraction that afternoon, Dude thought, It's the calico fever again, and he put an arm around the old man and said, 'Let's ease over to the Elkhorn and sink a few. What do you say, Uncle?'

'If you say so.'

Shug Neely was there, telling a horse story, and Dude bought him a drink and the old-timer said, 'Word has spread. Be a big crowd here for the race. There's already considerable money on your horse.'

'When Flying Tom's the favorite? I don't savvy that.'

'It's against Boots Kell and his bunch.

I wish N.A. would clean house out there.'

'Why hasn't she?'

'Kell has pulled the wool over her eyes, and you don't fire a trainer who's never lost a race for you.'

Uncle Billy listened without comment, and when he declined a second round, the partners left. They were coming out of the saloon when a two-seated buckboard occupied by three dusty men dashed past them.

Dude stopped, giving the three a casual glance, only to straighten on a surge of recognition. The driver was the bowler-hatted man of Roseville and Lightfoot, blinking as he drove.

Uncle Billy seemed to freeze. When the driver continued on toward the Drovers' House, the old man turned in the opposite direction, keeping Dude between him and the buckboard.

Dude was silent until they reached camp. 'Wouldn't happen to know that bird in the bowler hat, would you, Uncle?'

'Now, did I say?' No more was said.

Friday was quiet for a prerace day. There were lookers, of course, among them farmers and ranchers coming in for Saturday's big attraction. By now the burs had been picked from the Judge's mane and tail, and though curried and brushed, he still stood with hanging head, a seeming lethargy he would shed the moment he felt the light racing saddle being cinched up.

Uncle Billy kept to himself throughout the day. When strangers approached, he would give them a watchful look, then make a wide circle to Hap Gary's office. He also declined Dude's invitation to go to the Elkhorn, an unheard-of refusal that set Dude to puzzling again. After supper, the old man seemed to emerge from his pensive shell, saying, 'I don't trust this Kell fella any farther than I could throw a bull by the tail uphill against a stiff wind, so we'd better stand guard tonight.'

Dude nodded. 'You take the first

watch, then Coyote, then me. We'll halter the Judge at the wagon with the other horses.'

Uncle Billy's usual keyed-up fervor before a race was lacking, Dude sensed. He seemed on the verge of melancholy, and Dude, thinking of the Hathaway woman, understood and felt a deep sympathy for his gruff old mentor, as if he had found his true love too late in life for fulfillment.

It seemed but a short time to Dude until Coyote touched him awake. He pulled on his boots and scrambled out to stand by the wagon, rubbing his eyes and flexing his arms. Afterward, he walked around the horses and sat in Uncle Billy's cane-bottomed chair, aware of the changing night as clouds moved across the sky. Ideal cover, he thought, for somebody slipping in to fix an honest horse.

Now and then he got up to look at the horses.

He was still on the alert when a sliver of copper light pierced the eastern sky, and nothing had happened. Why? And then it came to him. What chance did 'an ol' cow horse' have against a fancy Thoroughbred? Why bother to try and fix a horse that was obviously outclassed? That was Kell's uppity reasoning, and not without foundation. Wasn't Flying Tom unbeaten?

On that sobering thought, he got up to make morning coffee.

Reflective and somber all morning, Uncle Billy appeared more so as post time neared and he finished harnessing Amos to the buggy. 'I have to get something off my chest,' he said. 'It can't wait any longer.'

Dude was startled. 'What do you mean?'

'This. There's no fool like an old fool when it comes to a pretty woman younger than he is. I don't intend to repeat the mistake.'

'I don't agree with you,' Dude said earnestly. 'She likes you.'

'No fool, Grandfather,' the loyal Coyote Walking said. 'Wise you are, like Owl Person.'

The old man shook his head, plainly sick at heart. 'I'm too old for a woman that young. I was a fool to think so.'

Dude was surprised at the size of the cow-country crowd as he rode Blue Grass to the track, followed by Coyote aboard Judge Blair. Wagons and buckboards and buggies and horsemen and spectators on foot lined the track from the starting line on the other side of the track to the finish line. The race course was another stretch of smooth prairie, a pole marking the five-furlong start and one on each side of the finish line. There was no grandstand or paddock.

Near the finish line in a buckboard sat N. A. Hathaway and Hester Thomas. Branch Thomas stood by the buckboard, talking to the women.

Dude saw Uncle Billy glance at the Hathaway woman, rest his eyes on her for a heartsick moment before turning away.

There was a rising buzz of voices down the track. Turning, Dude saw Kell on a pony horse leading Flying Tom and jockey onto the straightaway. Hoodoo Roup cleared a path through the crowd.

Making a visible effort to shake off his thoughts, Uncle Billy said, 'Dude, you and Coyote hold up till Kell takes his horse to the starting line. Let 'em sweat a little. I believe you can outbreak that Thoroughbred, Coyote, pardner. Dude, I told Hap Gary about our swinging break and that we'd demand a flip for the lanes. Take the inside if you win the toss. I'll be at the finish line.'

Stepping down from the buggy, he moved through the crowd and past the Hathaway buckboard without as much as a glance her way. Dude saw her start to wave at Uncle Billy. When he didn't look up, she let her gloved hand drop, her eyes hurt and puzzled.

When it was time to go, Dude ponied Judge Blair through the milling crowd to the track. Coyote's attire, without the war paint this time, brought a chorus of exclamations. Dude led onto the other side of the track.

Waving jockeys and pony riders over,

Hap Gary said, 'It will be a walk-up start. When you come to the line even-Stephen, I'll bring my hand down like this and yell, 'Go!' Now, we'll flip for lanes.' Producing a silver dollar, he said, 'McQuinn, you call it in the air.' He flipped and Dude called, 'Heads,' and Gary let the spinning coin fall to the ground. It came up 'heads.'

Mindful of when Stub Tate had forced Coyote outside on the turn, Dude said, 'We'll take the inside.' For once, he thought, we've won the toss.

Kell shrugged as if it didn't matter. At the same time he was studying Judge Blair with unusual interest.

Gary's voice hurried them. 'Jockeys get ready to take your horses back and walk up to the line.'

Kell spurred over for a final conference with Cat Curry. It was brief but emphatic, judging by Kell's gestures.

'Good luck, Coyote,' Dude said and released the lead shank.

Curry nodded to Kell and swung back. Together he and Coyote turned their horses, Flying Tom commencing to prance, the Judge quietly walking, always a quiet horse until the break.

Curry, a wizened little man, rode hunched, outwardly half bored, his manner cocky and intimidating. Dude guessed him no heavier than ninety pounds. No wonder Kell had agreed to catch weights! The afternoon sun on Curry's seamed face suggested the likeness of cracked leather. He kept eyeing Coyote, as if that would unsettle the young Comanche. When Coyote ignored him, Curry blustered, 'Injun, this big Thoroughbred don't like bein' crowded, understand? Stay clear or he'll squash that short horse like a bug!'

Coyote's dark eyes glittered amusement. 'Indeed,' he said. 'White man, you better worry about catching this short horse first.'

'I'm warmin' you — stay clear — or we'll run over you!'

Smiling from the teeth, Coyote shook his Comanche quirt, a short cedar handle decorated with brass tacks set in patterns of horse tracks and from which dangled lashes of braided rawhide. 'Grab not my saddle or crowd my horse. Do — off your arm I will cut — like this!' And he snapped the quirt downward.

They were nearing the starting line, Gary's arm poised. But just before the horses reached the line, Curry, obviously set to break an instant before the signal, jumped Flying Tom away.

Coyote merely walked his horse across, while Gary yelled, 'Come back! Come back!' Even so, Flying Tom ran some seventy-five yards before Curry could take him in hand.

Kell voiced his displeasure in an undertone when Curry rode back.

'Be no start till you're even-Stephen,' Gary sang out. 'Come again.' They moved toward the line once more, evenly enough. Curry silent this time. Gary, intense, rigid, swung his arm downward and yelled, 'Go!'

Coyote's whoop, usually reserved for later in a race, sounded a fraction later. Judge Blair, in the swinging break,

jumped half a length in front, charging out of the inside lane. Flying Tom
ducked out a little at the break. Curry
batted him on the right side, straightened him, got him going.

Running smoothly, Judge Blair
quickly opened up a length lead on the
backstretch and held it sprinting into
the turn. The crowd there, packed along
both flanks of the track, was yelling full
voice.

Dude, watching from the starting line,
suddenly went cold when a bottle sailed
out of the crowd and struck Judge Blair's
neck. The startled gelding jerked and
slowed a little. Coyote settled him, soon
had him running full stride again, but
not before Flying Tom surged up beside
them.

The horses swept into the homestretch,
firing head to head, Curry cleverly bearing in to save ground.

Dude spurred Blue Grass across the
track's infield to the finish line.

Coyote's whoop carried like a war cry,
and Dude, standing in his stirrups to

watch, saw the Judge tear ahead of the dark bay Thoroughbred. Half a length. Now a length.

Dude's hopes soared. Coyote and the Judge were goin' to win it, God bless.

Then, in disbelief, Dude saw a burly man stagger into the inside lane, weaving like a drunk. Dude froze. Insight flashed. The man wasn't drunk. It was planned — deliberate — to make the Judge swerve or break stride.

For a breathless tick of time, Coyote seemed to rein his horse away from the man. But just that little, for Flying Tom was rushing up on the outside. Coyote reined back, riding straight at the man. He stood on the track and waved his arms. At the very last he plunged back into the crowd. Hands grabbed him and smashed him down.

But that threat, Dude saw with a groan, had cost the Judge and Coyote precious ground.

Running powerfully, Flying Tom drove to the Judge's hip, to his withers, now to his head. The two dark bays were racing head to head, hooked, as old horsemen said, neither horse giving to the other.

Dude glimpsed Curry's desperate grab for Coyote's saddle, saw him miss by inches when Coyote raised his quirt and slashed.

The duel continued unchanged, stride for stride, heart for heart. Dude thought: A dead heat, neither horse giving or able to nose ahead. And then, as he had so many times, he realized that he was waiting for something.

It came: Coyote's screeching whoop. And quickly another whoop, primeval and stirring, a Plains Indian calling on his horse for more run. A Comanche and his horse. *Run, horse, run. Run like buffalo horse. Run.*

The crowd jammed at the finish line pushed back when the horses bulged like flying demons, eyes walled, nostrils wide, ears laid hack.

'Come on! Come on!' Dude was shouting.

He heard Coyote lift one final curdling whoop. And then Judge Blair seemed to leap ahead in the last two jumps.

The roaring crowd lost voice, spent, eyes following the horses easing up into the first turn. Dude saw Coyote raise his quirt and bring it down, the Comanche sign for 'finished,' 'done' — this for Curry to see. The jockeys turned their horses, trotted toward the finish line. Coyote waved. Curry trailed the victors, his weathered face hardly changing even in defeat.

There was a new and sudden movement in the crowd. A man came out on the track and pointed to Flying Tom and two men ran and seized the bridle and motioned for Curry to dismount.

Dude stared. What was going on?

The pointing man wore a black bowler and he was blinking against the sunlight. Kell was there also, protesting the seizure of his horse, Hoodoo Roup in step beside him.

'Are you Adam Kell, also known as Boots Kell?' the bowler-hatted man asked.

'I am. What of it? Release my horse.'

'I can't do that, Mr. Kell, because he was stolen.'

Kell hesitated. 'Who are you?'

'C. W. Pratt, of the Pinkerton Detective Agency. I have a warrant for your arrest, Mr. Kell.'

A hush had settled over the spectators. Kell spread his hands and looked around imploringly, an appeal of injured innocence. 'What for? I'm foreman of the Hathaway Ranch. Ask these folks.'

Heads nodded.

'For stealing the Thoroughbred Royal Road from the Royal Farms, Cass County, Missouri, two years ago. That is Royal Road there.'

Kell had to laugh. 'That's Flying Tom.'

The Pinkerton man eyed the stallion again and frowned, flustered but determined. 'It's Royal Road.'

'Prove it,' Kell mocked.

'Hold on,' a gruff voice interrupted. Dude gave a start when Uncle Billy stepped from the crowd.

'Why, hello, Billy,' Pratt said, staring. 'Long time no see.'

'If you will hold on just one minute I believe I can help you.' With that, the old man darted through the crowd to the buggy. He was back in seconds, clutching a bottle and a rag.

'What's that?' Pratt asked, impatient. 'One of your potions?'

'Turpentine. You always were in too big a hurry, C.W. Just hold on, will you?' The old man soaked the rag, stepped to the stallion, and began rubbing the dark bay forehead.

The spectators gasped when a spot of white appeared. And more white, and still more, until an irregular blaze shaped like a question mark was exposed, Dude saw, dismounting for a closer look.

Uncle Billy said, 'There's your horse, C.W. There's Royal Road.'

'It is,' Pratt said. 'That unusual marking fits the exact description. Mr. Kell, you are under arrest. I also have warrants for one Jonas Roup, alias Hoodoo Roup, and one Morg Curry, alias Cat Curry, for aiding and abetting the theft of Royal Road.'

While a bystander held Royal Road's reins, the two detectives handcuffed Kell and Roup and Curry and marched them away.

Everything had happened that fast, Dude thought wonderingly. Like the long-missing pieces of a puzzle suddenly found.

'I thought that was Royal Road all the time,' Pratt was telling Uncle Billy with satisfaction, 'but I couldn't quite prove it.'

'You *thought*,' said Uncle Billy, bantering. 'That's the trouble with you, C.W. And you *thought* I had a hand in Royal Road's theft because obviously somebody with a fine touch had to cover up the markings of the best-known Thoroughbred in Missouri to sneak him out of the state. I left Missouri so I wouldn't be falsely accused, you know.'

Dude nodded to himself. That fit as well. Explained why Uncle wouldn't campaign Judge Blair in Cass County. Why he had come to Texas in the first place. Yet there remained many unanswered questions about the old codger's life that Dude realized he would never know, and perhaps it was just as well.

'I did have a warrant out for you,' Pratt admitted, his tone sheepish.

Uncle Billy said curiously, 'I can read you like a schoolboy's primer, C.W., except for one little wrinkle you pulled. How did you know to track Royal Road here?'

'I didn't — for certain. Call it a hunch, maybe. But when I heard about an old gent with a white beard and a horse that was pure forked lightning cleaning out everything in southwestern Missouri, I thought they might lead me to Royal Road stashed somewhere. Trouble was, you kept disappearing. Only lately did I come across evidence that linked Kell and the others.' He held out a hand, blinking rapidly. 'That wraps it up, Billy. So long — and thanks.'

'So long, C.W. Keep thinking.'

A slab-bodied man shuffled out of the ebbing crowd. A jubilant Lige Swink. 'Brother Lockhart, the Good Tidings ladies have raised the money for Avalanche,'

447

he announced, waving his arms, and lowered his voice. 'Ordinarily, I would not condone this means. Yet it only goes to prove that the Lord works in mysterious ways. You see . . . the ladies bet the pie supper money on Judge Blair, and not only do we have enough now to buy Avalanche, but enough to build the Sunday school room.' He fluttered his hands. 'When can I get my horse?'

The old man hemmed and hawed and fingered his beard and caught his cherry-red lower lip between his teeth and kicked at a tuft of bluestem. Cocking an eye at Dude and Coyote, he hesitated, then said, 'Maybe I'd better think about this some more, Parson.'

'You mean you don't want to sell the horse?' Swink's anticipation evaporated all at once.

'Could be. Could be.'

Branch Thomas was waiting. He said, 'I believe there's a lady over there who wants to see you, Dr. Lockhart.'

Uncertainty seemed to come over Uncle Billy, and for a space Dude feared he was going to refuse. But in the end he took a tug at his shirt collar, pulled on his string tie, tilted his hat at an angle and walked straight over to N. A. Hathaway.

'Nancy Ann,' he said, bowing, 'would you mind leaving your buckboard with the Thomases? I want you to know what it's like to ride behind my drivin' horse.'

'I think that would be very nice, Billy.' Just the way she said it was enough.

Whereupon he held out his arm and escorted her to the buggy and in, and he climbed nimbly to the seat after her, and took up the reins and chirruped, 'Gid-dup, Amos.'

We do hope that you have enjoyed reading this large print book.

Did you know that all of our titles are available for purchase?

We publish a wide range of high quality large print books including:
Romances, Mysteries, Classics
General Fiction
Non Fiction and Westerns

Special interest titles available in large print are:
The Little Oxford Dictionary
Music Book, Song Book
Hymn Book, Service Book

Also available from us courtesy of Oxford University Press:
Young Readers' Dictionary
(large print edition)
Young Readers' Thesaurus
(large print edition)

For further information or a free brochure, please contact us at:
Ulverscroft Large Print Books Ltd.,
The Green, Bradgate Road, Anstey,
Leicester, LE7 7FU, England.
Tel: (00 44) **0116 236 4325**
Fax: (00 44) **0116 234 0205**

*Other titles in the
Linford Western Library:*

VULTURE WINGS

Dirk Hawkman

Infamous low-lives, the Strong brothers will do anything for a quick buck — but this is going to be no ordinary kidnap. They are paid to abduct two young men, and don't ask too many questions when their paymaster gives them some unusual instructions. Then, as the boys' father races to rescue his sons, he realises that their snatching is linked to dark secrets from his old life as a bounty hunter.

REUBEN'S REVENGE

Ben Ray

Reuben and Grace Chisholm led a happy, almost idyllic, life on a small homestead — until the day that was to change their lives. In the saloon, Reuben heard that their closest neighbours, the Carver family, had been murdered and their home destroyed. His first thought was for Grace, and he set off to return to her. But he was too late. The house had been burned to the ground and there was no sign of his wife. Now he must find her . . .

THE DEUCE OF DIAMONDS

Charles M. Martin

Roaming Reynolds and Texas Joe find themselves helping out a couple of old ranchers who are being plagued by rustlers. Reynolds suspects that local cattle baron Griff Tyson, owner of the Deuce of Diamonds spread, is behind the trouble. But Tyson is quite a gunfighter himself, able to shoot playing cards out of the air. Will Reynolds and Joe prevail against him?